MW0817006

WINTERFROST MARKET

TALES OF MIDWINTER HAVEN BOOK ONE

Jenny Sandiford

VELIKOR
PUBLISHING

Contact: jennysandiford.com

Cover Designer: Fay Lane

Map Creator: Melissa Nash

Editor: Mandi Oyster

Proofreader: Amy McKenna

ISBN (ebook): 978-0-6459796-3-3

ISBN (paperback): 978-0-6459796-4-0

ISBN (hardcover): 978-0-6459796-5-7

First Edition: October 2024

For anyone in need of a hot cup of tea, a cozy blanket, and a magical escape.

WELCOME

Welcome to Midwinter Haven, a secretive town with mysterious residents. In this cozy, winter wonderland you will walk side by side with witches, fae, elves, werewolves, dwarves, vampires, and even the occasional mortal.

Beyond the borders of the human realm, Midwinter is where you will find what you are looking for: good company, hot tea, enchanting magic, and plenty of fireside stories with a touch of romance.

CHAPTER 1

ELSIE

T he smell of cinnamon and fresh bread drifted through the air as Elsie darted between market stalls, her focus set on Sammy's bakery. She had to get there before the crowds hit to prevent another disaster of a day. Her desperation had hit a new low—bribing the new girl at the tea house with cake.

She took in a deep breath of crisp morning air. Today was going to be good. The morning was at its finest: the market coming to life, the fresh air filled with the tempting scents of baked goods, and the cheerful bustle of people—

"Oi, watch it." A man barged past her, lugging sacks of what could only be putrefying rubbish.

Elsie sidestepped. "Good morning to you, too," she mumbled, determined not to ruin her mood. A chill crept across her toes, and she glanced down. Great, she was standing in an icy puddle.

"Oh, sugar," she muttered to herself. And just after she'd polished her boots this morning. She pulled a clean handkerchief from the pocket of her red coat, a Midwinter present from her mum the year before, and wiped the icy scum from the worn black leather. Her throat constricted at the sudden thought of her mum.

How had three weeks passed so quickly? Her mother had never been more than a day late from her trips before, yet now she was a week overdue and in Midwinter Haven of all places.

Perhaps she had just found a good lead for the rare spices she'd been hunting for and got caught up tracking them down. That had to be it...

Elsie, her sister Marie, and their mother Tia had only arrived in Winterfrost a month ago, and Elsie had been doing her best to push aside her concern about their mother's sudden departure, especially at this time of year.

"Good tidings, young Elsie. Don't mind Peter, he's in a right foul mood," Fred called from a nearby stall; a fellow market-vendor and rosy-cheeked old man who Elsie was very fond of.

Elsie pocketed the hankie and wandered over, tucking loose strands of black hair that slipped free from her plaits behind her ears.

Colorful nesting dolls stood in neat rows in front of Fred. "Morning, Fred. I see your new designs are selling brilliantly." She nodded at the blue, white, and silver winter-themed dolls.

"Ay, that they are. Still two weeks until Midwinter. I best get cracking and make some more, don't ya think?"

Ten days, not even two weeks. She kept the panic to herself. "Might be wise." She smiled. Fred was so proud of his creations and rightfully so.

"How are you all holding up without your ma?" He dusted around the dolls, keeping his eyes down.

"Fine thanks, Fred. The tea house has been busy, but we're expecting her back any day now." She clenched her gloved hands in front of her.

"Good, good..." His words drifted off as he focused on dusting under a doll.

She sensed his discomfort and forced a smile. The people in Winterfrost never spoke about Midwinter Haven, nor the magic folk that lived there which only made her more concerned. It was only about a day away through a steep mountain pass, or a week's ride the long way round. Yet few ever journeyed there. "Have a good day."

"May the season's blessings be with you." Fred gave a sharp nod.

"Same to you." She resumed her path for Sammy's, past the stall selling amulets and charms (not real magic, of course), the candle store, and the grumpy woman who sold cheese and never said hello back.

"Good morning, Mrs. Clark."

...Nothing. Not a word.

Elsie rubbed her gloved hands together, not yet acclimated to the higher elevation winter town, but was glad she, her sister, and their mum had returned a month ago. More than anything, she wanted to stay in this town and make it her home.

She arrived at Sammy's stall, a wooden market hut adorned with evergreens and red ribbons that matched all the other stalls, and poked her head around the back since the shutters were closed at the counter.

"All is well, Sammy?" Elsie inhaled the heavenly aroma of freshly baked pastries as she eyed them on the counter at the back of the cozy bakery. How Sammy whipped up so many treats in such a tight space she'd never know. Their own tea house wagon was a similar size, but they didn't need large ovens and stacks of trays, though their ingredients and tea collection rivaled Sammy's pantry inventory.

"Elsie! So lovely to see you." Sammy's smiling face popped up from the cupboard she was rummaging through. Her red hair was stuffed under a tight cap but spilled out the side in a frizz and bounced as she stood up and rested her hands on her rounded hips. "I s'pose you're seeking fruitcake before the crowds?"

"I am indeed. For Clara. She's not handling things well, so I thought I'd get some to cheer her up."

"Sweet of you. But I fear the cake won't be ready till this afternoon. Would you care for mince pies?"

Elsie's heart sank. Clara, their new assistant at Tia's Traveling Teas, had a strange obsession with this particular fruit cake, and Elsie needed her to stick around for the Midwinter rush.

"Not to worry, mince pies would be lovely. I'll take three please." It would have to suffice. Clara might not be happy, but Elsie's mouth watered thinking about them. These pies were her and her sister Marie's favorites: mini golden brown, butter pastries filled with plump dried fruits mixed with chopped almonds and walnuts and coated in warm spices like nutmeg, cinnamon, and clove—and the mixture steeped in brandy of course.

Elsie's stomach growled. When had she last eaten?

Sammy handed her the pies wrapped in brown paper in exchange for six coppers, and they wished each other a good day.

Hopefully, Clara had everything set up at the tea house. Not that Elsie expected that to be true. She upped her pace as she took to Main Street which ran parallel to Winterfrost Market Square.

The established shops and cafes along Main Street were already bustling with Midwinter tourists. They flocked for the cozy winter vibes, quaint village, and the lively ambiance of the Midwinter Festival. Elsie's mother brought them here every few years for a similar reason. Plenty of tourists meant plenty of tea, which is why it was odd that her mum hadn't yet returned to help.

It was time to start worrying.

After work she would follow up on her lead from a kind stranger, a traveler, she'd met at the butcher when buying soup bones. Apparently, he was the only person who was willing to talk about Midwinter Haven.

Elsie tried to push those thoughts away. Being patient was hard. Her boots clacked over cobbles as she passed thatched roofs and small piles of snow neatly shoved to the side. Horses trotted by, drawing grand carriages likely bound for one of the many inns.

"Els!" Nell called from across the street.

Elsie waved as her friend, who worked at a local inn, dodged a gap between two passing carriages.

"Bloody tourists blocking up the streets." Nell bustled up with handfuls of bags and drew Elsie into a hug.

Pressing her face into Nell's white cap that barely contained her blonde hair. Nell wore a plain wool dress with a brown cape over top, same as every day and same as the other servants at the Good Tidings Inn.

Unlike Nell, Elsie had a few dresses to choose from, at least. Today, she'd chosen her favorite green woolen dress which fitted her nicely at the top and was cinched at the waist. Yet, it was the red coat that she wore overtop she loved the most—it made her feel warm and at home anywhere.

Elsie leaned into Nell's warmth, savoring the embrace. "You'll get knocked over one of these days. You ought to be more careful."

Nell's cheeks were flushed red from the cold, likely matching Elsie's. "I am careful." Nell dropped one of her bags, then picked it up again.

Elsie took two of the bags out of her hands. "It seems we are both in a rush, can you walk and talk?"

Nell was already walking. "We ran out of linen. The inn is so full. I spotted you and wanted to check how you are faring. Any word from your ma?"

Elsie couldn't seem to escape talk of her mother, perhaps it was a sign. "No word. But I was chatting with Hob, the butcher, and a customer there overheard and gave me the name of a man who might be able to help."

"That's brilliant, Els! What does the man do?"

"I am not certain. Some sort of tracker, I suppose, but the lad said he'd be at the White Fox the next few nights if I want to meet him. Word is he's heading to Midwinter Haven."

Nell stopped and spun Elsie around to face her. "Midwinter Haven! Have you lost your wits? You're actually considering meeting a strange man in a pub who's going there? And the White Fox of all the dodgy pubs?"

Elsie dragged Nell to the side to dodge the chestnut cart they'd stopped in front of and apologized to the owner. "If he is the only person going to Midwinter Haven, I can't exactly be fussy now, can I?"

"I don't know. Seems unlikely anyone would journey so far north at this time of year. It's dangerous Els, all that magic and the *creatures.*" Nell shuddered.

Elsie did her best to hide the concern in her voice and linked arms with Nell to start walking once more. "I'm sure it's not that bad. People travel there all the time."

"Not people from here."

Elsie might not know a lot about magic and the north, but something about it made her curious. She'd met a few magical folks, witches mostly, while traveling around the Celestial Isles, though only in human towns. The witches tended to keep to themselves, and she could see why. People in Winterfrost were overly superstitious and close-minded, but surely the stories weren't all bad. "No, but traders and travelers journey regularly from the Eastern Road and make it back unscathed," Elsie said.

"My cousin's neighbor heard a tale from a solider who escorted a messenger to the Springfae Kingdom." Nell paused.

"And?" Elsie knew how these 'whispers on the wind' type stories changed with every telling. Especially when they got to Nell.

Nell shook their linked arms enthusiastically. "And he said that the King of the Winterfae Kingdom is ruthless and cruel, and he cut off the wings of a visiting fae for no reason at all."

Elsie nibbled her lip. Her mother had always told them tales of the fae; she even blamed them for Elsie and Marie's father's disappearance, but as far as Elsie could tell, there was no real evidence. They weren't even sure where he went missing, though, in the last year, their mother became convinced he'd disappeared in Midwinter Haven. Another reason to be concerned.

Nell continued, "I also heard that the Winterfae King sent his sons out on dangerous quests, and one of the princes hasn't returned. Folks are saying the king set him up to be murdered."

"Where'd you hear that one?" Elsie did her best to listen, but her mind was partly focused on what lengths her mother would go to to find the truth.

"From Lilly, the seamstress who heard it from Sid at the mill, who heard it from a traveler from down South."

"Well, I'm sure there is truth to it," Elsie said diplomatically.

"All I know is magic is too strong around this time of year to be messing with. If your ma is in Midwinter Haven still, I'll be praying to the angels for her."

"Thanks, Nell," Elsie said. Nell's heart was in the right place. "She's probably just delayed. Found a good spice dealer or something and is haggling them for a bargain."

How Elsie wished that were true.

"Or maybe she found a man and got swept up in a torrid love affair!"

"You've been reading too many romance books," Elsie said, not believing that would ever be an option. Since her father disappeared, Elsie's mother had never shown interest in other men. She was obsessed with their traveling lifestyle and her endless hunt for rare spices and teas, or what Elsie only worked out recently was a cover for finding out what happened to Elsie's father.

But after all this time, Elsie suspected it was delusion or wishful thinking. So much time had passed, and it was causing a rift between her and her mother. That and Tia didn't understand why Elsie wanted to live in one place and try to have a normal life.

"You never know." Nell winked.

Elsie was glad she'd found a friend in Nell.

Elsie shrugged, but her stomach clenched as she tried to block horrible thoughts of what might have really happened. "You never know," Elsie agreed. Nell was trying to make her feel better. She appreciated it, but she knew in her gut her mum was in trouble.

They turned down Fleetfoot Alley and stopped at the side door to the Good Tidings Inn. "You'll be careful, won't you?" Nell dropped a bag and pulled Elsie into a hug, which was nice of her. Hugs always cheered Elsie up.

"Course I will." Elsie's stomach growled at her again.

"You get some food in you. Can't have you wilting away." Nell picked up her bag, and Elsie piled the other two into her hand.

Elsie continued down the alley and was back at Winterfrost Market Square. She hastily unwrapped one of the mince pies and bit into the flaky pastry, savoring the butteriness as she darted between the rows of stalls. The fruit and cinnamon sent a comforting warmth through her as she dodged between busy vendors rushing about as they set up.

She neared their tea house, which was at the end of the row of market stalls—a perfect spot. It overlooked the southwestern corner of the square with a view of the giant evergreen tree at the southern edge, decorated with ribbons, dried oranges, and bells. At night it was lit with candles. South of the tree and the square was a man-made lake of ice that people loved to drift around on sharp blades attached to their shoes.

Tia's Traveling Teas wagon, painted with images of bright cups of tea and flowers, was parked behind the market stall they rented. Once they opened, there would be chairs and tables set up in front of the wagon around stone fire pits. Why hadn't Clara started setting them up?

Elsie ran when she noticed the black smoke pouring from the air vent in the top of the wagon, and a distinct, sickly smell of burned spices singed her nostrils.

Not again! Elsie broke into a run. Clara had burned their precious winterspice mix for the tea that people specifically came to them to try. There was nothing else that compared to its euphoric effect and comforting warmth of unique spices. How many times had she told her to only lightly cook it for fragrance? Twenty seconds! Not till it was black.

"Clara! What have you done!" Elsie flung open the door of the wagon.

"So sorry, Miss Elsie," Clara called from inside. "It's under control!"

"Oh, Clara. Not again." This day was not off to the start she had hoped for. *Keep it together, Elsie.* All she had to do was make it until tonight when she could meet this tracker and make a plan.

CHAPTER 2

KIT

"When I said I needed to go to town, I did not mean I wished to attend the healer. I need to order the box for the stone." Kit followed Thomas down the wooden staircase, careful not to let his left arm bump the railing. The pain in his arm was his constant companion, and he knew Thomas was right; Kit had put off seeing a healer far too long. But he wasn't sure a mortal healer was the answer.

"It'll be fun," Thomas called back. "You can order the box after."

Kit stretched his fingers making the tight flesh on his forearm burn even more. "Somewhere along the way, your idea of fun became warped," he jested but was glad Thomas forced him out of his room.

"Ay, *your* idea of fun is sitting on a cold rock looking for a rare double-breasted warble-garbler," Thomas said as they bypassed the busy pub on the ground floor. Kit stared in the door as they passed. A pint of ale would go down rather well right now. Instead, Thomas

13

led them down a darkened hall and heaved open the door to the slush of snow on the back porch of the White Fox Inn.

"I believe it was a double-banded Denison finch." Kit stepped outside and had to shield his eyes against the late afternoon sun. He breathed in the smell of civilization: wood-fire smoke, horses, freshly hung washing, and dampness. It had its own charm, not entirely unpleasant.

"Whatever it was, it wasn't fun." Thomas looked around.

"Pepper!" Kit called and let out a shrill whistle. They stood for a moment, waiting. The giant white wolfhound lumbered around the corner of the old inn, tail wagging, her black eyes wide with excitement when she spotted Kit. He couldn't help but smile; that was a face that always cheered him up. She'd most likely been out back waiting by the kitchen door for scraps. The White Fox might be a crappy inn, but at least the people were nice.

Pepper barked.

"Yes, we're going for a walk." Kit ruffled her head as she shoved up against his leg, then set off in two giant bounds. She stopped and looked back to make sure the two men were following.

Kit took a deep breath as they started walking. His 10-hour sleep hadn't done him much good. His magic was draining fast, so fast he could feel his glamour flickering.

Thomas was right. Kit needed help.

He'd worn a fur cap that covered his ears, just in case. Other than that, his appearance was almost mortal. The only thing that could hint he was fae were his eyes which inconveniently changed color with his surroundings. Right now, in normal outdoor light, they should appear blue like a blue jay.

Pepper barked back at him, checking he was still okay. He nodded to her to continue.

Another non-mortal problem was his facial features. He was careful with his appearance. His glamour took the sharp angles of his cheekbones and jawline and smoothed them to be more rounded, more friendly, more mortal. He was fortunate to be short for a fae, it allowed him to pass as tall for a mortal.

They walked in companionable silence up the alleyway watching Pepper investigate every pile of half-melted snow and rubbish she came across.

Kit adjusted his hat. His brown hair which he kept shoulder length was unkempt and tousled from being on the road and could do with some soap and a wash, but it allowed him to fit in with the mortals. When not wearing a hat, he tied the top half up with a piece of leather to cover the top of his ears, letting the rest fall to his shoulders.

He supposed in a few weeks' time he wouldn't have to worry about any of that anymore, that was if the healer could fix his arm. He suspected it was the wound causing his magic to drain.

Turning up at Snowspire Palace weak and wounded was not an option. According to his father's ultimatum, Kit had to return by Midwinter's Eve, which left him with a mere ten days of freedom. Freedom he now suspected would be dedicated to healing his arm. Time that would be better spent finding a way to keep the Bloodgate Ruby from his father.

"Thanks for doing this," Kit said as they turned onto Norfolk Street. A knot formed in his stomach as they neared the healers.

"Don't mention it. You put it off any longer, you'd be half dead on your way to Midwinter Haven," Thomas joked, but he might not be too far off.

They took a left onto Main Street. Kit did his best to keep up with Thomas and Pepper, but the pain in his arm mixed with exhaustion had him wanting to sit down for a rest already.

Pathetic. He'd traveled far across the Celestial Isles, all the way down the east coast and across to the Dwarf Kingdom in the south, and now that he was nearly back and this close to the end, he could barely manage the last stretch. He wondered if some of that might be in his mind but preferred to blame it on his arm.

Horses and carriages rumbled by, and tourists, here for the famous market, strode about as if they owned the place, looking for their next indulgent snack. Every direction he turned decorations caught his eye: evergreen garlands, bells, wreaths, red ribbons, candles. The mortals certainly tried, though it couldn't hold a candle to Midwinter Haven.

Kit walked right into Pepper and nearly tripped over her.

"We're here," Thomas said cheerily as they arrived at the healer's office, a large brick building with a black door.

Kit stroked Pepper's soft ear. "Best get it over with, then." But he didn't make a move to go in. His father always said he was a coward, weak; Kit hated proving him right.

"Want me to come in? I can tell it, just like it happened." Thomas crouched down and stabbed at the air with an invisible knife.

Kit smiled and shook his head. "As wonderful as your retellings of dwarf fights are, I think I'll be fine."

"No worries. Me and old Peps will grab a bite from that lovely pie saleswoman down the market. Right, Peps?"

Pepper barked; her tail slapped against the cobbled path.

Kit stepped into the healer's office. Fortunately, the healer had an opening, and he only had to wait ten minutes in the waiting area that smelled of herbs and vinegar.

He followed a woman wearing a white robe into a pokey room that had a round potbelly stove crackling in the corner. It was stifling hot.

"Take off your coat and hat, lovey," the healer instructed.

Kit closed his eyes for a second to shore up his glamour, took off his hat and his long oilskin coat lined with sheep's wool, and placed them on the spare wooden chair.

"I'm Healer Marberry. What might your name be, my dear?" she asked as she washed her hands in a basin near the stove.

"I'm Kit. Just Kit. Sorry." She didn't need more detail than that. Kit did not sit. He was too nervous. He focused his energy on investigating the many jars and contraptions around her room. "What are all these?"

"Herbs and medicines. I make most myself." Healer Marberry turned around. "Please put that down, sir. It is a delicate instrument."

He frowned at the metal device as he placed it down. Perhaps he should have tried to push through to Midwinter Haven, where the healers had magic. This whole setup looked rather primitive.

"Let's get to it. What brings you here today, lovey?"

"A wound by a blade. It occurred weeks ago but has not yet healed." Kit rolled up the sleeve of his shirt, revealing the linen bandage on his forearm.

He did his best to sit still as Marberry unwound it, her fingers expert and gentle, but the burning sensation grew stronger as she peeled off the bandage covering the wound. It was sticky, and the skin was angry red, like the sun was glowing out of it.

"This is no normal blade wound." The healer leaned in close, not repulsed but interested.

He winced. "I'm impressed you recognize that; few—" he was about to say mortals "—healers, would know it."

"I have seen many things and worked in many lands." She glanced up at him with a knowing look. "That is how I know you are fae." She grinned at him and threw his bandage in a pail on the ground.

His free hand went to his ear. No, still mortal.

"Your glamour holds true, young fae. But I have better eyes than most, and I saw it in the way you walked when you entered."

"Great, now I have to find a new way to walk," he joked. But a stone dropped in his stomach. Hoping she wasn't one of those mortals who enjoyed gossip or exposing fae.

She went to the shelf and reached for jars of herbs, lining them along the wooden bench. "No need to make yourself ill at ease. I won't tell a soul."

He cleared his throat, suddenly aware of the danger he was in and how much he needed her help. "What is it about my walk that is a giveaway, might I ask?"

"It's the confidence. For someone dressed as a traveler, you walk with an air of grace and elegance one would not normally possess from traveling the hard roads north for weeks."

He didn't feel as though his walk was graceful or confident. He felt like he might topple over any minute. It was an unfamiliar state to be in and deeply unsettling. Oh well, no secrets now. A strange stillness settled over him, a relief from someone knowing after a year of hiding who he was. "It wasn't my glamour, at least. The problem is it's been failing. I thought it might have something to do with the wound."

She paused. "What blade were you struck with? Did you get eyes on it?"

"It was a dwarfish blade. The little bastard came out of nowhere." Anger flushed through his blood. It had been his own fault; he wasn't fast enough.

She shook her head, put two jars back, and went to a cupboard under the bench. "I'm sure that would have been a sight to see. Cursed perhaps?" She turned his arm at different angles, studying it with narrowed eyes.

He had been refusing to admit it was cursed. Kit did his best to sit still in the hard wooden chair and not look at his arm. Disgusting. The blade had sliced clean across his forearm that Thomas had neatly stitched. It was not large, but what it lacked in size it made up for in highly distracting pain. He usually healed quickly, and this was a weakness he couldn't afford, not when he was returning to court.

"Have you treated it in any way?"

"I attempted to use a healing crystal, but I assumed it was depleted, as it did not work. Other than that, I've been going through swathes of bandages that my friend has been kind enough to change."

"I will wash the wound and make up a poultice for you to put beneath the bandage each day. Do you have someone to help with this?"

"Yes." For now, he had Thomas at least.

"I hate to admit this is beyond my healing skills."

His heart sank. "I need a fae healer, don't I?" Exactly what he didn't want.

"I believe so. You are from Snowspire, the Winterfae Kingdom I assume?"

"Indeed, but I prefer not to go there. I could go to Midwinter Haven instead." Midwinter Haven was just over the Sylan Mountains, usually a day's walk from Winterfrost, but in his current condition, perhaps longer. Even though Midwinter Haven held a special place in his heart, it bordered the Winterfae Kingdom, and as soon as Kit stepped foot in the town, his father would find out that he'd returned.

Kit watched as she pulled jars from the shelves. "Is there a way I can recover my strength before I leave?"

"I can give you some herbs for tea that will restore your strength. I would suggest rest, but I think getting to someone with expertise in such matters should be a priority."

"I hadn't planned on leaving for another week."

"I recommend you go tomorrow." She glanced at his arm and went back to pounding something green in a large stone mortar.

Oh dear, so soon. He should have heeded Thomas' advice earlier. Just thinking about the trek over the mountains made him feel exhausted.

"May I ask what magics you possess?"

Kit checked his ears once more. "Could that have something to do with it?"

"No idea. I'm just curious."

"The usual ice and water magics of the Winterfae. Basic glamours." He left out the plant magic he got from his mother's side. No need to make it too obvious who he was.

After a stinging bath of strange liquid to his arm, Healer Marberry slathered on her green gooey poultice that smelled of mint and spooned the rest into a jar for him to take away.

With his arm wrapped in a fresh bandage, he gave the healer his thanks and paid her a gold piece, far more than the standard fee. Not as a bribe to keep quiet, but because she hadn't judged him or kicked him out.

He stepped onto the street and his hand slipped into his pocket, checking that the crimson stone was still there. It was that blasted stone that got him wounded in the first place and a burden that weighed heavy on his shoulders. Should he give it to his father as ordered? It was the whole point of his quest to Stonehelm in the Dwarf Kingdom. But now that he knew the true nature of the Bloodgate Ruby, that it was the key to breaking the protective wards of Midwinter Haven, he couldn't just hand it over. Even if he was bound by a blood oath.

In his father's hands, it could destroy too many lives.

CHAPTER 3

ELSIE

E lsie poured the fragrant winterspice tea into a rounded pottery mug. "That'll warm you up, Mrs. Baker. Enjoy." Their famous tea with the secret ingredient was known for its unique spicy warmth, perfect sweetness, and the calming, euphoric feeling that came after drinking it.

"The air's got that bone-chilling cold about it tonight. You best be careful, girl," Mrs. Baker said, looking around with narrowed eyes.

A cold shiver skittered down Elsie's spine. She couldn't help but think of her mum. But hopefully tonight she would have a plan. Just a few more hours till they closed up and she could go meet the tracker. She just had to find a way to tell her sister, Marie.

Marie was on top of things with customers for the after-dinner rush, so Elsie quickly set about washing more teacups and spoons before they ran out.

"We might need another batch of winterspice tea tonight. We're nearly out," Marie called over her shoulder.

Elsie dropped a cup but caught it just in time. That was the last thing she needed. "Oh, sugar, I was supposed to make that up this afternoon, but clearing up Clara's mess this morning threw my whole day out of kilter."

"At least she found a new pot in time to replace the ruined one." Marie wiped a strand of sleek black hair from her forehead with the back of her hand as she spun around gracefully setting a teapot on the bamboo tray.

Elsie searched the cupboards in their market stall, her two black plaits swaying in her face as she leaned down. She should have pinned them to her head earlier. Elsie and Marie had the same hair color, but Marie's was always much straighter. She preferred to wear it in a long braid that trailed down her back with two sharp strips that framed her face. Elsie preferred her hair in two braids, either left loose or circling her head like a crown.

Elsie sighed, she already knew what ingredient they were missing for the tea, and she wasn't going to find anymore here; hopefully, there was a little of the rare powder left in the wagon.

"Looks like we're out of ingredients for it." Elsie stood up too fast and felt the air rush by as Marie swept past her with another teapot.

"Careful, Els. You're all over the place today."

Elsie took a calming breath and gripped the bench wondering how to bring up the topic of the tracker with Marie.

"Sorry. I forgot to eat lunch; that might be it." Elsie glanced around, forgetting what she was doing next.

"Never mind the spiced tea for now. Can you warm two teapots for me?" Marie asked far more kindly than usual. Elsie really must look a mess if Marie was being this nice when ordering her about.

23

"Certainly." Glad to be given a task without having to think, Elsie ladled hot water, not quite boiling, from the large iron pot on the stove into their smallest-sized earthen pottery teapot and swirled it around. She watched Marie out of the corner of her eye as her sister took more customer orders.

Elsie recognized the worried expression on her sister's face that would match her own in a mirror. They had the same large brown eyes, freckled cheeks, and pouting mouth. At twenty-one, Marie was just a year younger than Elsie, and they were often mistaken for twins. Marie was slightly taller and thinner and did a lot less smiling than Elsie. They both had the same dark rings under their eyes.

Elsie tipped the water from the teapots and set them on the tray ready for Marie.

Marie spun around in the small space. "I wish Mum would hurry back. Her secret ingredient certainly isn't worth all this trouble." Marie measured a scoop of their dwindling winterspice blend and sprinkled it into the teapots.

Elsie used the small ladle to fill them with hot water and placed the earthen cap on the pot with a louder-than-intended clink while Marie placed cups on the tray.

"I want to go look for her," Elsie blurted out. There, she had said it.

Marie frowned but said nothing. Elsie didn't miss the forced smile as Marie added a small sand timer to the tray of tea and slid the tray to the customer.

"There you are, sir. When the sand runs out, the tea will be perfect to pour."

As soon as the customers were gone, Marie spun around, hands on her hips, looking a lot like their mother.

"You want to find Mum? To go to Midwinter Haven?"

Elsie swallowed. "Yes. I have the name of a man who might be going there."

Marie grabbed a tea towel and began drying teacups a little too enthusiastically. "No. No. You cannot go there. It's too dangerous."

Elsie went back to washing cups while there was a lull in customers. "We don't know that. Most of the stories about the North are just that, stories. No one knows what it's like there because of all the ridiculous gossip."

"But there are witches...and werewolves...and vampires... and *fae*. How could that not be dangerous? And Mum hasn't returned when she should have been back by now?" Marie paused. "What if she was right about Father; what if he really was taken by the fae all those years ago?"

"We can't know that. Mother's stories seemed so far-fetched before. It's hardly the time to start believing them after all these years." Though Elsie stiffened at the thought of her mother being right. What if the fae had taken him? What if they had their mum now?

"We have to be logical, consider it. I can't lose you too." Marie slammed down a teacup and looked away.

This was suddenly far too real. Were they really considering the stories were true? "You won't lose me, Marie." They never spoke such thoughts aloud. Elsie moved before she realized what she was doing and snatched the tea towel out of Marie's hand and hit her with it sending bubbles flying around them.

Marie batted the towel away and shook her head like she pitied Elsie. They often fought, minor tiffs mostly, but this time Marie wasn't rising to the challenge. "You can't make promises like that."

Elsie checked there were no customers before she spoke, lowering her voice. "Just because Father disappeared, doesn't mean she will too. She simply went looking for the ingredient for the spiced tea."

"Same as Father. Apparently, the same place too." Marie threw her hands up. "I don't know what Mum found out, but she kept it from us trying to protect us, and you can't go after her."

Elsie shook her head. "It might not be true. She's been looking for that bloody ingredient in every town for years; it might have nothing to do with Father."

"What if she found him? What if she decided she wanted a new life wherever he was? She's always saying how staying in one place means trouble in the long run."

Elsie froze, realization washing over her. Could that be true?

"What is it, Els? You're as white as a snow goose."

"Before she left. I told her I wanted to stay in Winterfrost. We argued because I wanted a dog and a cottage and a real tea shop, not even a tea shop on Main Street, just a small tea shop. I saved up my coin for the rent, even." Elsie took a deep, pained breath. "She said just that, how staying in one town meant trouble."

Marie was silent for a moment. "It's not your fault, Els. She wouldn't have left on a whim because of that. If she planned it, she'd have known for a while."

A customer came, and they worked in silence setting out cups, measuring lavender and chamomile, and pouring water as the tension between them rose like a kettle about to boil over.

As soon as the customer walked off with their tray, Elsie got in first. "I'm going to go meet this man tonight—"

"No!" Marie cut in, setting the teapot she was holding down with a clatter.

"If you let me finish." Elsie took a breath giving Marie time to focus and glower at her. "I will just talk to him. See what he has to say then speak with you regarding a plan."

Marie's shoulders lowered, and she leaned against the back bench in front of the stove. "Fine. But you must promise me you'll make no agreement to go with him. You can't leave me here." Marie turned away.

Elsie noticed the fear in Marie's voice she did well to hide, but Elsie knew her too well. "I'll make no such promise, but I will do my best to get him to find her."

"Good." Marie nodded as she busied herself finding fresh candles.

"You'd be fine if I left you here. You can manage the tea house with Clara, and we have other applicants you can hire." Elsie gripped her tea towel, watching Marie.

"I know that perfectly well. I'd just rather not have to."

Elsie nodded, wishing it didn't have to be this way. But she had every intention of returning, and Marie would be safest here. "I know."

"You will be careful, won't you, Els?" Marie didn't look up from the counter where she switched out the old candles.

"Aren't I always?"

Marie laughed and shook her head as she wiped the bench around the fresh candles. "No, you are far too friendly. You need to be more wary, especially of strange men you meet in the pub."

Elsie forced herself to sound light-hearted so as not to cause any more worry. "I've met many men in pubs before. This isn't my first time."

"I know, and I'm not entirely convinced you know what you're doing," Marie said. "That last one was very odd."

Elsie grinned and put away some of the clean teacups on the hanging rack above her head. "Anyway, you needn't worry about me. I am not getting tangled up in any fruitless dalliances in this town. I want to stay here." That shouldn't be too hard. Elsie had far more important things to concern herself with anyway. Like finding their mum.

Marie snorted. "How long will that last?" She set about making tea, presumably for the two of them since there were no customers.

"It will last until I find the right man. I am perfectly capable of being happy on my own." Elsie set two cups in front of Marie.

Marie poured the steaming liquid into the teacups. "Good luck with that, then. But you're a lodestone for the unattainable or those wild-at-heart, mad types."

"I am not." Elsie crossed her arms. How dare Marie know her so well?

Marie sipped her tea. "Whatever you say. How about you go grab a bite now while it's quiet? We're well past dinner. Who knows, your dream man might be out there now," she teased.

"Perhaps he is." Though Elsie wouldn't know it. The only man she needed to be thinking about was the one who would help find her mum. Elsie sipped her tea quickly. She could do with a bite to eat, something to tide her over until she went to the pub.

CHAPTER 4

ELSIE

Elsie stood in line at the sausage stand. The man at the front was arguing about how much sweet mustard was the right amount for a sausage, and the woman beside him seemed to think sauerkraut was the only way to go.

Resigned to a longer-than-usual wait, Elsie sighed. Marie was wrong about their mum. She knew it. She would never have stayed away without telling them. But Elsie would do as she said, and after they packed up for the night, she would meet this tracker at the pub and see if he would search for their mum on their behalf.

Her stomach rumbled. Maybe another food option would be better tonight, one without a line. She turned and crashed into an extremely large white dog behind her.

"Sorry about that." She suddenly felt silly apologizing to a dog. The dog didn't react, and despite its formidable size, it had a friendly face and perked up a giant floppy ear.

Elsie looked around. No one was standing with the dog who appeared to be waiting in line behind her. "Do you have a master about?"

The dog, who was some sort of wolf hound with a shaggy white coat, stared up at her, its tongue hanging out with drool dripping from its enormous mouth.

"Anyone lost a dog?" Elsie called out. The five people in line turned around and all shook their heads, several frowning at the dog. No one walking by stopped.

"I'm certain your owner will be back soon." Elsie stayed in line, and when it got to her turn, she ordered a sausage that came in a small bread roll that was easy to grip. She spooned some sweet mustard on top, coating it in just the right amount.

"Thanks, Lyle, see you tomorrow."

"Have a good one, Elsie," Lyle replied and leaned over the counter. "That your dog?"

She shook her head. "I think he's hungry, though."

"Ay, looks like he could eat a horse, that one."

The dog gave a tiny whine as he eyed Elsie's sausage. "I don't think I should feed you. Your owner may not approve." She took a small bite of her sausage to subdue the hunger, then spotted a leather collar around the dog's hairy neck.

"May I read your collar, please?" She walked a short distance from the sausage stall so as to not be in the way. The dog followed and sat in front of her on the cobbles where she held out her non-sausage hand for it to sniff. "I'm Elsie, pleased to meet you. Can I see your collar for a moment?"

The dog seemed satisfied with the introduction, and she gave it a pat on the head to test the waters. The dog looked up at her with sweet brown eyes and wagged its tail when she stroked its head. "You're just a big softy, aren't you?" She leaned over to reach the collar and twisted it but couldn't find any name. As she stood back up, the dog let out a booming bark, and Elsie jumped back. Her sausage slid from the bun, and she jerked her hand, splashing mustard down her beautiful red coat. The sausage fell with a plop onto the hard cobbles.

The dog was already on it and gulped down the meat in two bites.

Elsie groaned, but it had already disappeared. Her stomach growled in response. She ought to remember to eat earlier in the day. Perhaps that was the lesson here.

"You there! Step away from my dog!"

Elsie glanced around, trying to work out where the angry voice was coming from. Then she spotted him. A man in a long oilskin traveler's coat pointed right at her. He stormed up to them. His hair was tousled and unkempt but suited his rugged traveler look. As did his tall, lean athletic build that might be that of a warrior if he weren't dressed so poorly. And gosh, those blue eyes... Had she ever seen such a vivid color before?

Elsie! Focus.

Elsie stood her ground. She wasn't about to be bullied for trying to help. "Is this your dog, sir? He ought not be left unattended like that."

"*She* was not unattended. I told her to wait outside the craftsman's wagon for me." He tapped his leg, and the dog trotted over and sat at his side.

"Well, you can't expect a dog to wait patiently where there are all these temptations about." Elsie held up her empty bun.

"Not when there are people like you willing to feed her and lure her away."

"Excuse me, *sir*. I'll have you know she tricked me into dropping my sausage, and I wasn't about to run off with her."

"I saw you luring her away with that sausage."

"I was doing nothing of the sort." Elsie's voice raised, and she consciously lowered it. "She was all sad and hungry with those big eyes. I was going to try to find her master."

"Well, here I am. Thank you for the noble gesture," he said sarcastically as he looked over the dog as if Elsie might have done something to her.

"Perhaps you should look at getting a rope to tie her." She locked eyes with him, and, really, such a shade of deep blue should be illegal; it was so distracting.

He glared back at her as if a leash was the most insulting thing he'd ever heard. "How would you like to be tied up? I would never lower her to such treatment."

Instead of the flare of indignant anger she was expecting, a curl of warmth threaded through her belly. She paused in confusion for a second. No, Elsie! Stay focused.

She cleared her throat. "I am certain I would not enjoy that." It did not come out as assertive as she intended. "But dogs become accustomed, and it is for their safety."

He went to cross his arms, then winced as if in pain, holding his arm to his chest. "Pepper refuses to be restrained, and I respect her wishes."

"Pepper told you that, did she?" Elsie scoffed.

"She did." His face was dead straight.

"Well, isn't she so clever," Elsie said. Pepper smiled up at her with a lolling tongue as if she'd done nothing wrong; that was a face that was hard to say no to. She fought the urge to ignore Mr. Arrogant and ruffle the dog's head, but in the interest of self-preservation, she didn't, thinking Pepper's master wouldn't take too kindly to that.

The man shook his head. "You've got mustard on your coat, by the way. Come, Pepper." He turned and walked off with Pepper right at his heel.

"Nice to meet you, too," she mumbled. As Elsie looked down at her stained coat and the sad empty roll in her hand, tiny snowflakes fell on it, melting instantly. She let out a heavy sigh. What an unpleasant man.

"I think I'll be needing another sausage, Lyle," she called out and turned to see Lyle shaking his head. He had been watching the whole time.

"You were just trying to help. Nothing wrong with that. It's on the house." He held up a steaming sausage in his tongs.

This day really was not going as planned. Hopefully meeting the tracker would turn things around.

CHAPTER 5

KIT

K it slid into the hard chair at the White Fox Tavern, and Pepper lay down at his feet. No one had said she couldn't be in the pub, so it seemed acceptable, and after her recent trauma, he wanted to keep her close.

"There you are!" Thomas called from the doorway and bounced into the seat across from Kit, slamming down his pint of ale.

"You're rather chipper. Good day?" Kit asked.

"It certainly was. I've managed to get myself a last-minute stall at the market. Can you believe it?"

"I'm very glad to hear it will work out. I told you it would, didn't I?" He meant it. Thomas was more dedicated to his cause selling buttons and sewing goods than anyone he had ever met.

"Ay, that you did, Kit." Thomas frowned. "Got that medicine tea of yours?"

"I've ordered a teapot of water to brew the herbs the healer gave me." He patted the bag of herbs on the table.

"And that old barkeep agreed to that? You must've worked some magic on him." Thomas took off his wool hat, released his tangle of red hair, and took a large drink of his ale.

"No magic whatsoever," Kit said honestly, not that he had a choice in that matter. Fae couldn't lie, and his magic couldn't persuade people to do anything. Unlike his brother, Anders, who had a knack for controlling others.

Thomas didn't know Kit was fae, or if he did, he had never bought up the subject. They'd met at a pub in Middlemarch and had traveled together since. Thomas joked about magic as if it were normal. Most mortals weren't that easygoing.

"However, I promised I would buy dinner and a pint later, so he agreed to it," Kit said.

Thomas glanced up at the dinner specials: beef stew or cabbage soup. "Dinner sounds like a fine idea. Though he's taking his time boiling that water. Probably no one's ever ordered a teapot in here before." Thomas chuckled.

The room was full of drunks already, happy ones at that, but Kit doubted they ever ordered tea. Looked like locals mostly.

"While I remember, I was talking with the butcher. Mr.... can't remember the bloke's name, but when we were talking, a lady came up asking about a tracker." Thomas took a large swig of his beer.

"Was there more to this story?" Kit asked. Thomas had a tendency to go off track.

"Ay, there was. I told them you were a tracker."

Kit clenched his teeth. "Why would you mention me? I'm not a tracker."

"Well, you tracked down that rare stone for your dad well enough."

"I already knew roughly where that was."

"And you found our way up here when we had to go off the track and take the back path due to those blokes trailing you."

Kit shook his head. "Again, I'd done my research and knew there was another way."

"Ay, but you've got an instinct for it. I can tell. Like how you're so good at spotting birds."

Kit let out a slow breath. Thomas had a tendency of over-enthusiasm, not to mention a loose tongue.

"What was this woman wanting to track?"

"Can't recall exactly. I was eying up some fine bones for Pepper at the time."

"Try." Kit did his best not to get cross at Thomas. He was always trying to help. But Kit didn't need extra people involved in his affairs right now. Not when it might put them in danger.

"It was something about Midwinter Haven. I said you were heading up there. She was looking for something... or was it someone? I forget. Anyway, I said we were staying here."

"So, she's coming here?" Kit wished he had ordered an ale.

"I told her we would be here if she wanted to stop in." Thomas shrugged but seemed more concerned with seeing what food the neighboring table had ordered.

This day hadn't been the best, and he didn't want to make it worse by getting angry. He would just have to see if she turned up. The pain in his arm made him short-tempered. Where was his blasted tea?

"How did you go at the market?" Thomas asked.

Kit's hand went to his pocket. "Good. I got the box for the stone, but I had a rather unpleasant encounter with a woman who tried to lure Pepper away."

"She did not!" Thomas slammed down his drink; he had the best overreactions, and Kit couldn't help but smile.

"She claimed she was going to find her owner, but I swear she fed Pepper a sausage." Pepper's ears perked up at her name, or perhaps it was the word sausage. Kit reached down to stroke her ear.

"I'm sure it would have been a misunderstanding. Was she a pretty lass?"

"That's neither here nor there."

"Perhaps she was trying to gain your attention?"

No, that couldn't be the case. Though she certainly was pretty, her cheeks rosy from the chill of the night, and the way she smiled at Pepper, a bright smile that went all the way to her eyes. He shook his head.

"I doubt that. She looked at me with such a glare." He saw her brown eyes still right there at the front of his mind, piercing into his soul, accusing him of mistreating Pepper. As if he ever would, Pepper was everything to him. She had been a gift to his father from the Elven Kingdom when he was a child. And when Kit realized no one wanted her, he gladly adopted the tiny snowball of a puppy as his own.

The old barkeep marched over, a teapot in one hand and a chipped cup and saucer in the other. "Found these, it's the best you'll be getting here, I'm 'fraid." He slammed the teapot down next to Kit.

"Very kind of you, sir. Much appreciated," Kit said as the man muttered something under his breath and walked off, gathering empty tankards from neighboring tables as he went.

Kit opened the small leather drawstring bag of herbs and took a sniff. He wrinkled his nose.

"Bad, are they?" Thomas said.

"I'll be needing an ale to wash it down." Kit shook out about a tablespoon of dried sticks and unfamiliar flower buds, into his palm. He took off the teapot lid and dusted them in with his finger. Now to wait. Should he order an ale now?

"So, what's your plan then? Heading back tomorrow, I suppose?" Thomas said, his voice hinting concern.

"I have little choice, according to the healer." He didn't want to worry Thomas any further with the truth of how terrible he felt.

Thomas nodded along. "Best to listen to the healer. She knows what's what. And no need to worry about me here. I'm all set now."

"I've been grateful for your company, Thomas. I wish I had more time here, and I'm not sure when I'll be traveling south again."

"Well, you let me know when that wonderful bird book of yours is finished. I'll be happy to tell people I was there with you when you spotted all them birds. Even if I didn't know what half of them were."

"I'm going to do my best to complete it." He was most determined. Though if he stayed in the palace, it would be difficult, his father had no tolerance for 'wasteful childish fancies'. And that encompassed Kit's two major passions: bird watching and drawing. The book he was putting together, a compendium of all the bird species of the Celestial Isles, he'd tried to keep secret from his father, which had not worked at all.

Pepper's tail was hitting Kit's leg. He glanced down at her to see where she was looking. His stomach sank as he caught a flash of a red coat, a very familiar coat he had seen not so long ago in the market.

"Pepper, calm down." He hissed and gave her a few firm pats on the shoulder, hoping the woman wouldn't turn around from the bar.

Thomas turned to see where they were looking.

"Oh, that's the lady. The young miss looking for a tracker." Thomas sat up straighter and attempted to comb down his hair with his fingers as he nodded to Kit.

Kit shook his head at Thomas. "That's her. The woman from the market."

"Oi, Miss. Over here!" Thomas called out before Kit could stop him.

"Blast it," Kit muttered under his breath.

CHAPTER 6

ELSIE

E lsie stomped her boots at the door to get off the caked snow and wandered into the pub cautiously. She hadn't been here before but knew locals and seasoned travelers frequented it, rather than tourists who preferred the fancier inns and upmarket restaurants on Main Street for their late supper.

Still, it was warm and light and seemed to have a jolly atmosphere. No one was fighting, but plenty of loud drunks yelling their stories over one another, and a strong smell of beer and pipe smoke hovered in the air.

Nerves fluttered in the pit of her stomach as she walked toward the bar. She kept her conversation with Marie at the front of her mind; she would act professionally so the tracker would take her seriously, and she would ask him to find her mother. All she could do was ask. How hard could that be?

"Evening, Miss. What can I get ya?" the large barman asked through his bushy mustache.

"An ale please, just a small one," she said. It felt like an ale kind of situation. Tea or even sweet mead wouldn't cut it here; a little liquid courage was always a good thing. That's what people said, did they not?

The barman nodded and set to work.

Elsie dusted some lingering snow from the shoulder of her red coat. Glad she had managed to remove the mustard stain from earlier. She cleared her throat. "I'm here to meet a man. I believe his name is Kit. It was Hob who said he might be here," Elsie said.

"That's 'im over there." The barman nodded past Elsie's shoulder as he cleaned a silver mug with a rag, and she turned to see where his gaze landed. Elsie stifled a groan. Of course, it was *him*. The man from the market with the blue eyes, adorable dog, but unfortunate personality. He was staring into his cup and hadn't seen her. "You are certain?" Her voice came out as a squeak.

"Ay, that's Kit. One with the teapot next to 'im."

Oh, sugar. How important was it that she found her mother? Perhaps her mother was walking in the door of Peony Cottage, where they were staying, right now and would have a go at Elsie when she got in for being all uptight and worried. It could happen...

"Can I change that order to a pint, please?"

She counted the five coppers and handed them to the barman, then watched as the golden liquid filled the tankard, leaving a layer of soft foam on top.

The barman slid it over to her, and she sipped the bitter ale, waiting for the liquid to hit her stomach to build up that courage. How long would it take for the buzz of warmth to reach her mind? She needed it to soften her racing thoughts if she had to go over there and talk to that disagreeable man. Was he truly the only tracker around?

She glanced around the room. Hob had said she'd be lucky to find anyone traveling north to Midwinter Haven, and she knew he was right. No one in their right mind wanted to risk going beyond the human borders this close to Midwinter. It was only two weeks away, and even this far south, there was a hint of magic in the air. She tried not to think about what it might be like beyond the border—better not to.

She glanced over her shoulder. Chances were, he was going to refuse her straight away, anyway. Even if she were giving away their special spiced tea for free, she suspected he would refuse her. *Go on, Elsie. Just act professional and stick to the facts. Get it over with so he can be gone as soon as possible.*

"Oi, Miss! Over here," a voice called out, and she spun around. It was the young man she'd met at the butcher's.

Her heart jumped a little when she saw Pepper under the table. The cheerful dog's tail slapped against the hard chair and into her master's legs.

Eek, she had been spotted! This was it. She had to go over there now.

She walked up with her shoulders back and smiled at Pepper, but didn't dare reach down to pat the dog. "Hello, again."

"It's you," the man, apparently named Kit, said.

"Yes, it is me." She kept her expression neutral but had a few choice things she'd like to say to him about his manners and dog ownership.

The man with red hair she'd met at the butcher stood up. "What my friend means to say is welcome and please join us?" He pulled out the chair next to him with a genuine smile.

She very much wanted to turn around and walk right back out, but out of politeness and her desperate need for answers, she placed her ale on the table and lowered herself to the chair as she thanked the man.

Pepper stood up and licked her hand, then lay down next to Elsie's chair. Elsie stroked the dog's head, a small victory.

"I'm Thomas, and this is Kit." Thomas gestured to Kit across the table who was pouring himself tea. A strange thing to be doing in a pub, but she was all for tea and was not one to judge.

"Nice to meet you both, officially. My name is Elsie Fielding." She resisted the urge to tuck her stray hair behind her ears and look down. Instead, she focused on Thomas.

"I believe you two also met earlier this evening," Thomas said with a cheeky grin on his face.

"Yes." Elsie sat up straight. She would take the high road on this, not because she needed Kit's help, but because she was a good person. "An unfortunate misunderstanding. I apologize, sir. I was not trying to steal your dog."

He looked up from his tea, his eyes the same midnight blue as before, but now they had speckles of gold that danced with the firelight. She hadn't noticed that the first time.

"If you say so. I apologize for being so rude. It has not been the best day." His voice was sharp.

"I'm sorry to hear." That wasn't the answer she had expected. She had been expecting a fight. She clasped her hands in her lap.

With a softness in his eyes, Thomas looked at his friend. "Kit's arm's been giving him trouble."

Kit glared at Thomas as if he hadn't wanted to share that personal detail, but Thomas remained oblivious.

Kit took a sip of his tea and scrunched up his nose. "By the gods, what is in this vile concoction?" He wiped his mouth.

"May I?" Elsie asked. Anything tea-related and her curiosity always won out.

Kit nodded and pushed the teapot toward Elsie. She plucked off the lid, raised the silver basket of tea above the porcelain edge, and sniffed it. "It's got white willow in it. The bark makes it bitter. It will take away pain."

It also had several other medicinal ingredients she was familiar with, but she didn't want to appear a know-it-all. She lowered the basket back in and put the lid on the teapot.

"By the Ancient Mother, it is certainly bitter." But he drank the rest of his cup and poured another.

An odd expression. A follower of the old gods of the land, perhaps. Most peculiar.

"Are you a healer?" Thomas looked at her in awe.

Elsie smiled and shook her head. "By the angels, no, nothing like that. My mum owns a traveling tea house, Tia's Traveling Teas. You might see it in the market. I know a lot about tea, that's all."

"How wonderful. I myself am a marketman as of this afternoon." Thomas took a large swig of his beer and puffed out his chest.

"What are your wares?" Elsie asked.

"All your sewing needs, buttons in every color, fine threads, and the sharpest needles you ever did see."

"One can never have enough buttons. I'll tell my sister, Marie, to seek you out. She has a great love of sewing," she said. Winning Thomas' favor might help her with his unreasonable friend.

"Grand idea," Kit said. "But I need to get this taste out of my mouth. Thomas, Miss Fielding, would you care for another ale or a meal? They have a fine stew tonight," he asked, overly politely, as if it were an obligation, not a genuine offer.

"I'll go for a stew please, Kit," Thomas said right away.

Elsie was never one to pass up a free meal. "A stew sounds lovely, thank you. And please call me Elsie."

Kit stretched out his fingers as if testing his arm as he stood up. "Very good, *Elsie.*" He drew out her name in a way that gave her goosebumps in a pleasant way.

"Then we can get down to the reason you're here," Kit said as he turned to the bar.

CHAPTER 7

ELSIE

Elsie rested her hands in her lap, doing her best not to show how uncomfortable she was, though she relaxed a little when Kit left to go to the bar to order their meals.

"Don't mind him. He's upset because he has to leave tomorrow. Thought he'd 'ave another week here, but that arm of his needs seeing to."

"Is it that bad?" Elsie watched as Kit leaned on the bar. He was keeping his arm close to him.

"Ay, quite bad. The healer gave him these herbs, but he needs more than that. The wound's cursed, you see." Thomas nodded sincerely and took a swig of his drink.

Elsie didn't know whether to laugh or inquire further. "Truly, a cursed wound? I've never heard of such things to be true."

Thomas stared into his drink for a second as if thinking, then looked up. "It's true enough. He got the wound on a quest retrieving a particular stone for his father. But perhaps I wasn't supposed to mention it. Best keep that to yourself." He glanced in Kit's direction and muttered something to himself that sounded like a scolding.

"You mentioned he was going to Midwinter Haven?" Elsie asked, determined to get as much information before Kit returned to the table.

"'Tis true. That's where the best fae healers are. They've got all the healing crystals there."

"Healing crystals?" Perhaps she should be even more wary of him if he associated with the fae.

Thomas nodded and looked like he was trying to busy his lips with drinking, so he didn't talk more.

Even if he did know fae, she couldn't be fussy. Perhaps that would even help. "Do you think he'd be willing to look for my mother? I'd pay him, of course."

"That's something for you to discuss with him, miss. I could not say."

"Could not say what?" Kit appeared next to the table; his boot steps so silent Elsie hadn't even heard him approach.

Thomas' cheeks glowed red. "I was telling you before, Elsie here might be needing some help."

Kit placed a brown bottle and three pewter goblets on the table. "Thomas told you I was a tracker."

"He did." Elsie nodded and squeezed her hands together on her lap, sitting as straight as she could.

"I am sorry you have been misinformed. The only thing I know how to track is birds." Kit poured the amber liquid into the three goblets.

Elsie's chest squeezed tight. "But you *are* traveling to Midwinter Haven?"

Kit eased into the chair. She noticed it now, the subtle pain behind his eyes. He slid the two drinks to Elsie and Thomas and downed his in one go. "Yes, I leave at dawn tomorrow."

Elsie nibbled her lip. "That soon?" She took a sip of the drink to be polite. The sweet burn of brandy slid over her tongue and down her throat, and she did her best not to cough.

Kit nodded in recognition and poured himself another cup of his medicine tea and drank it down, followed by a chaser of brandy.

Elsie wasn't sure he was supposed to mix his medicine with drink but would not be the one to bring it up.

She took another sip, for courage. "It is not so much a tracker that I require. Rather, someone familiar with Midwinter Haven. You know the town?"

"I do."

"I was just hoping, since you are already going there, would it be possible for you to make some inquiries for me?" Her heart was racing. This was her one shot, and she was sure she was saying all the wrong things by the scowl on Kit's face.

"What sort of inquiries did you have in mind?" Kit leaned in.

"It's my mother, you see. She's gone missing, and I need someone to find out anything they can about where she might be."

"No," Kit answered abruptly.

Thomas sat there quietly, though he looked like he was holding himself back, wanting to speak.

Elsie held Kit's glare before it was cut off by their food arriving. He didn't need to be so rude. They thanked the servant who delivered their steaming wooden bowls of stew, a standard brown affair with a few rogue carrots and onions among the copious gravy and sparse chunks of meat.

Elsie waited a good few seconds before everyone had had their first bites. "What do you mean, no? Can you not hear me out before deciding so decidedly?"

The servant came back and plonked a bread loaf that sounded as hard as wood into the center of the table and retreated once more.

"I am not a detective. I can't find missing people. You ask too much." Kit ripped off a piece of the hard bread.

The panic was building in Elsie's chest. "I have no one else to ask. You are the only person I have heard of traveling north." She hated to sound so desperate, but at this point, she didn't care.

"So, I was your only option and last resort. How flattering."

"I would not have asked if I was not so desperate." She took in a shaky breath, determined not to let her frustration with this stubborn man get the better of her.

"The answer is no." Kit dunked his bread into his stew and didn't look up.

Elsie fought the sting of tears at the corner of her eyes, and instead of showing him how much he upset her, she ripped off a piece of bread and slammed it back down on the table.

"Now let's not ruin a perfectly nice meal. Elsie, how about you tell us about your ma?" Thomas glanced between the two of them. He was a sweet thing trying to get them to get on, but she feared it was a hopeless cause.

"My mother traveled to Midwinter Haven several weeks ago. She was seeking spices for our tea house, a rare ingredient we have nearly run out of. And a contact said she might find it at the Midwinter Haven market since we are yet to find it in the lower lands." It was best to leave out the parts about her father or the fae, she didn't want to come off barking mad right away.

Thomas nodded for her to go on.

Elsie lowered her spoon to rest by her bowl. "She said she would be no more than two weeks, but it is well past that now, and I fear something might have gone wrong—she may be in danger."

"What makes you say that?" Kit said.

"Because she always returns on time and, and—"

"You believe Midwinter Haven to be dangerous?" He leaned away.

"I don't know myself, but people around here say it is."

"Does the name *Haven* give you any reason to believe it is dangerous?"

"Names can be misleading."

"I assure you. It is not. Midwinter Haven is safer than anywhere in the huma...lower lands." Kit set his spoon on the edge of his bowl.

Elsie narrowed her eyes. He spoke very oddly. "And what makes you an expert?"

"I grew up near there."

"You did?" Elsie wasn't sure how to respond to that. She'd never heard of normal people living in the magic lands. His parents must be strange indeed. She composed herself.

"You know it well, then. Could you not make inquiries about my mother and send word back to me? I can pay you."

"It is not a matter of money."

Thomas leaned in. "What Kit means to say, is that we're sorry to hear about your ma. But with his arm and all, he's in great need of getting to a healer and has a special task for his father he needs to fulfill."

Kit rubbed his hand on his forehead. "What did I tell you, Thomas?"

"To stop blabbing your life story to strangers." Thomas didn't look the least bit sorry that time.

"He's right though," Kit continued. "I am otherwise engaged and will return to work for my father immediately."

"But you said your father isn't expecting you 'till Midwinter eve." Thomas slurped his stew.

Elsie bit the inside of her cheek to stop herself from smiling. Thomas was either really good at putting his foot in it, or he was trying to help her.

"Maybe you could take Elsie with you. You said yourself you wanted someone to travel with, and you need someone to bandage that arm. Elsie probably knows how to make that tea taste better, too."

Elsie sat up straight and shook her head. "Oh, I couldn't possibly go." Marie would not like that one bit, though part of her knew it was the right thing to do.

Kit smirked and leaned his good arm on the table. "Why not? You'll have me do your work, but you aren't willing to look for your mother yourself?"

"It isn't that. I would happily go, but I promised my sister I would not." Though finding her mother herself would be faster, and no one was more motivated than her. But to go with this man...

Kit paused, and a strange expression spread over his face. Like he knew something she did not. Her scalp prickled.

"I'll do it," Kit said, his gaze lingering a moment too long.

Elsie's heart skipped a beat. "You will?"

"On one condition." He leaned in closer, almost like he was challenging her.

Her breath hitched, and she struggled not to be drawn in by his intense stare. "And what might that be?"

"That you will accompany me."

A shiver ran down her spine. She had told Marie she would not go, but if this was her only chance, shouldn't she take it? She couldn't pass it up just because she found the man disagreeable.

She paused. It suddenly clicked in her mind that he did not believe she would go. He was attempting to call her bluff; merely challenging her for his own enjoyment.

"Certainly not." She met his stare, his challenge, and her cheeks warmed as she clenched her hands on her lap. Two could play this game.

"Why not? It is a fair request. You are the person who knows your mother best, therefore the person best to find her. I am offering to be a guide. More than generous, if you ask me, and I don't have to meet my father until Midwinter's Eve."

"Ay, a generous offer," Thomas piped up.

She considered it and knew she had to take him up on the offer. First, she needed to test him to see if he actually knew about Midwinter Haven. "I can't go on a journey with a stranger. And there are werewolves, and vampires, and witches, and *fae*!"

He laughed. His smile might have been charming under different circumstances, but he was laughing at her expense. Her eyes drifted to his arms, the muscles beneath his shirt were clearly defined. At least he would be able to protect her from whatever creatures they encountered, even if he was irritating.

"What? There are, are there not?" She glared at him. That was a perfectly reasonable question. He wasn't even taking her seriously, and she actually wanted to know if the fae were dangerous.

Kit shook his head looking strangely offended once he stopped laughing. "You've read too many fairy stories."

She drank the rest of her brandy in one gulp and set the goblet back down. Not that she was trying to impress him or anything.

"I'll have to discuss it with my sister, Marie. She doesn't want me to go." Marie would be fine without her, she knew that. It was just a matter of convincing her. The truth was, Elsie wanted to go. She wanted answers, but also to see the lands to the north before she settled in this town. She wanted to know if the stories of the fae were true.

"You're afraid," he stated. Not in a mean way this time, more like it was a fact.

"Of course, I am." The mix of brandy and beer was warming her blood quite nicely, making her bold, impulsive. "I've made up my mind. I want to go. But I need to speak with my sister first." She stared at him, seeing if he would backtrack and admit what he was doing. That he had no wish to take her along.

He stared back, the tension between them rising in a silent battle, and the air suddenly felt stifling hot.

"You know it will be an all-day walk, two if we are delayed for any reason." He reached for his cup as Elsie leaned forward.

"I am aware." She was also aware of how close his hand was to hers curled around her cup.

"And that we cannot bring a horse because of the steep crossing at the ridge of the Sylan Mountains."

She had not known that but wasn't about to back down. "I am accustomed to walking."

"Very well. I leave at dawn. You best start packing, unless you're afraid of a little adventure." His eyes lingered on hers. Another challenge.

She smirked internally. So, his pride won out, and he would be stuck with her, which she was certain he did not want. *Excellent work, Elsie.* Though it dawned on her that now she would actually have to go and somehow would have to explain it to Marie.

She leaned back in her chair, clutching her neglected ale that had lost all its foam, and took a few sips to think. This was her one shot, her chance to find her mum. If she passed it up, she would never forgive herself. She could do this.

"I'm staying at River View Cottages in Peony Cottage. I'll be ready at dawn." Elsie withheld a smirk.

Kit rubbed his temples. Oh, so he hadn't expected that. It was worthwhile solely for that delightful moment. Kit blinked slowly, his striking blue eyes drawing her in once more. She looked away quickly. She would need some sort of remedy against their effect.

"Good show." Thomas beamed as if he'd organized the whole setup.

CHAPTER 8

KIT

Snow fell lightly on the windowsill, bright against the midnight sky, and it was indeed after midnight according to the clock on the mantle in Kit's room at the White Fox Inn.

Kit closed his eyes to massage his temples, but a vision of that woman appeared, clear as day. Damn that woman for messing with his sleep. Why had he agreed to take her? It was almost as if his pride had tricked him. Or had she tricked him? Either way, this was not the position he wanted to be in. Guiding a mortal—he was a fool.

Squinting in the low light at the gear laid out on his narrow bed, Kit tried to ignore the pain in his arm, though it had been dulled by the tea.

The soft clatter of buttons clicking together merged with the crackle of the fireplace in the background as Thomas sorted his wares into small woven baskets in front of the fire. Kit didn't ask why Thomas did that there, but he knew his friend was worried about him and suspected that hovering around was his way of checking Kit was well.

Ah, there they were. Kit spotted the wooden box of elven water-color paints he was worried he'd lost. They were his first gift from the elves, and to that day he cherished them. They were special paints that never ran out and would be impossible to replace.

He placed them on top of his bird journal. That confirmed, he lit two extra candles. He might actually be able to see what he was doing now.

He glanced over at Thomas before opening the large leather drawstring pouch and slid the contents onto the bed. The long shards of crystals were each wrapped in velvet, and most had lost their glow already. Only two charged warding crystals remained, and four healing crystals—though, despite being charged, they had failed to work on his arm. Still, the warding crystals would be enough for one night in the wilderness if they needed them, and with any luck, they would make the walk all in one day. It all depended on how well Elsie could handle the trail.

"How are the wares, Thomas?" Kit tested his arm, stretching it out.

"Very well. I have enough to keep the crowds happy with these new styles the likes have not been seen in the North! These mother-of-pearl buttons are exquisite."

"That they are. Folks will appreciate the trek you made to source them."

"How goes the packing?"

"Well enough." Kit slid the crystals back into their individual tubes, padded with felt to keep them from touching.

"I can't believe you agreed to take Elsie with you. It's very good of you, Kit. I was sure you would say no. May I ask what changed your mind?"

Kit slid the watercolors into his bag, but his thoughts drifted to Elsie. The way her brown eyes sparkled with warmth when she laughed along with Thomas, and the playful smile that danced at the corners of her lips, waiting to shine through.

He scowled, frustrated he had let her take over his mind. He gripped his bird journal. The one thing he couldn't lose, he'd put far too much effort into it. "I may have messed up there. I had a thought, but I acted too quickly on it. In my heart, I didn't believe she would agree to come, anyway."

"She's a tough one, no doubt."

"Indeed."

"Well, tell me then." Thomas stopped his button sorting, his focus on Kit.

"What?"

"The brilliant thought you had about why you suddenly wanted her to go."

Kit sighed as he ran his palm over the leather of his journal. "I'm sure saying it aloud will sound more ridiculous."

"Spit it out."

Kit placed the journal on a piece of felt that still smelled of sheep's wool. Everything here did. "I thought that perhaps if I entered Midwinter Haven with her at my side, it could be a sort of disguise for me."

"So your father won't know you were back?"

Kit narrowed his eyes. Thomas picked up on far more than Kit liked to give him credit for. "Something like that."

Though after the way his father treated his last lover, he'd have to be extra careful, for Elsie's sake. This would not be a repeat of Marella.

"Is it because you're fae? You think as a pair of humans walking in, your father will never put it together that it's you."

Kit blinked as Thomas went back to sorting his buttons. "How long have you known?" And how was he so calm about this? From his experiences, mortals reacting to the fae was never positive.

"Long enough. No one carries around that many crystals like you do. It's a dead giveaway."

Kit shook his head. He thought he'd been so careful.

"You're a wonder, Thomas. Most would have run for the Kingswood by now if they'd found they'd be traveling with a fae."

"Most would. But I've met many folks in my time, and fae have never done me any wrong. I figured you'd be a useful companion with those crystals and all."

"Using me for my crystals. A wise move," Kit joked. His heart warmed knowing there was no tension between them on the subject.

Thomas looked up and grinned. "You'll protect young Elsie. I knew she'd be safe with you."

"You set this up, didn't you? You wanted her to go with me," Kit said, certain Elsie was a similar age to Thomas, perhaps a few years younger than Kit's twenty-five years.

"Ay, you need someone to watch out for you when I'm not there. You pretend to be all strong, but I see what the wound is doing to you."

Kit tipped his head in acknowledgment. Thomas knew a lot more than he let on. "It has weakened my powers considerably." He hated to admit it. Spoken aloud it made it more real somehow.

"And if something happens to you, at least she can go for help. It's all I ask. Even if you want to use her as a decoy for your father," Thomas said with a notable hint of disapproval.

"I won't use her. Just having her present will be enough. It will give me a week to think about what to do with the stone. Maybe I can find a way not to give it to my father." All he had told Thomas about the Bloodgate Ruby was that it was a rare object his father had sent him to find. He mentioned nothing of its unique magical properties to break wards.

"You'll know what's right when the time comes." Thomas stood up, admiring his button sorting.

"You're a good friend, Thomas."

"I know. Now I'll go get some hot water for you so you can make a tea before bed and rest like the healer said."

"Thank you," Kit said, feeling like a child with a nurse maid.

"At least Elsie will be able to make your tea right," Thomas added as he walked out the door.

CHAPTER 9

ELSIE

Ice crunched beneath Elsie's boots as she turned up the curved laneway toward the river. The snow glowed yellow from the oil lamps behind her, and she pulled her red coat tight around her.

The short walk to Riverview Cottages felt much longer in the dead of night. The bell had tolled midnight before she left, and guilt churned in her gut for staying out so long. Marie would be waiting up.

She turned under the archway over the gate. The skeleton vines of slumbering plants that covered it were adorned with red and green Midwinter ribbons.

At Peony Cottage, Elsie stamped her boots on the coarse mat to dislodge the caking snow and brushed off her shoulders.

The door swung open. "You're back," Marie said with relief.

"Sorry, I am later than I expected to be."

Marie pulled Elsie inside into the entryway. "Stop letting the cold in."

"You didn't have to wait up." Elsie shut the door behind her.

"I couldn't sleep worrying about what you were talking about with the tracker. Did he agree to it?" Marie hugged a blanket around her shoulders, her nightgown and slippers peeking out underneath.

Elsie peeled off her coat, and Marie grabbed it impatiently and hung it on the hook next to Marie's dark gray one while Elsie shuffled out of her boots and socks, swapping them for her sheepskin slippers that were waiting at the door.

"How about some tea?" Elsie said. Tea always eased bad news.

Marie walked over to the fire, poked some embers around angrily, and hung the kettle at the edge. Elsie removed her scarf and hung it over her coat, then moved to the small living area.

She went straight to the armchair by the fire and held her hands out to absorb the warmth back into her chilled blood.

Marie prepared tea at the kitchen bench against the back wall. Elsie trusted her to pick a good night blend.

She better get this over with. "Don't get cross with me, Marie, but the tracker offered to take me to Midwinter Haven, and I agreed to go."

Marie shook her head, her eyes darkened. "No. No way, you promised."

"I made no such promise, Marie. You must understand this could be our only chance at getting help to look for Mum."

"I'd rather have you here than lose both of you. What if the fae did take her and Father?"

"I don't have any plans to do anything dangerous. I will simply ask questions and find out where she might be."

"I can't believe you're doing this to me." Marie stormed to the other side of the small room and stared out the window.

Elsie sighed to herself, then got up, and using a cloth to grip the handle of the kettle, she lifted it onto the bench and poured water into the teapot, swirled it around then tipped it into a cup. She glanced at the tea blend Marie had picked: chamomile, lavender, valerian root, and passionflower, then scooped a large spoonful of the mixed flowers and bark into the teapot.

Neither of them spoke, but Elsie got two oat biscuits out of the tin on the bench, walked over to Marie, and handed her one.

"I have to do this, Marie. She might be in danger."

Marie nibbled the edge of the biscuit while Elsie went back to the kitchen area and poured two cups of tea. She placed them on the small table by the armchairs and nearly jumped out of her skeleton when Marie appeared beside her.

"You need to be careful in Midwinter." Marie broke the silence.

"I will be. I promise," Elsie said softly, relieved Marie had come around to logic so quickly.

"I mean, you need to be prepared. You need protection against the fae." Marie pursed her lips.

"What do you suggest?" Would she really be in danger if she was surrounded by people in the town?

"Wear iron to ward against the fae so they can't mind control you." Marie furrowed her brow. "And just to be safe you should bring a silver cross and garlic against vampires. Don't look a witch in the eye or she can steal your soul, or was that elves?" Marie mumbled to herself.

Elsie didn't want to hear more for fear of talking herself out of it. "I'm sure Kit will tell me what I need. I can go shopping before we leave."

Marie sat down and pulled her sewing onto her lap, clutching it in her hands. "Kit. Is he the man you are going with?"

"Yes, and I believe he will honor his word and protect me." Elsie hoped as much was true.

"I want to meet him." Marie made no move to start her sewing.

"He wants to leave early and will be at the cottage at dawn. You can meet him then. I promise. I will not go with him if you do not approve," Elsie said. "Though he is an unpleasant sort of fellow, I admit."

"I will be the judge of his character. We can't trust you with such things." Marie picked up her tea.

Elsie leaned back in the chair and took a sip of tea. She closed her eyes for a moment and reality hit. An image of Kit at the table paraded across her vision, his vivid blue eyes staring into her soul like he already knew her, challenging her with that infuriating smirk.

Her eyes shot open. Was she really going to go through with this? Follow a strange man through a mountain pass into a mysterious magic town. It had seemed like such a good idea earlier. But what if she didn't come back either?

She couldn't think like that. What she needed to do was start packing.

CHAPTER 10

ELSIE

The sun wasn't yet up when a loud knock sounded at the door.

"He is here this early?" Marie let her spoon drop in her porridge.

"I am mostly ready." Elsie set down her bowl and stood up from the table. He was rather early. Was she ready? Had she packed enough? She smoothed out the skirt of her fawn-colored woolen traveling dress.

Too late to concern herself now. She ran a hand across her head to flatten the strand of hair that refused to sit in the braid. No need to be nervous.

Pulling open the door, she forced a smile on her face.

"Good morrow, Kit, Pepper." She couldn't help but smile when she saw Pepper's enthusiastic dog grin. Her gaze shifted to Kit, and she almost forgot how to breathe. Even in his plain traveler's coat, he was undeniably dashing. He was far taller than she recalled from last night, or perhaps it was because they were standing close. So close she caught the earthy aroma of his oilskin coat mingled with the faint scent of sheep's wool.

He rubbed his angular jawline marked with dark stubble, and she realized she was staring.

"Morning, Miss Fielding." A noticeable awkward pause lingered in the still air. Kit averted his gaze down quickly, busying himself with adjusting the leather tie in his dark chestnut hair that kept half of it up, and the other half fell in unruly waves.

Elsie remained in the doorway and Kit on the narrow path between lines of freshly cleared snow. Behind him, the forest across the river remained black with night, but a faint wash of pink seeped onto the horizon behind it.

"Oh, will the snow affect our journey?" Elsie glanced at the extra foot of snow that must have fallen overnight and blanketed everything in a clean layer of whiteness.

"I'm hoping not. Have you decent boots?" Kit glanced down at her boots beside the doorway.

"No, she does not." Marie marched up beside Elsie, arms crossed and glaring at Kit.

"You must be Marie. Pleased to meet your acquaintance." Kit bowed slightly and aimed a very charming smile at Marie.

Elsie blinked. Was this the same man she met yesterday? She was impressed he remembered her sister's name and slightly jealous of that smile.

"I take it you are Kit. And I'll have you know I do not agree with Elsie journeying with you in this manner. It's quite improper."

"I assure you nothing improper will take place." Kit's hand rested on Pepper's head.

"Are you carrying protection?" Marie demanded.

Kit looked a little bewildered. "I carry a small knife, but we are not going to war. It is a simple journey through the mountain pass. Though at this time of year, the path is easily lost; I assure you I know my way."

"I mean against the creatures of the North. The witches and vampires and werewolves and fae."

Kit tilted his head as if he were trying to tell if it was a joke. "I don't believe such measures are necessary."

"Thought you were the expert. Shouldn't you know these things?" Marie's hands went to her hips.

"I grew up in the Midwinter Haven area. I assure you I know what I'm doing. We will not need such things in a peaceful town. I know it well and can take your sister to the places she needs to enquire about your mother."

"Would you care to come in?" Elsie asked to break the tension.

"Thank you, but Pepper and I are fine out here. Are you ready?" He didn't appear at all cold, no red cheeks, or sniffly nose the way Elsie got as soon as she stepped outside.

She nodded. "I believe so." She glanced at Marie who gave a subtle nod in approval. Elsie couldn't help but launch herself onto her sister in a big hug. "Thank you," she whispered into Marie's hair.

"Be careful. Be smart," Marie whispered back, and she pried Elsie off her.

Elsie slipped on her red coat and was instantly too hot. She quickly pulled on her old boots. They might be old, but they would get her there and back well enough.

"She will need some decent traveling gloves too," Marie stated.

"Mine are quite fine," Elsie scolded. Her sister was certainly doing her best to embarrass Elsie in front of Kit. She pulled her thick wool gloves from her pocket; there was nothing wrong with them.

"Your sister is right; you need leather gloves. These will not be waterproof or warm enough."

She sighed. Another expense to take away from her shop savings. "Very well, let's pick up gloves before we leave." Elsie arranged her traveling cloak around her shoulders and tied the cord at the front.

"I know a shop that opens early," Kit said.

"Good. Then I believe I am ready." She settled the knapsack on her back, adjusting the two straps.

"Please take this," Marie blurted out and untied the long ribbon from her own neck.

"Oh, Marie, I couldn't," Elsie protested but let Marie drape the ribbon with the tiny iron star amulet over her head. If it made her sister happy, she wouldn't argue. This was Marie giving her approval to go.

"It will protect against the fae. It is iron." Marie straightened the collar on Elsie's coat.

"Does that work?" Elsie asked Kit, unsure which of Marie's stories were ever true.

"Ay, it does," Kit said a little too quickly and looked away. "Now let's get moving."

Elsie wasn't sure if he said that to appease Marie, or if it was true. She would have to ask later.

Marie shot her a look with raised eyebrows that said *I saw the way you looked at him.*

Elsie shook her head and mouthed the word 'no' very clearly and pulled Marie into another hug, a goodbye hug this time.

"I will be back with Mum before Midwinter. We can decorate the log together, okay?"

Marie pulled away and nodded. "May the road rise up to meet you," she said with kindness in her voice, and she kissed Elsie's cheek.

"May Astriel watch over you." Elsie squeezed the iron star and tucked it into her dress as she stepped out the door to follow the handsome stranger.

Elsie and Kit made their way up the lane in silence while Pepper bounded along up ahead. The snow on the road had already turned to slush from the carts and horses that had already passed through.

She glanced at Kit. His face didn't give away anything. Was he regretting bringing her along already? Was he glad of a companion for the trip? She wondered if the medicine he'd had last night put him in a better mood.

She couldn't take the silence any longer.

"We don't need to worry about the gloves and boots. I understand you were bullied into saying that by Marie. I'm sure these will do quite fine." She'd manage. Plus, she didn't want to spend money unnecessarily.

"If you want to make it there without frostbite, you'd be wise to take up my offer." His voice lowered to a teasing tone. "Part of the service, let's say."

Angels, even his voice was attractive. *No, Elsie, stop noticing things like that!* He was off limits, her temporary guide who she could not get attached to.

Though he did have a point. She didn't want to freeze her feet off halfway; that would be embarrassing. She supposed he would add it to her bill at the end. Yes. It would be wise to agree, and she didn't want to be difficult.

"If you insist." She flashed a quick smile.

They took a shortcut through Winterfrost Market, and Kit bought some flatbreads and a few other food items for the trip. Elsie greeted all the usual early morning market folk setting up as she went.

"You certainly know a lot of people here," Kit commented.

"We've been coming to the market for a few years now." Elsie adjusted her bag, very aware of Kit's presence beside her.

They walked in silence to Blackmore Shoes on Main Street, and Elsie was fitted for boots that Kit deemed appropriate to weather the mountain pass and gloves with a lining softer than anything she had felt before.

It felt nice that someone else was looking out for her for once. She was so used to looking after Marie, her mother, the tea house. She chided herself for enjoying it and followed Kit out the door.

His footsteps were graceful, like a cat effortlessly navigating a narrow brick wall, and she wasn't the only one to notice it. The shopkeeper and his assistant's gaze followed Kit as he glided down the steps and out onto the street.

She wondered if he noticed or if it bothered him.

They stood out on the street. "Is there anything else you need to buy?"

"No. But I did want to speak with my friend Nell."

He groaned. "Why did I agree to this?"

She resisted the impulse to touch his arm. "I was just teasing. But I was wondering the same. Why did you offer to take me when it is such an inconvenience for you?" She shuffled her feet, wondering if he would give a straight answer. She hated being a burden on anyone, but in this case, she did need help.

He paused, tucking a strand of unruly hair behind his ear, his finger brushing lightly along the top as he did so. "It is good practice to never pass up a chance to make coin on the road, and I was already going this way."

She studied his face. He seemed genuine enough, though his expression revealed very little. "Very well. I am ready if you are. Let us begin the journey."

"Ready as I'll ever be."

Her stomach fluttered with uncertainty. What was she walking into?

CHAPTER 11

KIT

Kit breathed in the fresh winter air and felt a lightness trickle over him. Being in a town always put him in a bad mood, but once outside it was like he was a bird set free. If only he could stretch his wings. It had been too long.

Fresh snowfall masked the path that meandered through the larch forest, but the wooden markers every so often were easy enough to spot, and with the trees bare of needles, the morning sun shone through brightly.

Elsie's footsteps sounded behind him. He pictured her boots, then his thoughts turned to her trying them on, seeing far more of her leg than he meant to.

Whenever he tried to think, she was there, either chattering away or invading his thoughts when she was silent. Though to give her credit, she had not complained once and had kept pace as well as Thomas would.

A redpoll, a small finch with a red forehead and chest, flitted onto a low branch near his head. A sign. "Redpolls are my favorite bird," he offered a piece of information about himself. He didn't like sharing personal details, but he wanted Elsie to be comfortable around him.

"It's adorable. It has a friend!" Elsie exclaimed as a female joined it on the branch. The tiny birds darted to a tree ahead of them.

As a child, he would sit at his window watching the tiny finches come and go over the walls. How he envied them. How he wanted the freedom of a tiny redpoll.

"Are there many humans living in Midwinter Haven?" Elsie called from behind him.

"There are a fair few," Kit replied. He checked his glamour was still in place, lifting a hand to his ear, then dropping it.

"Why do they live there?"

"They like it, I suppose. Life is easier there," Kit called back. At least the medicine had revived his energy, hopefully enough to make the walk without incident.

"Oh." She sounded surprised. He held back a chuckle. She might not be from Winterfrost, but she seemed to have heard one too many stories there.

"What makes it easier?" she asked.

"Magic. It makes everything better. You'll see."

"Is it dangerous though? No one can seem to give me a straight answer."

He stopped and turned around. "Let's clear up one thing before we go."

She came to a halt in front of him. Her cheeks were rosy from the exercise. He hadn't noticed the fine sprinkling of freckles dotting her cheeks before.

No, he was trying to prove an important point. *Stop getting distracted.* "Magic is not dangerous, and you can't be saying that around anyone there. Got it?"

"No." She glared at him. Staring a little too closely at his eyes, like she was studying them. The hair lifted on the back of his neck.

"I don't understand. I've heard so many stories about magic, good and bad, but I don't know what to believe."

"Magic is a good thing. I know you've been told a load of crap by other people, but it is nothing to fear. It is used to improve life, make things easier," Kit said sharply as Pepper nudged his hand. Had he been too harsh?

"I'm sorry. I've just never heard that before." She looked at the ground. "But I would like to learn more."

Pepper went to Elsie and nudged her. Elsie slipped off her new glove and ruffled the mass of white fur covering the dog's head.

"Keep an open mind, and you will do just fine." He turned around before he stared too long and started walking again.

Kit didn't want to admit to himself he couldn't walk much farther. It was a weakness. His arm was throbbing, and he was growing unsteady on his feet in the dimming light. The elevation had risen in the last hour as they'd moved into denser pine forest where the light no longer reached the forest floor; the sun was already dipping behind the ridge.

"We aren't going to make it much farther," he said between heavy breaths, pausing a moment for Elsie to catch up so they could walk side by side on a wider section of the path, with Pepper plodding along in front.

Elsie's eyes were wide as they darted to the surrounding trees. "You mean we have to sleep out here?"

He noticed she was limping, probably blisters from her new boots. He had been enjoying the companionable silence and hadn't thought to ask how she was faring. She appeared so capable. He chided himself for not paying better attention.

"There is a cave close to here. If you can make it another ten minutes, we should reach it before we need extra light."

She brushed past him, and the smell of cinnamon drifted over him as Pepper bounded up to her. She looked back as Pepper bounced around her. "Let us make haste, then."

He almost told her to slow down, but his pride couldn't quite bring him to it, and she looked so happy.

He kept up with her well enough, knowing they were near the end of the day's walk, and in less than ten minutes, Pepper stopped at the familiar rock next to a path off to the left.

"Good girl, Peps. Up that way." He nodded to the path, then turned back to Elsie who was sticking very close. "Grab any kindling on the way up if you see it."

She nodded as they trudged onto the snowy path.

A few minutes off the track and with a small clamber up some rocks with arms full of dryish firewood, and they were at the cave.

Kit nearly lay down from exhaustion and relief. This was the first time he wasn't sure he'd make it this far. He'd always at least made it halfway, and he'd like to blame their slow pace on Elsie, but it was all him. Checking the small cave was clear, they dropped their bags without speaking and both went out to gather more firewood so they wouldn't have to go out in the dark.

Kit returned before Elsie and grabbed the two protection crystals he'd stashed in his bag pocket. He set them at the entrance out of sight and ready to activate.

"Do you think we'll be warm enough in here?" Elsie rounded the entrance as he stood up.

"Warm enough if we get this fire going. The wind is passing us by, and the cave is small enough to hold heat." He dusted some dry leaves and sticks out of the way and eased himself onto the ground of sandy material. "You're not from Winterfrost, are you?" he asked as Pepper plonked down next to him, panting happily.

"No, but I'd like to live there. I'm still getting used to the cold." She pulled out her own tinderbox and started arranging the kindling.

"Let me do that." Kit reached for the wood.

"No, you stay put. I can see that arm of yours is giving you grief. I'll get the fire lit and make some of that tea of yours."

"You don't need to go to the trouble."

She waved her hand as if that were nonsense. "We both need to warm up. Nothing's better than tea for that."

He couldn't argue and didn't have the energy for it. "I'll prepare some food. I have a small pot if you need it."

"I have this." She pulled her knapsack across the sand toward her and removed a small iron kettle wrapped in a shawl.

"You brought a kettle with you for a one-night journey and a stay at an inn?"

"You need to take your medicine, don't you? I wasn't sure you would think to bring one."

"That's why you brought it?"

"No, of course not." Her face flushed red beyond her already rosy cheeks. "I never go anywhere without tea-making equipment. You can never trust an inn to provide the right quality."

He'd never known an inn not to have tea-making services at all hours, but he wasn't about to say that. If she'd done it for him that was extremely thoughtful, though she seemed to be that friendly with everyone. He scowled at the thought.

Elsie got the fire roaring in no time and went outside with her kettle to fill it with snow.

While she was outside, he pulled out a package of waxed cloth and laid it on a flat stone by the fire that someone had placed there for that very purpose. His mouth watered despite the unexciting selection of food: salted pork, hard biscuits, flatbread he'd bought that morning, cheese, and a jar of pickled cabbage he'd also got that morning while waiting for Elsie at the market. At least the flatbread was fresh, not a week old after traveling.

As Elsie walked back through the cave mouth, he mumbled the activation for the crystals, and a small pulse of energy rippled through him in response. No one would bother them tonight.

"What was that?" She shivered, placing the kettle down by the fire. Her plaits, black as raven feathers, cascaded over her scarlet coat as she straightened. Her warm brown eyes, flecked with orange from the firelight, sparkled with a soft glow.

He shrugged. "I'm just feeding Pepper." Sometimes diversion was the best method when one couldn't lie. He set out a pile of dried meat for Pepper to gnaw on. Pepper drooled over the meat and took a piece in the corner of her mouth, chewing loudly.

"Did you want some cheese?" he asked.

"Oh, yes please." Elsie used a stick to shove a burning log over to reveal a small stand of stones within the fire pit and set the kettle on them without a second thought. It was clear she was well accustomed to life on the road.

He handed her a flatbread with a few pieces of pork, some pickled cabbage, and cheese on top. She peeled off her gloves and grinned as she took it.

"Lovely, thank you. We don't usually eat meat while traveling."

Her manners surprised him, and he realized they had fallen into some sort of comfortable traveling companionship. She wasn't nearly as annoying as he initially thought her to be, based on their first meeting. Perhaps this wouldn't be so bad.

"What do you usually eat?" he asked.

"When we travel up and down the east coast and to the south, we eat a lot of salted fish, or fresh fish, if we can catch it. But mostly we have lentil or barley soup with whatever is in season." She ripped a piece of pork in half with her teeth. "When we get to a new town, our mother always treats us to a meal at an inn where we can order anything we like."

"That sounds like a lovely tradition."

"It is. We look forward to it every time." Elsie's shoulders slumped, probably thinking about her mother.

"Will you tell me about her, your mother? It may help in finding her." Pepper came over to join them and flopped down by the fire.

Elsie nodded as she finished a mouthful. "She went to buy spices. We are running short on several of the rarer items and thought it would be a good time to find them before the rush of Midwinter."

"But she failed to return."

"Yes, and it's most unlike her. Plus, it is in the north. If it were any other town, I was familiar with, I'm sure I wouldn't be so worried."

The food turned dry in his mouth. She needed to stop talking about Midwinter Haven like that. It was his sanctuary, his home away from home, and the people who resided there did not deserve such talk.

"I have a picture if that helps." She shuffled to access her pocket in the folds of her dress and pulled out a silver locket in the shape of a book.

She handed him the chain hesitantly. Their fingers touched as he clasped it, and she pulled away. "You may keep it until we find her."

"I promise to look after it. Thank you, this is most useful." He studied the miniature. The woman at the center looked a lot like Elsie. He glanced up at her: long straight black hair with a sheen like a raven. He studied her face the same way he identified birds. It was the details that counted.

Elsie's cheeks had a light sprinkling of freckles, her nose was proportional to her face, and her lips looked soft as they slightly parted.

"You're staring," she whispered.

"Sorry if I made you uncomfortable. You look a lot like your mother. I was trying to note details in case I see her." He tried to cover his tracks, he had been staring, yes taking in detail, but he also hadn't wanted to look away.

"Very well, since we are speaking of appearances. I noticed your eyes are a different color than this morning. I thought I imagined it at first, but now I am sure of it."

"Indeed?" He set the locket down and took a bite of cheese. She'd notice such detail? He wasn't sure if he should be flattered or concerned for his identity. He glanced at Pepper, wishing she was awake to distract Elsie.

"They were near white this morning, blue so pale it was like ice. Tonight they are midnight blue like the night sky after dusk." She shuffled to sit cross-legged. Every rustle of her skirt caught his attention as she settled it across her knees.

He cleared his throat. "You are quite detailed in your observations. You would make a good bird watcher." He tried to change the subject. He didn't want her to be a bird watcher. If anything, he wanted less in common with her. Getting attached to her would only put her in danger with his father.

"Did you know your eyes did that?"

"Yes, it is a family trait. Quite harmless, I am told."

"Interesting."

He cleared his throat. "I'm sure. Tell me more of your mother, what she is like, anything that might help."

As they finished their meal, Elsie told him many things about her mother. He suspected something strange about the woman. No one went to Midwinter Haven to buy spices. They were the same as any market in the Celestial Isles as far as he knew, but he kept this to himself.

After eating, Elsie pulled out two teacups from a small wooden box lined with velvet as well as two little metal cages on chains. She started spooning tea from a linen pouch into one.

"Pass me your medicine tea, please."

He dug into the bag and pulled it out, and she spooned the mixture into the other little cage and poured hot water into his teacup, then her own.

Placing the kettle back down on the stones, she looked over at him. "What really happens if fae touch iron? Have you seen it?"

Did she know about him? For a second, he had an urge to show her who he really was. But that would do no good. No, some secrets were better kept secret.

He remained calm, though all his muscles tensed. "I've seen it, yes. Their skin burns like a hot brand." He ran a finger over his ear but, when he noticed her eyes following his hand, lowered it.

"What about iron alloys?"

"To a lesser extent, but they still burn."

"And glamours? I heard fae can conceal themselves."

"That's right. It's mostly for vanity reasons." Though in his case it was identity protection. Not only did he have a human glamour, but also a royal glamour. The face everyone knew him by as a prince, a beautiful, desirable face. His true face was a secret from most, something he kept for when he could be himself and his disguise whenever in Midwinter Haven.

"Interesting." She raised her tea holder up and down in the water. "You should let yours steep for longer than mine."

He busied himself by opening a package with dried fruit, figs, and apricots.

"Dessert?" He held out the bundle.

CHAPTER 12

ELSIE

E lsie woke up next to a warm presence at her side and froze for a second, but turned to see Pepper sprawled next to her, sound asleep. Holding her breath, she realized that Kit's head was just inches away from hers. He had clearly tried to get closer to the fire, the same as she had in the night.

Sitting up as quietly as she could, she added the last of their kindling to the glowing embers, then placed a small log on top once she saw flames. The cave had stayed surprisingly warm overnight, and she felt well-rested, considering she had slept on the ground.

She studied Kit as he slept. His hair draped over his face, and she fought the urge to brush it aside.

What color would his eyes be today?

Wait. She shouldn't be thinking about things like that. Just because he had been pleasant most of the previous day didn't mean it would continue. He was there to do a job and so was she. She would not let her feelings get clouded and mix things up.

She prepared black tea to break their fast, and Kit stirred just as it was ready, the sun bringing color back to the sky.

"I see Miss Peppermint has taken sides," he grumbled as he sat up. Pepper was happily lying next to Elsie with her head resting on her paws, watching Elsie make tea.

Peppermint. She liked that. "Smart dog, this one."

Once there was enough light to make out the path, they were on the road. Elsie observed Kit. There was something off about him. He was certainly knowledgeable when it came to comments about magic or the fae. Perhaps she was paranoid, or perhaps it was his arm wound. She was concerned. When he had re-bandaged it and replaced the poultice this morning, it looked worse than the night before, and she would be glad when he got to a healer so she wouldn't have to worry about him dropping dead when she was the only one around.

They climbed to a considerable elevation over some hours. Kit only spoke to point out birds he spotted. It seemed to be his way of distracting himself from the pain, and she welcomed anything to take her mind off her burning leg muscles, blisters, and the steep climb. She now saw why people took the much longer eastern road around the mountains to get to the north. But that took up to a week, a week she didn't have. She never would have been able to keep to the track without him.

So far, she had learned about three new types of finches and spotted a glorious eagle owl, larks, warbler, woodpeckers, falcons, and shrikes. She'd even joined Kit's excitement every time they saw a hoopoe, a beautiful cinnamon-colored bird with black and white wings and a funny crest on its head.

The forest was alive with movement, not just in the branches, but in the undergrowth, too. Squirrels scurried between trees, chipmunks poked their heads from fallen logs, and they'd even spotted a white fox in the distance with a rabbit in its mouth.

Seeing all the creatures was delightful, but every creak or rustling bush made Elsie jump. Could it be a werewolf this time, a vampire? They were so close to the northern border it could be anything, and the forest was certainly strange. It remained winter nearly all year round, like most of the north, and the wildlife had adapted. Apparently, many creatures remained all year round instead of migrating like they did in other lands.

She stuck close to Kit and Pepper, her heart racing, not only from the uphill path but because she was about to go farther north than she'd ever dreamed of traveling and wasn't sure she wanted to know the truth about magic. What if it was as horrible or as dangerous as people said? Maybe they could go back to the nice, cozy cave.

She quietly hoped they would just bump into her mother on her way down.

But the few travelers they passed hadn't heard of her mother, nor seen her. They were traders on their way back to Winterfrost for Midwinter and were happy to chat, but she noted Kit's frown when she mentioned her mother.

They stopped for lunch, eating the remaining flatbread and more salted pork, and sat at a lookout point at the top of the ridge of the mountain range. Pepper chose to sit next to Elsie, and she shared her pork willingly.

Kit said it was the lowest point in the range where they could safely pass through, but it was the highest Elsie had ever been. The trees spread out like a carpet of green and white; Winterfrost was not even visible beyond the woodlands.

Kit's pace was slower as they made their way up a steep section of rock with no clear path. Elsie was glad of her new gloves after having to use her hands for many difficult sections.

After an hour or so of rough climbing, they made it to a narrow pass between two vertical walls of rock. The path was flat, and the last two hours were easy compared to their hike up, but Kit needed rest more often, and he hadn't written in his bird book in some time or named any birds even if they were right in their path.

"Are you okay, Kit? Do you need more of your medicine?" Elsie asked cautiously, not wanting to overstep.

He leaned against a tree trunk and closed his eyes. His face was pale.

Elsie reached into the side pocket of his bag, pulled out the water skin with cold tea in it, and forced it into his hand.

He took it without question and downed the liquid down without even complaining. His eyes were now a dull gray.

"How far is it?" she asked.

He glanced around. "Not far, only half an hour. Maybe a little longer at this pace."

"And you thought I'd be the one slowing us down," she joked but had genuine concern she might have to drag him the rest of the way or go on without him to get help.

"I can make it," he said with determination in his words.

They set off again.

Elsie walked behind Kit. He was barely going straight and his steps even slower than before. But true to his word, they made it to the edge of the forest, and suddenly they were back in civilization.

The North.

Elsie's hands grew sweaty as people came into view, not people, but creatures. She stuck very close to Kit, who seemed to verge on delirious as their path neared a dirt road.

Elsie did her best not to stare and was glad Pepper was on her other side.

Tall people with metallic skin and pointed ears glided by so gracefully she might have thought they were floating if she couldn't see their feet. Some ordinary-looking people passed by, pulling carts or herding goats, and she felt a sense of relief knowing there were at least a few humans around.

She almost gasped aloud when two people with double sets of wings right out of their backs neared them.

Kit linked his good arm into hers and whispered close to her ear. "Don't stare, it will piss them off."

A pleasant chill tracked down her spine at his closeness. She wasn't sure if it was for her benefit or to keep himself upright. She didn't protest. In fact, she hated to admit she felt a little safer at his side.

"Hail," Kit said to the strangers as they passed. "Praise the Ancient Mother."

The strangers with wings were dressed in fine silks that couldn't be very warm in this weather. Elsie wondered how their wings went through the backs but didn't dare turn to look.

The pair tipped their heads in acknowledgment. "May her wisdom guide this day."

A little shiver ran down Elsie's neck. "What are they?" she whispered back, trying to keep her gaze set forward and not grip him too tightly. She hated she felt so far out of her depth here.

He waited for them to pass before speaking. "They are fae."

Elsie gasped and risked a look behind her. "I didn't know they actually had wings." She half expected him to laugh at her ignorance. He might be right to. There was so much she didn't know, and they appeared harmless enough, but appearances could be deceiving.

"You will learn quickly enough." He was leaning on her now, so she suspected he might need the support as much as her. Pepper moved to his other side as if she intended to catch him should he fall.

He was too sick to argue, even with the pain prompting him. That must be a bad sign.

"I hope so. I should hate to offend anyone."

The forest path became a dirt road that ran around the outside of the walled city, well, not so much a walled city, but a town with a chest-height interlocking dry stone that looked quite neat and picturesque with the row of quaint cottages and taller thatched buildings behind it.

They neared the sculpted stone archway with a bell hanging at the center and an engraved sign that read *Welcome to Midwinter Haven*.

Gripping the iron star at her chest, she stepped toward the archway.

"Let's find you a healer."

CHAPTER 13

ELSIE

Elsie survived the short walk up one street of Midwinter Haven, doing her best not to stare at the people she learned were elves (the metallic-skinned sorts), and the fae (ones with wings or horns). Easy enough to remember. But according to Kit, witches, werewolves, vampires, and even fae could look like any normal person. She would have to be highly vigilant.

"We just need to get to The Fae's Folly Inn, and my friend, Liri, will find the healer." Kit's foot nipped a cobble and jerked forward.

Elsie caught him by his good arm just in time. Pepper barked supportively as they stumbled along, and thankfully, around the next corner a sign came into view, *The Fae's Folly,* written in elegant letters surrounded by carved flowers painted in bright colors.

A bell chimed as they stepped into the pub, and Elsie lowered Kit into the first booth she came across and went straight to the bar leaving Pepper to guard Kit. The man at the bar had curled horns creeping from his head and golden wings folded behind him. She was about to talk to a fae.

Her throat was thick. "Excuse me, sir. Is someone called Liri here?" She didn't dare look around for fear of catching the eye of a fae.

"Liri!" he called over his shoulder. "People here be wanting you!"

Elsie stood there speechless after his unexpected bellowing.

"She'll be right with you," he said softly as a crash came from beyond the swing door behind the bar. "Can I get you a drink, lass?"

"Um, yes, please. A jug of small beer if you have it and two cups." The last thing Kit needed was strong ale. At least small beer, a weak low-alcohol beer would get some liquid in him. It was never wise to order water from new places.

"Certainly. Six coppers," the man said. She couldn't help but stare at his shiny curled horns; she'd been told the fae could have many looks and disguises. That part of the stories was true. What else was?

She counted the coins with shaking fingers and thanked him as she took the tray with the jug and two wooden cups.

She let out a breath as she settled into her seat. She'd survived her first encounter with the fae, and it wasn't so bad, in fact, a lot friendlier than many other taverns she'd been in. Kit was leaning his head against the wooden booth with his eyes closed.

"Your friend should be out soon. She'll know what to do." Elsie hoped anyway. "Drink this."

She poured a cup of small beer for him and forced it into his hand. It wouldn't help any of them if he was dehydrated, and if he got any sicker, she would be on her own finding her mother. A prospect she didn't want to face.

Elsie sipped the watery beer, letting the mild hoppy flavor play across her tongue as she swallowed. She hadn't realized how thirsty she had been.

She took the opportunity to look around as subtly as she could and was pleasantly surprised. It wasn't a dingy pub by any means. Warm light streamed through the pane-glass windows that had live sunny, yellow daisies on the windowsills and intricate swirled carvings around the frames.

A fire crackled at the far end of the wide room, the floor was well-swept, and there was a pleasant smell of fresh bread mixed with something like sweet mead or wine. No one was looking at her, and though most of the patrons appeared to be fae, they were quietly chatting away like anyone in a normal pub.

She hoped it wouldn't be too expensive to stay here, it was certainly nicer than pubs they usually went to.

"Kit!" a voice called.

Elsie choked on her drink when she spotted who it came from. A fae woman with wings like shimmering copper fluttered behind her, protruding from her tight leather outfit covered in buckles and pockets. Her face was intimidatingly beautiful with high cheekbones, full lips, and eyes bright with green and gold.

"Liri," Kit groaned and didn't get up.

"Is that you, Kit?" Liri squinted at him. "We've quite forgotten what you look like around here."

"Of course it is," Kit grumbled, opening his eyes and holding her gaze. "I haven't been gone that long."

"Oh, how silly of me. You never used to look so dirty." She laughed and walked around the table, carefully offering him a one-armed hug, avoiding the arm he was clearly protecting. The extra-long hug made

Elsie even more uncomfortable when Kit whispered something in Liri's ear. She couldn't help but wonder what he didn't want her to hear. Or perhaps they were lovers. Could a human and fae be lovers?

"Good to see you back, Kit. Now tell me, what's wrong with you?" Liri moved back to stand at the table edge with her hands on her hips while Kit leaned back in the booth, clearly struggling to keep his eyes open.

"He needs a healer. It's a wound on his arm," Elsie said after Kit didn't speak.

"I see." Liri focused on Kit. "Does anyone know you're back?"

He shook his head.

"We just got in and came straight here." Elsie gripped her cup.

"And you are?" Liri narrowed her eyes, looking Elsie up and down.

Elsie swallowed but kept her shoulders back and lifted her chin with fake confidence. "I'm Elsie. Kit is supposed to be helping me find my mother, but he needs urgent help."

"What happened to him?"

"A cursed blade, I believe. The wound will not heal." She pointed to his arm.

"Oh, is that all?" Liri slid into the booth beside Elsie. "I thought he might have been poisoned or something."

"It seems rather serious." Though poisoning seemed equally serious.

"Healer August will clear it up in no time. Sorry I was so rude, I thought it was something else. I'm Liri. Pleased to meet you." She held out her hand to Elsie.

Elsie took it, sure her hand was all sweaty. Her first time touching a fae. She held her breath as she shook Liri's hand firmly, not wanting her to think she was weak. Nothing happened. No buzz of magic, no curse of the fae. She collected herself quickly as she pulled her hand back. "Why did you say he had been poisoned? Who would do that and why?"

"His father I expect."

"Enough." Kit slammed his hand on the table, glared at Liri with a look of warning, and gave a subtle shake of his head.

Elsie ignored him. "Why would his father poison him?" Who would poison their own son, and wasn't he here to bring a stone of some sort to his father? Surely, he would want him alive for that.

Liri didn't answer her, taking Kit's warning. "Finish your drinks while I contact the healer for the Prince of Dramatics over here, then I'll see you to your room."

"Room? Is it possible to get two rooms?" Elsie asked, clasping her hands together tight in her lap. She blinked at Liri. Was she blinking too much? Did she look strange? Oh dear, she was starting to feel hot.

"My apologies, I assumed you were together. I've had a room saved for Kit these past few weeks, but I'll see if another is available."

"We'd appreciate that," Elsie squeaked, poured more small beer into the two cups, and took a large swig of hers. Hopefully, another room would come up. She should not be staying in a room with Kit, no good could come of it.

Liri didn't seem too concerned either way, which only increased Elsie's unease.

The fae woman pushed out her chair, went around the table, and kissed Kit on the forehead. "It's nice to have you home, Kit."

He smiled at her. "I missed you."

Elsie's stomach clenched. She had traveled all over the Celestial Isles but never felt more like an outsider and out of her depth than right in that moment.

CHAPTER 14

ELSIE

"Only one room available, sorry," Liri said as she slung Kit's arm over her shoulder and hauled him up. He was barely conscious now. Should she make more medicine tea? Would this fae healer know more than a human one? Could they be trusted? What if they couldn't help him?

Liri didn't seem worried about Kit. Apparently, it was an easy fix, but Elsie couldn't quite believe it. *Wait, one room?*

Elsie's breath hitched.

"Will there be another soon?" She heard her voice go high.

She swallowed back her apprehension and followed Liri, who was carrying Kit up the stairs with the help of another barman who looked human but was abnormally tall.

Pepper nudged the bottom of Kit's feet like she thought she was helping. Elsie carried Kit's bag in front of her after Liri dismissed her offer to help with Kit.

"Should be one before nightfall if some guests leave. I'll come get you if one comes up."

Liri pushed open the door to a room halfway down the long hall, dropped Kit onto the bed, and removed his boots before swinging his feet onto the top of the blankets. It seemed like she might have done this before.

Elsie set the bags next to the wall, which was as bright as if it had been whitewashed the day before. A circular rug with patterns of deep blue spirals and stars took up most of the room and went all the way under the bed, which was made of heavy-looking wood with tall posts at the corners and an elaborate headboard carved with vines and leaves.

Pepper sprawled out by the fire that had already been lit and was smoldering away.

On either side of the bed were two nightstands with strange, frosted orbs sitting at the center of each. She had to investigate.

"What is this?" She kept a safe distance and looked at the back and the front. There was a tiny lever sticking out on one side.

"You can switch it on. The healer might need more light," Liri said as she opened the curtains that appeared to be made of luxurious heavy wool for insulation.

"It is a light?" Elsie asked. She followed Liri's lead in ignoring Kit.

Liri lifted an eyebrow. "Have you never been to the north?"

"No, I mean, not north of Winterfrost. I've been to the Southern Witchlands, but only the human district in Old Port. Is this magic?" She knew she should fear magic, but her curiosity was getting the better of her.

"It's a fae light. It has a crystal inside it." Liri leaned over and flicked the tiny lever and light bloomed within the globe.

Elsie gasped forgetting her fear of the fae woman for a moment. "That is brilliant." How useful it would be to have light at the touch of your fingers.

Liri laughed. "If you're amazed by this, wait till you see the shower."

Shower? Was that one of the things Kit mentioned? Whatever it was, she wanted to know. "Is the shower here?"

"Right this way." Liri grinned.

Liri was right. Elsie loved the shower instantly. It had hot water that came from a sprinkling device that created hot rain from above a bathtub. Elsie had to try it immediately. Liri also showed her the toilet that was indoors and flushed away waste with water. It didn't even smell! What a wonder.

Liri left her to explore the bathroom, and she decided this particular fae woman was not so bad at all. Elsie locked the door and put aside her fears for the sake of cleanliness.

The hot water sprinkle was heavenly. Elsie scrubbed all the road dirt off every inch of her with lavender-scented soap and even washed her hair despite it not being hair-washing week. The towel she dried herself with was white cotton and oh so fluffy, something she had never owned herself but was just as amazing as the magic she had seen so far.

Dressing in her nice green dress and wool stockings made her feel like she had been reborn into a strange new world where magic was acceptable and, so far, not as scary as she had been led to believe.

When she left the bathroom, Liri was opening the door to the healer, so Elsie quietly seated herself in the armchair by the window, hands folded on her lap. Pepper remained by the fire with one ear flapped over her head, either listening or trying to block out the light.

The healer, a fae man with silvery wings folded at his back and a gray mustache, waved something under Kit's nose, and Kit woke with a start.

Kit blinked in confusion but seemed to recognize the man and relaxed. Elsie tried to pay attention to what the healer asked Kit, but she was so distracted by his wings. Since his back was to her, she had a clear view of how they came out the back of his coat. It had specially designed slits where the material bunched around his wings, presumably to keep drafts from entering the holes. A brilliant design. The tailors here must have quite advanced skills.

Elsie couldn't see as the healer removed the bandage. He tut-tutted at the wound, then had Liri fetch a bowl of hot water.

Elsie's curiosity won over, and she moved closer to watch.

The healer removed the poultice they'd put on that morning, and when Liri returned, he washed the wound while Kit winced, but to his credit, remained silent.

It was all over quickly. He gave Kit a potion in a vial to drink, then sprayed something on the wound in a mist that smelled like fennel, then sprinkled some sort of dust on the wound.

"What is that?" Elsie couldn't help but ask.

"It is ash from a yew tree. It counteracts the curse if I pair it with black tourmaline." The healer explained as he held a long, black, rod-like crystal over the wound.

"Isn't yew poisonous?" Elsie asked, her eyes flicked to Kit. She rubbed her chest. It was hard to see him like this even though she barely knew him.

It sounded like dark magic indeed, but the angry redness dissipated from Kit's skin, and the wound turned fresh pink, like it was a week healed.

"Not when used in this manner," the healer replied, apparently not offended by her questioning.

"I've never seen anything like that."

"You must be new around here," the healer said. "My advice, stay away from this one. He's trouble." He said it kindly, but it also felt like a real warning.

"I'll have you know I've been very good at keeping out of trouble," Kit croaked but didn't open his eyes.

"Clearly." The healer snorted a laugh.

"One mishap with a dwarf."

The healer packed up his equipment. "I take it you'll be seeing your father soon?"

Kit shook his head. "I am yet to decide. I have a week, and I promised Elsie here I would help her find her mother. Please don't mention I'm here."

"Sounds like an excuse to distract yourself. You do not do yourself any favors hiding out."

"Thank you for your advice, Healer August, but I am fine the way I am for now," Kit said through gritted teeth.

Elsie looked between them, trying to understand the hidden meaning behind their words.

The healer placed several vials on the nightstand beside the orb.

"Take one of these a day, and reapply the yew ash and tourmaline every day for a week. You may use the poultice too. If it doesn't heal, send for me at the palace."

A palace healer? He must be expensive. Since Kit kept dozing off, Healer August explained the instructions to Elsie. Once they were all clear on what to do, the healer gave Kit a potion that made him fall asleep instantly. He hadn't even waited for Kit to pay him but didn't seem concerned.

Once he was gone, Liri headed for the door. "Did Kit say anything to you about his father?"

Elsie shook her head. "No, I admit I know little about him. I only met Kit two days ago."

"You are quite fearless, traveling somewhere so foreign with a stranger."

"Desperate, more than fearless. If you haven't noticed, I'm quite out of my depth."

"You appear to be doing just fine."

"Thank you for saying so." Though she was sure Liri was just being kind. "Can I ask you some questions?"

"Are they about Kit?" Liri asked, her wings flattened down her back tightly.

Curious. "No, about my mother. I'm trying to find her and was wondering if she might have stayed here."

"It's unlikely; we don't get many mortals staying here. But do you have a picture?"

"I do." She went to Kit's bag and took out the locket from the front pocket. She supposed she shouldn't be surprised about this inn. Most of the people in the tavern had been fae as far as she could tell. But why did Kit like to stay here?

She showed Liri the miniature and glanced up at her hopefully.

"Sorry, don't recognize her."

Elsie's brief hope came crashing down.

"But the Blue Lantern often takes mortal travelers, plus a few other ones around town. You might try there, but I'd wait until tomorrow when Kit can take you."

A spark of hope flickered. "Why? Is it dangerous?"

"It's safe, but since you're not so familiar with the ways of Midwinter Haven, it might be best to have a guide."

"You've known Kit a while, haven't you?" Elsie couldn't help but ask as she grew bolder around Liri.

"Yes," Liri said.

"And fae can't lie. Is that right?" Elsie said.

Liri looked nervous. "It is true, but you should be careful what you ask around here. You might not get the answers you're hoping for."

Elsie wasn't sure if that was a threat or not. "Is there anything about him I should know? Like you said, I'm putting a lot of trust in a stranger."

"You are safe with Kit. You needn't worry, but don't get too close to him. His life is not his own."

"You mean his father?"

"You'd be wise to stay out of it."

"But—"

"Don't ask me anymore. It is up to Kit to tell you," Liri said sharply, ending that conversation.

"I understand. Thank you for your help." Elsie was never one to stay out of anything. Friends and gossip always seemed to find her, but she always did her best to help others. Maybe Kit needed help. But she would take Liri's advice until she knew more.

"I'll send you up some dinner when I go back down."

Elsie perked up. "That would be wonderful. Thank you."

———❄❄❄———

Dinner was like nothing Elsie had ever experienced. Liri had the cook 'throw together' a salad, and it was almost impossible to believe they had such food here in the middle of winter.

She sat quietly at the table by the fire and watched the flames as she ate, periodically looking up to check that Kit was breathing.

The salad had foods she hadn't seen in months: fresh crunchy greens, sweet tomatoes, cucumbers, peppery radishes, and even fruits! It was topped with fresh figs and slices of pear with a sweet vinegar glaze of some sort over top.

She munched it down alongside a whole loaf of herb bread.

It was dark out when Elsie finished eating, and despite the early hour, she was ready to drop dead from exhaustion.

Liri hadn't come back, so she had to assume a room hadn't opened up. Her stomach tightened. What would Marie say if she knew Elsie was sharing a room with a strange man? Probably, *I told you so.* Well, she would prove Marie wrong and continue to be proper.

Kit was asleep, curled on one side with Pepper half under the bed beneath him. She paused, watching them both breathe in and out so peacefully, and envied them.

It would be so easy to curl up beside them. *Be a good girl, Elsie.*

She tiptoed across the room, carefully pulled the throw blanket from the end of the bed, and draped it over herself as she snuggled into the armchair that fortunately had very comfy cushions.

The room was lit with a pleasant soft glow of the fire, and she tried to piece together what Kit might be hiding. A mysterious stone he didn't know if he wanted to give to his father, a cursed wound, eyes that changed color, and that strange vibration she felt when their fingers touched.

How would he react to iron?

Perhaps it was paranoia and being in a new land of magic, but as her eyes slipped shut, her last thoughts were of Kit and his secrets.

CHAPTER 15

KIT

"Blast it!" Kit stumbled over his boot and hopped on one leg to avoid crushing Pepper.

Elsie sat bolt upright in the chair. Her dark eyes were wide and alert.

"Sorry, I was trying to be quiet." He kicked the boot he'd tripped over.

She blinked at him, probably confused about where she was.

Wait, she was still in his room? "Did you sleep in that chair all night?"

Elsie pulled back the curtain behind her. It was still dark out, but carts rattled by on the street below.

"Is it morning? I only meant to close my eyes for a moment." She yawned and stretched her arms. Her black hair was loose and spilled over her shoulders onto her green dress that nicely hugged her figure.

He looked away quickly.

"Sorry, you could have slept on the bed. I feel bad for taking it up." Liri must not have been able to find another room.

Elsie rubbed her eyes. "It's fine. You needed it more. You appear better today," she said, apparently holding no resentment against him.

He truly was the worst guide. Not that he was actually a guide.

Kit ran a hand over his ear in the dim light—glamour still in place—he flexed his fingers on his wounded arm. All he felt was tightness in the wound, no pain. Thank the Ancient Mother for magic and Healer August. He didn't know how mortals did anything without magic.

"I'm feeling very well. Thank you for looking after me." *Well* was an understatement. He felt like a new man. He hopped over Pepper and crouched at the fire with no fatigue, no slowness, and the chill of his magic returning through his veins. With a wooden-handled poker, he prodded the remaining embers and tossed another log on top.

"I'm glad for you. You looked like a washed-up merman yesterday, that's how green you were. Well not actually green, but you know the expression." Elsie brushed the curtain aside to look out the window.

"Seen a lot of mermen?" he teased.

"Well, no, but folk do often say how green they are."

"That's one story that is true. I happen to have seen a merman, and he was quite green."

Elsie's lips tweaked at the edges to a small smile, and Kit's heart raced. He reminded himself he had a job to do, which did not involve getting attached.

Kit braced to avoid being bowled over as Pepper jumped up to lick his face. He stood and scratched behind her ears, avoiding more of her sloppy kisses.

Elsie cleared her throat as if suddenly realizing she was in a room with a strange man. She stood up and ran her fingers through her hair, trying to straighten out the already sleek locks.

She was lovely, her hair natural like a forest spirit, and the vision strengthened by her green dress. All she needed was a flower crown on her head, and she would fit in well here.

He twisted away, guilt rising that he had made her uncomfortable, and wondered what to say to break the forming tension.

But Elsie was the one to do that.

"How long is it since you've been here?" Her voice faltered.

"Nearly a year," he answered, continuing to scratch Pepper, who nipped his hand whenever he stopped.

Elsie folded the blanket that she placed back on the bed. "Why didn't you want to return? It's lovely as far as I've seen."

As she walked past, he caught a whiff of lavender and soap. "This isn't the part I don't like," he admitted, trying not to react to how lovely she smelled. Speaking of which, he should probably shower.

"Oh."

He could tell she wanted to ask more. She was practically bursting to keep in her questions and remain polite. He decided to put her out of her misery.

"My father, he's the part I'm not looking forward to."

"I suspected. Otherwise, you'd be staying at his house. It's about the stone Thomas mentioned, isn't it? Why don't you want him to have it?"

She went all in once she had an opening. He would have to be careful of his words with her.

"It's a very long story. I think we best focus on trying to find your mother." The more she found out, the more danger she would be in. Best they found her mother and sent them both back to Winterfrost as soon as possible.

He stood up to face her; her hand rested on the corner of the bed. She was about half a head shorter than him, much shorter than fae women, but oddly he couldn't help but notice he liked it.

"Do you have any ideas of where we should start?" Elsie's eyes wandered to his half-open shirt.

They stepped back at the same time, and he turned away, looking for his bag and some fresh clothes. "Where's my bag?"

"Over in the corner." Elsie moved to the window. "Liri mentioned an inn that people go to, humans I mean," she said loudly, as if to make it obvious she wasn't facing him.

"Very well. Might as well kill two birds with one stone and break our fast there. I could eat a bear." He stood up with a clean shirt in hand.

"They eat bear here?" She turned around and scrunched up her nose.

"No, it's just an expression, and I don't kill birds either, in case you were wondering." Kit grinned. He flexed his hand once more; his arm didn't even hurt. It had been weeks since he felt this good.

"Never would have guessed." She rolled her eyes.

He supposed he had talked about birds a lot on the way here. But what else was there to talk about? It's not like he wanted to get to know her further. That sort of thing only led to disaster, and he wasn't about to risk a repeat of what happened to Marella. No, he would never let his father anywhere near Elsie, that much he was certain of.

CHAPTER 16

ELSIE

This pub wasn't as nice as The Fae's Folly, but it was clean enough, and with every footstep on the hay-strewn floor, Elsie caught a fragrant whiff of mountain thyme.

While they waited for their porridge, Elsie spoke with the innkeeper, a gruff woman set on getting on with her day, not messing about with questions and records. She'd not seen Elsie's mother and was most certain of it.

Kit came back to the table at the same time as Elsie after speaking with the servant boy he'd spotted in the hall. As Elsie well knew, servants often saw more than their masters, but this boy was certain he hadn't seen Tia Fielding either.

"Perhaps we should ask about her in some other inns as well as the market and some local shops," Kit said.

"I just thought we would get lucky here. I had a feeling." Elsie sat up straighter, not wanting Kit to see her disappointment.

They ate their porridge in silence. Elsie sprinkled a generous amount of sugar on hers from the large bowl provided, an unexpected luxury for a simple pub. It felt strange without Pepper there. Kit had insisted on leaving her at the inn. But Pepper was their buffer, and without the dog's presence, she felt awkward around Kit.

"What exactly was your mother buying here? It may narrow down our search." Kit took a sip of his black coffee.

Elsie took her time swallowing her mouthful. She didn't want to lie to Kit, but she wasn't ready to tell him about her mum's crazy stories about the fae and her father or the rare spice her mum claimed to be hunting.

"She was buying spices." Elsie took a sip of the bitter coffee. Everyone here seemed to drink it, so she copied Kit's order to see what the fuss was about. Something in it had her heart racing and made her limbs all jittery. She wasn't sure she liked the feeling.

"But you had traveled up the east coast, and you said you started in Middlemarch. Did you not have enough spices to replenish on your way to Winterfrost?"

A heat rose in Elsie's neck. She felt Kit's eyes on her but didn't look up to see what color they might be. She couldn't look at him, and she was not fae, so she could most certainly lie. "In Innesdale, we had a rather busy time and underestimated our supplies. By the time we realized, we were already on the cliff roads and halfway to Winterfrost so couldn't buy more."

"And your mother had been here before?" If he suspected anything, it didn't show in his voice.

"I believe so." She forced her gaze up to meet his. His eyes were vibrant blue, azure, like a kingfisher Kit would have said if he could see his own eyes. "She came here with my father many times before me and Marie were born. Then when we were young, my father would come here to buy spices." She left out the part where he might have gone missing here. She wasn't even sure she wanted to know what happened to him. It couldn't have been good.

Kit stirred his coffee. "If she knew the area, it is unlikely she became lost. We can make our way through the markets. There are several spice sellers we can question." Kit stared past her in thought while sipping from the pottery mug.

Light snow fell as Elsie turned up the collar of her coat and pulled her wool hat down over her ears. She fast-walked to keep up with Kit as they left a tree-lined street and crossed toward the enormous square. It was half taken up by a glimmering market with walkways made entirely of glass that looked like ice.

"It's glorious," Elsie said as they neared the shimmering entranceway sculpted out of real ice blocks with little lights inside.

"It's warmer inside," Kit said as he passed under the archway, not even noticing how spectacular and clear the ice was.

It felt like they were entering an enchanted maze. Above, the walkway had a pitched ceiling made entirely of glass. Elsie stared upward, mesmerized by the falling snow gliding down the glass and falling onto the pitched roofs of the wooden market stalls below.

"How—" she started.

A firm hand wrapped around her arm and pulled her to the side. "We're blocking the path," Kit grumbled.

"But look at these lights. How is it staying warm?" Instead of candles, tiny baubles of lights hung from the edges of glass on strings so fine they were almost invisible, and warmth radiated down from the ceiling.

Kit sighed. "Magic. The crystals have energy that creates light and heat. The glass keeps it in."

"Magic," she mumbled to herself. It certainly wasn't all bad. So far, she hadn't seen anything bad. It didn't stop her jumpiness, but perhaps it wouldn't be so hard to get used to after all.

"We need to keep moving." Kit glanced around.

Elsie tried not to stare as they entered the maze of ice and glass. Creatures of all kinds, including witches in robes, elves with shimmering skin, and fae with wings in a myriad of colors, were selling all sorts of unfamiliar items at every turn. Some even sported peculiar horns, antlers, or flowers sprouting from their heads. She spotted her first vampire, or Kit said he was a vampire, but he looked like a normal human man selling books, and as promised, there were several humans selling their goods, no different to Winterfrost Market.

She couldn't help but stop at a shop full of trinkets and amulets. Smiling nervously at the young witch with flawless skin and black fingernails, Elsie made her first magical purchase. A palm-sized dream pillow for Marie, a Midwinter gift to give the user pleasant dreams. She remembered to ask the witch if she recognized the picture of her mother, but she didn't.

"That was a real witch! Did you see her?" Elsie resisted the urge to shake Kit's arm in excitement. She hadn't even tried to steal her soul like Marie said.

"Are you going to get this excited about every magical thing we encounter? You were terrified of magic two days ago."

"I know, but this is all so wonderful! Do you think it will work?" Elsie failed to restrain herself and bounced around in excitement as she tucked the sweet-smelling tiny pillow into her inner coat pocket.

"If the witch knows what she's doing, it should." The corners of his lips curled up like he was trying to suppress a smile. "She is a magic student here, from the Great Northern Citadel. You can tell by the badge on her dress."

Elsie grinned to herself. A magic student, how wonderful. "She didn't know anything about my mum." But was Kit, right? Was she too excited, too innocent, too ignorant when it came to magic? Maybe she ought to listen to Marie's advice and be careful.

"Neither did the palm reader over there." Kit tilted his head to a shimmery gray woman in a white flowing dress.

Elsie didn't let it get her down. She was in too good of a mood to be disheartened.

They wandered the market for hours, questioning every vendor. But no luck finding anything about her mum.

The spice sellers had stalls piled high with pyramids of red paprika, golden turmeric, powdered fennel, and so much more. She bought some packs of cinnamon sticks, star anise, and green cardamom pods, things they always needed more of. But the spice sellers couldn't recall her mother, or if they did, they didn't say anything.

She felt guilty for not being completely truthful with Kit, but she had wholeheartedly believed one of them would have seen her mother. This must mean her mother had gone out to collect ingredients herself. Just as Elsie had feared. She wasn't sure what to tell Kit or where to start.

If they hadn't found out anything more by tonight, she would have to tell him about the powder her mother went to the lengths of the isles to find.

They wandered up to a stall run by a tall woman whose arms were covered in silver bangles and her neck adorned with green gemstones set in silver circles that hung over her purple tunic.

Another witch.

Elsie was drawn to the colors and shiny gemstones, then noticed the simple cord bracelets, each with a tiny silver charm.

"Sir, buy a Midwinter wish for your lovely lady?" the woman sang out to Kit.

Elsie's cheeks heated. "Oh, he isn't—"

A rush of air shot into her. So cold and so fast it took her breath away and had her stumbling into the table, sending the bracelets and the tablecloth into a heap.

"Oi, get back here!" Kit bellowed, then shot off chasing after whatever caused the upset.

"I'm so sorry, I messed up your lovely display." Elsie stared at the shopkeeper who looked just as bewildered as she felt.

"Bloody thieves," the woman hissed. She came around the front and helped Elsie arrange the wish bracelets back in order.

"I didn't see anything." Elsie tried to copy the woman's arrangement technique.

"'Tis getting worse. The Haven Peacekeepers are a useless waste of space. Need to get in the Snowspire Guards."

"Snowspire Guards? Are they a policing force?"

"You been living under a rock girl?"

Before Elsie could answer, Kit was back, dragging a small boy with fluttering blue wings by the ear.

They stopped in front of the stand. "Give back what you took," Kit ordered.

"Do it or I'll curse ya," the witch added.

Elsie believed her. The boy quickly emptied his pockets of the gems he had taken, his wings vibrating like a mad hummingbird the whole time. Elsie almost felt sorry for the lad hooked in Kit's grasp.

"Do you want me to report him?" Kit asked the stall owner.

"I'll give him a warning." The woman leaned down and pulled the boy by the collar, so he was right in her face. "I know your face now, lad. You do this again and I'll tell the Snowspire Guards to come get you, and I'll curse you for good measure."

The lad nodded furiously. The woman released him, checked nothing else was missing, and nodded to Kit, who let go of him.

Kit leaned over to Elsie. "The Snowspire Guards are ruthless and not to be trusted," he said loud enough the boy would hear.

"And you know what they do to little boys who steal? They rip off their wings." The woman made a ripping noise as she tore an invisible wing in front of him, and he sprinted off down the path, crying, half running and half fluttering as he went.

The witch put the gems the boy had taken back into their places. "Thank you for that, sir. I've been trying to catch that little blighter for days."

"Not a problem. It's good of you not to turn him in."

Elsie had seen her fair share of pickpockets, but never any so fast and using magic of some kind. How in the heavens did Kit catch him at that speed? He was too fast, too knowledgeable about magic, too secretive. She was almost certain she knew what he was now—one of the fae. He probably had good reason to be hiding, but she didn't appreciate being left in the dark and planned to find out.

A gentle touch to her arm broke her thoughts.

She jumped. Kit's sky-blue eyes were suddenly in front of her, concerned, and trying to catch her gaze. "Did you hear me, Elsie? Are you hurt?"

Her neck warmed. "Sorry, I was lost in thought. I'm quite well." Kit pulled his hand away, and she found herself disappointed.

"For your heroics, I offer you one wish bracelet of your choosing for your maiden." The woman smiled at Kit and waved her hand above the selection.

"He isn't—" Elsie tried to say once more.

"I thank you." Kit slid off his gloves and selected one straight away, then turned to Elsie. "May I?"

Elsie nodded and held out her wrist to Kit. Shivers danced up her arm and down her spine as he slid her coat sleeve back to reveal the skin between her glove and her cuff. Warmth spread from his fingers as they grazed her exposed skin, tying a knot in the red bracelet with extreme care.

When his skin touched hers a second time, she glanced up with a start. She was sure he flickered.

"Did you see that?" she asked.

"What?" He was deep in concentration trying to tie the tiny knot.

"You shimmered for a second there." She felt silly as soon as she said it.

He casually dismissed it with a shrug. "Does it feel right?" he asked. Stepping back to admire his handy work.

She spun the red braid around to see the charm. The symbol showed a cup with a heart and a lightning bolt. "It's lovely, thank you." Perhaps she hadn't seen anything, or perhaps it was the glamour he said fae could have.

The woman smiled. "Good choice."

Kit thanked the woman and gave her a small candle from his pocket as they left.

"Why did you give her a candle? Was it not a gift?"

"It was a fair trade. Wishes aren't cheap, but by custom, she would not accept money. A candle to light her way is a fitting trade."

"You certainly know a lot about magic and such." Elsie rubbed the new charm between her fingers. If he was fae, could she trust him?

Kit turned down a new alley of the market. "I grew up near here."

Another suspicious fact. "What does it mean?" She spun the charm between her fingers.

"The symbols are the cup and heart for the Azure Sister and the lightning for the Ethereal Father. My wish was to 'find one's heart,' in the hope the gods will guide you to your mother."

Elsie's chest grew tight. That was the nicest thing anyone had done for her in a long time, even if he wasn't who he said he was.

Even if he was fae.

The thought had her stomach twisting in knots. But until she had proof she would treat him as the Kit she'd grown to like.

"Thank you, Kit." She bumped him playfully with her shoulder, and she swore he blushed ever so slightly as he turned and pointed to the exit on the other side of the market. She would wait for the right time to ask him what he was hiding.

CHAPTER 17

KIT

Kit ruffled Pepper's head. She'd collapsed in a damp heap by the fire as soon as they'd gotten into his room and was now snoring loudly. She was worn out, and no doubt happy to have had a decent run around outside in the snow once he returned from his excursion with Elsie.

Liri had managed to find a room for Elsie. At least she would be more comfortable in her own space. Though he felt oddly lonely when he looked at the empty chair by the window.

Night had already fallen, and the day of interacting with strangers and searching for clues had drained Kit more than he cared to admit. He ran a hand through his wet hair. He really should attempt to dry it and dress in something more than a towel. But after a long day of thinking he had recovered, his energy was back to zero, and he wanted nothing more than to lie down and sleep.

But his racing thoughts would not allow it. Standing by his bed, he stared at the Bloodgate Ruby just sitting there. His eyes were drawn in by the brilliant shine and deep crimson like dark wine and blood, mocking him with his own indecisiveness and lack of a plan. Its pretty exterior gave no indication of the destruction it could cause, especially in his father's hands. He sat down on the bed beside it considering his options.

At first, he thought the quest his father had sent him on an honor; if he came back with the stone, he would win a tiny amount of his father's respect. But on the road, he realized that was something he would never get, nor ever really wanted. What he wanted was to be able to live his own life, get out from the shadow of his father and brother. Funnily enough, the quest had allowed him to do that, to see what was out there in the world, and know he didn't want to be the spare prince any longer.

He stood up, not wanting to look at the stone, moved to the chair by the fire, and sipped the horrid tea he had been avoiding. Despite it being from a mortal healer, the fae healer had insisted it would help.

Still, the Bloodgate Ruby sat there, mocking him, wanting him to decide what to do.

His father was nothing more than a narcissist, a want-to-be conqueror who thought he'd been cheated of his rightful inheritance and wanted it back. The stone was the key, and Midwinter Haven was the prize he wanted to claim.

But after a day with Elsie in the market, Kit had spoken to more people of Midwinter Haven than he ever had in his life. He claimed to have grown up here, but the truth was he was an outsider. Elsie had made more friends in one day than he had in his life.

He forced himself to take another sip, willing the tea and the goddess, Azure Sister, to stabilize his magic and to balance his health.

Midwinter Haven was just that, a haven. Developed by a treaty between all the magic kingdoms over eighty years ago and set up on the land gifted by the Winterfae Kingdom, by his own grandfather to start a new city where all were welcome. The treaty was unbreakable unless all Kingdoms agreed to dissolve it.

However, the city wards were not unbreakable.

Kit clenched his fist. "Ow." Right, his arm.

He finished the tea in one horrible gulp.

A loud knocking sounded at the door. He glanced between the Bloodgate Ruby and his towel. The stone was more important.

"Just a moment, if you please," he called.

He wrapped the ruby in its cloth, tucked it into the wooden box, and shoved it into his bag.

He swung open the door, expecting Liri with news of his father.

What he found was a very startled Elsie staring right at his bare chest, and her eyes moved down to his towel.

"Oh, Elsie. Can I help you?" He tried to remain casual.

"I found something, may I please come in?" Her eyes were bright with hope, and she was holding a large bag.

"Certainly." He opened the door wider, and she walked right in and set the bag on his bed. "Is it about your mother?"

"It is." She nodded and chewed on her lip, not looking him in the eye.

Oh, right. No clothes, except the towel wrapped around his hips. "Please excuse me while I dress." He grabbed a clean shirt and semi-clean trousers and went to the bathroom to change.

When he came out, Elsie was sitting cross-legged at the end of his bed with the bag in front of her, staring at it.

"What is it then?" he asked as he adjusted a pillow and sat at the head of the bed, not sure if he'd get up again if he got too comfortable.

"It's my mother's bag. Liri found it." Elsie began chewing her thumbnail.

"How?" He couldn't help but be glad for Elsie that they had something to go on.

"Well, I went down to get a hot chocolate, and Liri was there. She said she'd done some asking around this evening, and one of her friends works at an inn on the outskirts of town. She said she had seen my mum." She took a breath. "So Liri went over there with her, and they gave her my mum's things to bring to me. Said she left one morning, well over a week ago, and never returned for her things, nor to pay her bill," Elsie spoke rapidly.

"Calm down, have a glass of water," Kit said, concerned she was going to pass out from speaking so fast. He poured her a glass of water from the pitcher on his bedside table and handed it to her.

She looked at it, then drank it all down. He had reassured her earlier the water was safe, though she was skeptical about a lot of odd things.

"We have a day she disappeared and a place. Let's check the bag and see if there is anything in there that can help us. Tomorrow, we can go to the inn and find out more."

Elsie nodded but didn't reach for the bag.

"Are you well?" He wasn't sure how to deal with this situation.

"I'm quite well. I can do this," she said, perhaps more to herself than him. She pulled the drawstring of the canvas bag open and began removing items and placing them on the bed. Kit forced himself up, despite his protesting body, and perched on the bed near her as she emptied the bag.

A few dresses, a hairbrush, tea-making equipment similar to Elsie's, some books about local plants and fungi in the Winterfae Kingdom—wait, that one was odd.

"This book." He passed it to Elsie. "Does it have any meaning to you?"

Elsie was silent as she held up a heart-shaped locket by the chain then clasped it in her palm and brought it to her chest. She tried to hide it, but Kit saw the tears creeping from the corner of her eyes.

"What is it?" He wasn't sure how to comfort her or what to say.

She swallowed, and thankfully, pulled herself together. "I think I know where she went." Her voice was fragile, like it might crack any moment.

"How do you know? Is there a note?" Kit asked.

Elsie shook her head, still clutching the locket to her chest. "She only ever took this off when we went walking in the forest or we went to the beach, anywhere she was scared she might lose it." Elsie flicked open the locket to reveal a picture of a man, presumably Elsie's father. On the other side were two little girls with jet-black hair, one smiling, one not.

"You think she went walking somewhere?"

"Yes, and I know what she was looking for." She reached for the book in Kit's hand, and he passed it over, not sure where this was going.

Elsie flicked through the book. "The ingredient she came here for wasn't a spice. She made me promise not to tell anyone, but it is the secret ingredient we use in our spiced tea."

Kit had a feeling he knew what she was about to say but waited, hoping it wasn't so.

"It was this mushroom." Elsie handed him the open book. "She must have tried to buy it, but I didn't see any at the market, and it only grows in one forest here, so she must have gone looking for it."

Rage threatened to bring his ice magic to his fingertips and blast something as he would have as a child.

"This is the sacred dragon's eye fungi," he said, then clenched his jaw to stop himself from overreacting.

Elsie leaned over him and frowned at the book. "It says here it is illegal to harvest. I didn't know that. I thought it was just a secret recipe."

Kit stood up and so did Pepper. "Down, Pepper," he yelled, and Pepper did as she was told, and he instantly felt bad. He paced the small space in front of the fire.

"What's wrong with you?" Elsie asked.

"The dragon's eye is sacred to the fae. It only comes from one forest in the world, from one stand of birch trees." He held his hands up, not believing someone would be so disrespectful to harvest the sacred fungi and for something as stupid as selling tea. There had to be more to it.

"I'm sure she didn't know that," Elsie whispered.

"Of course she did," Kit spat. "It's why she came here."

"Why are you so worked up? What is it to you?" She narrowed her eyes.

"It's only used for sacred ceremonies. The powder is so rare—" He shook his head; he didn't even have the words for how disrespectful this was.

Elsie stood up, her brown eyes shimmering with unfallen tears. "I don't understand."

Great, just great. He continued to pace while she stood by the bed with her arms crossed.

When he turned and got back to Elsie, her eyes were burning with rage.

"Hold this." She reached out her hand.

He instinctively opened his palm and caught whatever she dropped. White hot pain shot through his hand, and he released the item with a violent flick of his wrist and drew his fist to his chest hissing with pain.

"What in the Ancient Mother's name was that?" He opened his palm to see a perfect star burned into it—the same star her sister gave her.

He looked up slowly and met her eye.

"I'm not the only one who's been hiding something, Kit."

CHAPTER 18

KIT

K it shook his hand, doing a poor job of hiding the pain of the burn. "Elsie, I can explain." Pepper stood up from her fireside nap, looking between Kit and Elsie, confused. That made two of them.

Elsie picked up her iron star necklace from his bed where he had dropped it so suddenly, the burn still searing into the flesh of his palm.

She held up the amulet. "I might have lied to you about one thing, but this is so much bigger. You are fae. Aren't you? And you've been lying to me this whole time."

It had been nice while it lasted. "I've never lied to you."

"You are fae?"

"Yes. I am," he answered honestly. There was no other way. He thought he had been so clever.

She blinked but didn't move, perhaps scared he might use his magic on her. They both stood awkwardly at the end of the bed.

"It's a glamour," he said, unsure what else to say.

"I'm aware of that. But why? You are among the fae now. Why keep lying to me?"

"I always look this way here. I prefer it. The only difference is my ears and wings. People in Midwinter recognize me both ways."

"It wasn't to trick me?" She retied the ribbon around her neck and let the iron star fall to her chest.

He felt sorry for her. Everything her sister warned her about fae was proving true, and he was not helping the cause.

"No, I have no reason to trick you, Elsie. I wanted to tell you, but it was safer for you this way. You can trust me."

"Can I?" she snapped.

She'd done an excellent job of diverting the real problem at hand. He should be angry about her lying mother. He took a calming breath and walked around her to sink into the pillows on his bed and try to appear less threatening. She had a direct path to the door if she wanted to run.

"Of course." He closed his eyes, relaxing into the pillow. Perhaps he needed more of that potion the healer had left. He could feel her eyes on him still.

"What else are you hiding?" she asked.

He sighed and opened his eyes. "A good many things. Things I can't tell you, but I promise, there is no malicious reason behind it."

"Then why?" She lowered herself to the end of the bed and clutched her mother's dress.

"To keep you safe."

"From your father?"

"He is the main reason, yes." He couldn't tell her too much. The less she knew, the better.

She smoothed out her mother's dress on the bed and began folding it. "Very well."

"Very well? You're okay about me being fae, just like that?"

"I suspected it since we left Winterfrost." She looked around him as if trying to see his wings.

Oh, so he hadn't been as subtle as he'd thought. That and her detective skills were expanding by the hour it seemed. "I'm sorry I couldn't tell you. I wasn't sure I could trust you."

"And now you do?" She placed the dress back in the bag.

"I suppose," he said. Now she knew he couldn't lie. At least she could believe everything he said was true.

"Then take away the glamour, show me."

He paused at the unexpected demand, suddenly feeling like he was standing there in his towel all over again. If that was what it took to gain her trust once more, he was willing to do it. "Very well."

He eased himself off the bed and untucked his shirt from his breeches. "What are you doing?" Elsie stood up, clutching another of her mother's dresses.

He threw his shirt on the bed. "You wanted to see, didn't you?"

"Yes," she said stubbornly.

If she was afraid, she did a good job of hiding it. Closing his eyes, Kit removed the glamour for the first time in nearly a year. His shield, his mortal identity, all stripped away with a split second of magic.

He couldn't help but let out a groan of relief as his wings stretched from his back, and he stood up, letting them expand into this world once more. They were always there under the glamour.

He closed his eyes and rolled his neck at the pleasure of stretching, of being himself again. His ears grew pointed and poked through his hair that extended past his shoulders, transforming the brown tangled mess into soft and silky strands.

Elsie gasped. "Your face, it's nearly the same."

"You're not going to comment on my radiant wings? I'm quite proud of them." He swallowed, feeling her eyes moving over his true body.

She'd moved closer, though still at a safe distance near the end of the bed. "They are quite beautiful," she said in a hushed tone that sent goosebumps down his arms.

He turned so she could see his wings, and he glimpsed himself in the mirror over the dresser. He had to admit it felt good to see his wings, to know they were still there, the same wings as his mother: rich emerald green tipped with silver on the edges, rounded slightly, but long and graceful, and very different from his father and brother. Theirs were both sharper and more defined with the more appropriate light blue and silver—colors of the Winterfae royals as opposed to the Spring Court his mother hailed from.

"But why does your face look so similar?" Elsie asked, pulling him from his own wing admiration.

"You don't like my face? You certainly know how to compliment a man."

"I like your face perfectly well." She blushed. "You know what I mean, if you're supposed to be in disguise."

"I despise face-changing glamours. I simply needed to pass as mortal while traveling, so changed the bare minimum to be passable." This was the truth. This real face was his disguise, though few knew it. He didn't mention he also had a more famous royal face, the glamour for the public, and the palace knew him as Prince Christarel Whitewood, spare to the Snowspire throne. It was the perfect disguise. Even his own family didn't know his true face, neither did he know theirs.

"That makes sense." Elsie seemed convinced as she edged closer to him. "Can I touch them? Your wings?" she asked nervously.

He nodded and swallowed hard as she stepped around him cautiously and walked behind him. This was not what he had expected. Maybe it would have been better if she'd been afraid of him.

An involuntary shiver raced down his back as soft fingers traced the base of his wing and over the ridge.

She pulled her hand away. "Sorry, did I hurt you?"

"No, it's just rather sensitive there." He swallowed. That felt amazing. He snapped his wings flat on his back, and Elsie squealed, then stepped in front of him with a grin on her face as if she had just discovered magic.

"That is quite wonderful." She shook her head in disbelief then turned quickly and snatched her hand away when he moved.

Kit kept his wings flat across his back, not wanting to re-glamour them. He felt himself again.

Elsie avoided eye contact and continued packing up her mother's bag at the end of the bed.

"So maybe you don't hate the fae quite as much as you did before?"

"No." She locked eyes with him. "I suppose I don't. Though I won't forget you hid it from me."

"I won't forget you lied to me about your mother," he answered back quickly, though instantly regretted it as the smile fell from her face.

"I'm sorry I lied." She bit her lip.

"Would it be a step in the right direction toward rebuilding our trust if I said I might know where your mother is?" he asked cautiously. It wasn't good news.

Her eyes lit up as if she couldn't contain the hope that sparked. "It would be a good start."

"If she was caught in the sacred forest, she is most certainly in the prison at Snowspire Palace." Kit stretched his wings one more time, then snapped them down his back. He still didn't have the energy to reset the glamour, so he draped his shirt over his shoulders.

Elsie sank into the end of the bed, staring at her mother's bag for several seconds. "Then we must go to the palace first thing tomorrow."

"No. That would not be wise." He glanced over at Pepper, who had gone back to sleep by the fire, apparently not interested in their drama.

"We must find out somehow." She clasped the star amulet tight in her hand. "We need to go there."

"We need to be sensible about this. I have a friend. A guard. I'll send him a note tonight and see if he can find anything out tomorrow. Then we will go from there."

She stood up, then sat down again as if unsure what to do with herself. "But you said the guards can't be trusted."

"This one can. Just give me tomorrow to see what he can come up with. And I will take you to the sacred forest and see if we can find any clues ourselves."

"Very well. One day. But if your friend is useless, I'm going to the palace myself." She gathered the bag tight to her chest and stood up.

CHAPTER 19

ELSIE

E lsie hadn't realized how much of a trek it would be to the forest, or she might have taken up Kit's offer of catching a stagecoach. But she was the one who had insisted on walking in the freezing morning air. She was too restless to sit in a stagecoach, anyway. Not to mention having to sit that close to strange magical folks, or Kit, the word-twisting fae. She wondered what it would be like sitting that close to him, feeling his leg press against her as a carriage jostled them about.

"Are you listening, Elsie?" Kit said.

"Sorry, what was that?" She nearly tripped over a tree root rushing to catch up. That would be embarrassing, toppling over and tumbling down the bank onto the frozen lake. A frozen lake that apparently had a society of magical creatures or beings of some sort living within it. No, thank you.

His boots squelched in the muddy snow track of the many footsteps that had passed before them. "We're nearly there."

They'd followed the edge of the Veiled Waters all the way from Midwinter Haven. Kit said they were still in the Midwinter Haven Protected Zone, several hours away from the Winterfae Kingdom and the Vampire Realm borders that touched near the far end of the long lake.

She didn't admit how much her feet were hurting in her new boots, but she used the pain to drive away horrible thoughts about her mother in prison. She refused to think about her father and what his fate might have been. She could be walking the very path from where he disappeared. "Why is this sacred fae forest not in the fae kingdom?" Elsie tried to distract herself.

"It used to be. King Thedril, before the current king, King Valendor, gifted this land from the Winterfae Kingdom when they set up Midwinter Haven as a sanctuary for all."

"That was generous of him." Elsie wiped her eyes with her hanky; the cold air and brightness making her look like she was constantly crying.

Kit strode ahead, his footsteps barely breaking the snow and mud surface. "Indeed. It's the reason the current king is not happy. He wants to take back the land to gain control of trade in the town. He wants the taxes to fund his army. He believes it to be his right, and he might have a way to do it."

"But he can't do that, can he? There is a treaty in place. I read about it on the wall in one inn we went to."

"A treaty bound by magic. But some say he has found a loophole."

"What is it?"

He paused as if thinking his words over. Now that she knew he was fae, Elsie paid particular attention to his words, trying to work out what he was and wasn't saying.

"There is a way he can take down the protective wards on the borders and take back his lands the old-fashioned way."

That did not sound like good news for Midwinter Haven. She was growing attached to the place. Who would have thought? "Would he do that? How do you know all this?"

"This is the path." He pivoted away.

She had caught onto his diversion tactics now. "You didn't answer me." She followed him off the path bathed in sunlight and into a snow-covered way between trees with no footprints that was narrow like a deer track.

"I did not, because some things are better left not knowing."

A chill ran down Elsie's back. "Very well. But do you work for the palace? Is that how you know things?" It would explain why he had friends who were guards. Maybe the stone he collected for his 'father' was really for someone at the palace, and it was a code he used. She frowned. He couldn't lie, but maybe a code word made it true... Was she reading too much into this?

Kit stopped dead in his tracks and spun around so fast she nearly walked right into him. He needed to stop doing that.

"Yes, I do work for the palace." His hand went to his mortal-looking ear. He seemed to do that when he was nervous, though it didn't show on his face. "It is dangerous work. I do not want you involved for your own safety."

Her instincts were right. But she was surprised he hadn't dodged the question further. Perhaps he was beginning to trust her. She wondered if he was a spy or perhaps a tracker for the king, and birdwatching was his cover. Though his obsession with birds seemed real enough, as did the detail in his bird book he'd shown her on their journey.

Elsie took a sharp breath, realizing just how close they were standing. His eyes were icy blue, almost white. His expression softened. He didn't look away, and neither did she. She wanted to reach for his hand, to let him know he could trust her, but she didn't dare.

"I understand. I won't push, but I don't like to be kept in the dark." She crossed her arms and tried to repress the shiver that coursed through her.

"It was never my intention." He turned away quickly. "It's just up ahead. There is strong magic here, so stay close to me."

They passed a sign that read, You are entering a Winterfae Protected Territory. Entry permitted to citizens of the Winterfae Kingdom only. Trespassers will be imprisoned.

"About that sign back there..." Elsie's hands were sweating in her gloves.

"I suppose your mother didn't read it." He scoffed and turned around. But seeing Elsie's intentionally unimpressed look, he started walking again. He cleared his throat. "Don't worry. We'll be in and out before anyone can get here."

He must have believed that to be true, but if she ended up in prison alongside her mum, that wouldn't do any of them any good. She had to trust Kit knew what he was doing, and strangely enough, she found she did. At least the no-lying thing had benefits for her.

Ten minutes later, they were in a glade of scattered birch trees, their white trunks blending with the bright snow to create a scene of blinding white in every direction with the sparkling sun shining down through gaps in the canopy.

Breath misting in front of her, Elsie hardly noticed the cold, her limbs well warmed from the long walk. She slipped off her gloves and let them dangle from her wrists by the cords.

Kit waited until she was in step with him and leaned in close. "Do not be alarmed by the tree sprites. They will not hurt us if we do not threaten them." His breath whispered over her neck.

"Tree sprites?" she squeaked. There was no mention of tree sprites earlier. What was a tree sprite? She suspected she was about to find out.

A cackle of laughter came from behind. Elsie whipped her head around, but there was nothing there. She resisted the urge to cling to Kit's arm when a giggle erupted to her left.

"Is that them?" she whispered.

"We wish to speak with you. We offer no threat," Kit called out and held up his hands to presumably show he was unarmed. Elsie did the same.

There was a fluttering of wings, and two tiny figures appeared in front of them.

Elsie took a step back. The creatures, about a foot high, hovered at her eye level with wings beating so quickly they were a shapeless blur. Tiny round faces with wide eyes stared back at her, their teeth yellow, jagged, and terrifying with a grin that made Elsie's skin crawl. Their skin was natural camouflage, the same as the birch bark, contrasting with their dark spiked hair.

"We heard of an incident that occurred here and wanted to find out more." Kit lowered his hands.

"This one looks like her," one tree sprite hissed to the other.

Elsie couldn't tell the difference between them or if they were male or female. "Looks like who?" She could only hope they had witnessed what had happened.

"The thief. The one who asked too many questions," they hissed at the same time.

The sprites shot to a tree, their sharp claws slicing into the bark. Kit and Elsie exchanged a look.

"Are they safe?" Elsie whispered. Questions... that sounded like her mother.

Kit didn't answer straight away. "If you do nothing to threaten them."

"Would they have hurt my mum?" Elsie gulped. Not wanting to get any closer to these horrid creatures.

"Let's find out." Kit strode toward them.

Elsie followed at a safe distance, resisting the urge to pick up a stick to bat them off if they got too close. She suspected they might see that as a threat.

"What did you do to the thief?" Kit asked.

"She tried to take the prize. She wanted answers." They both stroked a lumpy black nodule growing on the trunk of the tree. The creatures' heads darted around like children who'd had too many sweets.

Unease prickled across Elsie's scalp. She had seen an illustration like this in her mum's mushroom book. These unappealing black growths were where the secret ingredients came from. She had to wonder if it was worth it and why in the angels' names her mother had gone to such lengths. Though deep down knew it was something to do with her father.

"Yes, but what happened to her?" Elsie demanded.

Their grins grew wider. "We scratched and scratched and buzzed and buzzed."

"You alerted the palace?" Kit asked.

Elsie bit her lip, her heart racing with the sickening feeling that something horrible had happened to her mother. She couldn't stand not doing anything. She set her gaze out over the forest floor, searching for anything that might indicate what had happened.

"The guards. They marched and marched and down she fell." The sprites both giggled.

"Was she injured?" Elsie was sick of this nonsense talk.

The sprites flew into the air, darting between trees. "Arrows all around."

One stopped on an arrow dug deep into a tree trunk.

Elsie gasped. "No."

Kit grabbed a sprite so fast Elsie didn't even see him move. "Speak, sprite, or I will freeze your very breath." Kit raised the sprite to the sky as the other hissed and flitted around his head, but Kit maintained a tight grip.

Elsie's heart raced as she witnessed the side of Kit that she was afraid of. But she stayed close, glad he was on her side as they moved closer to the tree with the arrow. There was no sign of blood, but the snow was fresh. Elsie kicked some with her foot, but there was nothing more than dead grass beneath the snow.

"The thief was alive, but bit by an arrow. Taken. Taken!" the sprite in Kit's hand screeched.

The other sprite threw acorns, or something equally solid, at Kit's head. He did well to ignore it. "Taken by the guards or taken from the light."

Elsie's breath hitched. Her mother had to be alive. It was the only option.

"Taken by guards. Stomp, stomp, away they go. Let me down!" Its voice grew higher.

Acorns rained down on Kit from above.

Elsie released a shaky exhale. "We can be certain they've taken her. Perhaps we best leave now." Elsie wanted him to let the creature go. No more good could come of this, and she knew where her mother was. She had to get to the palace. The sooner they got back, the sooner they would find out if Kit's friend had news from the palace.

"I think you're right." Kit released the sprite into the air, and it hissed at him and went straight to a tree and clung to it. "Thank you for your assistance," he said coldly.

The other sprite continued to buzz around, throwing acorns at Kit. "You lingered too long, marching, marching they come."

"Let's leave." Elsie was on the narrow path as Kit caught up to her, still under acorn fire.

"The guards do come. No, the mortals are not welcome in the land of the fae," the other sprite yelled after them as they cackled and buzzed obnoxiously in front of Kit and Elsie and darted out of reach.

Kit shot his hands out in front of him. Bright white magic blasted from his fingers, sending shards of ice into the tree canopy after the sprites.

Elsie ducked to the ground at the noise as snow clumps fell from the rattled trees above.

"Blast them!" Kit swore.

"What in heaven's name was that? Did you really need to do that?" Elsie stared at Kit in shock.

Kit spun around quickly. "Yes, it made me feel better, and we need to go right now."

She dusted the snow off her head and shoulders, not daring to look up in case more fell. "I gathered as much."

Kit reached for her hand and hauled her up. His skin was warm and soft, even after shooting all that ice out of it somehow. Despite her mind telling her she should be afraid, she didn't flinch or pull away; in fact, something inside her was drawn to him. Was he enchanting her?

Without a word, Kit set off at a run while hauling Elsie along. With her free hand, she pulled up her skirts and allowed herself to be pulled along, while her mind struggled to catch up. Her legs moved without her telling them to and whisked them out of the fae land. They were at the Veiled Waters lakeside in no time.

The sheet of expansive ice as far as the eye could see was a welcome sight.

Elsie fought to catch her breath, but Kit didn't slow down as they skidded into the lakeside path. His hand fell away from her, and she mourned the loss of contact. Then felt silly. She shouldn't be acting like a damsel in distress, she wanted to prove to Kit she was capable.

She kept his pace as they continued, suspecting it was slower for her benefit. But nearly slammed into him when he stopped.

"We need to get off the road. They're almost on us." His breath was heavy. She felt bad for the situation, forcing him to run while he was recovering still. Perhaps his medicine wasn't working as well as he'd said.

"Over there." Elsie pointed to a shadowed section of forest that had several large rocks among the thick-trunked pines.

Kit darted off the path with the grace of a cat, and Elsie lumbered after him, her dress dragging in the deeper snow.

"Our footprints," she called in alarm. They would be instantly noticeable.

"Never mind that." He ducked behind a rock, and Elsie lost sight of him.

She followed him into the shadows behind the large boulders where no snow had reached. Kit swapped places with her on the edge as she crouched in the bed of sweet-scented pine needles trying to still her rapid breath.

He held his hand out, aimed at the path they made in the snow, just as he did before.

Elsie stood up to see. Half mesmerized, half terrified by his power as a slow fog spread over their tracks and fell to the ground in a soft billow of white that curled up at the corners. The fog held for a second, then sank into the snow, leaving nothing but white powder. No footprints, no disturbance of any kind.

Elsie sucked in a breath. "That was beautiful." She stared at the ground, hardly believing such magic could be real.

"Thank you, I'm rather proud of my snow work. It doesn't come easily to me." He smiled a nervous smile.

It dawned on her that he was worried about what she thought. She wouldn't let him know she was a little scared. He had been so nice to her since their talk last night, and he didn't have to be.

Kit ducked and pulled her down beside him.

Voices sounded along the lake path, and Elsie did her best to ignore her heartbeat that was still thundering in her chest, sure Kit could hear it.

Neither of them looked around the rock, but the voices gave away the guards, though their footsteps were silent as cats.

Kit exchanged a look with Elsie that clearly said *stay quiet*. She had no intention of making any noise and focused hard on being still. As she did so, she became very aware of how close Kit was to her. His leg pressed against hers as they crouched. Their fingers so close to touching on the rock where they braced themselves.

His breath misted in the air mingling with hers. He must have had the same realization as her because he tensed for a moment. But Kit didn't turn away, instead a small smile stole across his lips.

Elsie swallowed, captivated by the intensity of his glacial blue eyes.

A shout startled her. She gripped the rock to steady herself.

She didn't look at Kit again. Focusing on the rock was better, and not moving, and especially not thinking about how soft his lips looked. Her fingers grew numb, and she wished she'd had time to put her gloves on before they'd started running.

After what seemed like an eternity, Kit moved, and she almost shot into the tree above in fright.

"You can relax," he whispered.

Elsie pried herself off the rock, feeling like a frozen oyster, and fell back to sit on the spongy pine needle carpet. All her energy sapped away.

Attempting to bend her fingers, she whimpered in pain as they burned with the movement. "Have they gone?"

He frowned and took her hand, rubbing his palms on either side of it. She winced as warmth spread through her skin, bringing sharp defrosting pains with it. As the pain turned to pleasure, she closed her eyes.

"You have heating magic too?" she said, opening her eyes as he slipped her fingers into her glove and moved onto her other hand. She stretched her gloved fingers which were now limber and back to normal.

"No, I just have a mix of winter and spring magic. But I don't get cold, so my body heat can be useful." He focused on her hand intently.

Elsie swore she saw a hint of blush on his cheeks. She was certainly appreciating his body heat now and admitted she enjoyed the closeness.

"What do you think the sprites meant about your mother asking questions?" Kit slipped her other glove on.

Elsie tested her fingers, not trusting herself to look at Kit. "I think she might have been asking about my father. I never believed her stories about the fae, but I think he might have gone missing here too."

The honesty felt good. It came out so freely and felt like a weight being lifted from her back.

Kit exhaled loudly. "And you never thought to mention it?"

"I never believed it was true. But I think she might have been right." Elsie's throat grew thick. Saying it aloud made it seem all too real.

"We better get back." Kit stepped back. Perhaps he sensed she was about to crack because he didn't press the subject.

She nodded, but her jaw was tight. She forced herself to speak, to hold herself together. "Yes. Now that we know what happened, we can make a plan to go to the palace."

Kit stood up gracefully, not like Elsie, whose bones were half frozen from crouching and tensing every muscle in her body.

"Let's see what Fenn has to say first. Let's hope it's good news," Kit said.

CHAPTER 20

KIT

Kit sat up straight in his chair in the corner of The Fae's Folly and scowled into his cup of bitter tea. He was envious of the neighboring table drinking elvish brandy, but glad to be out of bed after the afternoon of lounging around on healer's orders. Apparently, their morning adventures had caused 'too much exertion'. Healer August's words, not his.

The tavern was well-lit for the dinner crowds. Each table had at least two candles burning, and the smell of beeswax drifted off them, far more pleasant than the tallow candles that were all too common in mortal towns. He had missed the smells of Midwinter Haven.

The worst part of being an invalid and lying around was it allowed his thoughts to swirl in his mind, leaving him with too many unanswered questions: What should he do about the Bloodgate Ruby? How could he protect Midwinter Haven and fulfill his oath to his father? Why was his arm healing so slowly? But the one thing that kept popping to the forefront of his mind was Elsie. He couldn't shake the persistent feeling that he wanted to be near her.

But things kept growing more complicated. Her father had gone missing too. Very odd and unexpected. No good news could come of it.

Kit glanced up at the clock. Fenn should be there any minute now.

The thoughts were more than distracting. He pictured the way she smiled at everyone she met, her warm brown eyes, the way she made his tea before her own, the way she worried about him, even though she hardly knew him. It was rare to find someone with such generosity, always thinking of others before herself...

Stop this, Kit! He ordered himself and took another sip of tea. This was what too much lying around did and nothing good could come of it.

"There you are!"

Kit glanced up.

Fenn bounded across the room in wide strides, thankfully, wearing a nondescript tunic and brown worker's breeches, not his conspicuous silver and blue guard's uniform, and pulled Kit into a hug before he was out of his chair.

Fenn was the only one from the palace who dared hug Kit in that manner. He had been assigned to Kit when he was ten, and Fenn was only six years older and more like a brother to Kit than his actual brother, Andriel.

Kit beamed back. "By the Ancient Mother, it's good to see you, Fenn."

"You too, Kit, you too. It's been the talk of the palace when you might return."

"I wish I did not have to." Kit sank into his chair and gestured to Liri to send over another drink. She acknowledged him with a nod, eying Fenn as she went about her business. Unlike the others, Liri knew Fenn was a palace guard, not popular among the fae that resided in Midwinter Haven. Many of them had escaped the Winterfae Kingdom to pursue a life away from the control of the king.

"Know what your father means to do with the stone, then?" Fenn leaned back in his chair, glancing around, taking in the crowd with the eye of a guard.

Kit leaned in. "I don't plan on letting him do anything with it. That land was given over long before his time. You must agree?"

"Ay, many of us agree. But our job is to follow orders, and we are bound to King Valendor. He's withdrawn troops from the vamp borders, even the watch on Frosthaven Keep. He means to take Midwinter Haven by force and expects everyone to submit to his rule. It's happening soon."

Kit's chest squeezed. This was too soon. He waited for Liri to place their drinks on the table, thanked her, and waited for her to return to the bar before continuing. "But there is no army here, no defense force." The Haven Peacekeepers were just that, trained to keep peace and deal with petty crime. The wards would not let anyone with intent to harm others enter.

"The king knows how easy it will be. The only thing standing in his way are those wards; wards everyone has far too much faith in if you ask me."

Sweat beaded on Kit's forehead. He had no choice but to present himself to his father before Midwinter, but there was no way his father could be allowed to use the ruby.

"You must think long and hard about your next step. He will not be merciful to you."

"I thank you for your concern." Kit took a swig of the ale he knew Elsie would tell him he shouldn't drink with his medicine tea. "I've got six days. There is still time yet."

"There is to be another ball for Andriel two days before Midwinter. It is only a matter of time before he learns you are here. He has spies everywhere. Expect a summons."

Okay... four days.

Kit sat up straighter as Elsie entered the room. A hint of a smile appeared on her lips despite stepping into a room full of fae. When she spotted him, she waved, sending a flutter through his heart. What was this woman doing to him?

"Not another word of this to Elsie, she knows nothing of my position in the court or who I am," Kit whispered to Fenn as Elsie made her way across the room.

CHAPTER 21

KIT

"Elsie Fielding, please meet Fenn Silver of the Snowspire Guard. Fenn, this is Elsie, who I spoke of in our letter," Kit said from across the table.

"Lovely to meet you, Fenn." Elsie beamed as she shook Fenn's hand like she didn't have a care in the world, but Kit knew otherwise, and she was a master of concealing her troubles.

"Likewise." Fenn put on his low, charming voice as Elsie's delicate fingers disappeared in his bear-paw-sized hands.

They all sat down, and Liri came over to take Elsie's order for a small mead, and they ordered meals to share.

They made small talk for an appropriate amount of time while they waited for their dinner. Elsie shuffled in her seat but was too polite to start the serious conversation.

Kit's knee brushed hers under the table, but she didn't move away and didn't look at him. He held his breath, trying to focus on Fenn's description of his favorite egg tarts, but Kit's attention was all on her.

She pressed her leg closer, touching her knee to his without faltering in her conversation.

Would it be so bad if they got closer?

She was going back home soon enough. She wouldn't be in any danger once she left.

A servant depositing a large bowl in the center of their table interrupted his thoughts. The aromatic steam laced with cinnamon, peanuts, and coconut milk drifted over him, bringing back memories of the winter night he first stepped into this tavern when he was a young prince rebelling against his father by going into Midwinter Haven to see what life on the other side of the border was like.

"This is your favorite, is it not, Kit?" Fenn was already filling his bowl.

"I've missed it dearly." Kit nodded to Elsie's bowl. "Help yourself before Fenn eats it all."

Elsie picked up her bowl and peered into the clay pot. "What is it?"

"A peanut and beef curry, it's quite delicious. They slow cook the meat for a good eight hours until it's so soft it melts in your mouth." His mouth was watering just thinking about it, but he wanted to see Elsie try it first. Hoping it would bring her as much joy trying it the first time as it did to him.

Fenn relinquished the spoon to Elsie, and she scooped a large serving into her bowl.

She tried a small amount, and her eyes lit up.

"That is amazing." She took another spoonful and stared thoughtfully into nowhere.

Fenn laughed. "Looks like another convert, young Kit."

"You like it?" Kit asked as he helped himself to the delicious curry, for some reason hoping she loved it as much as he did.

She nodded excitedly. "I can taste cinnamon and star anise, and is it coconut? How would they even get that here?"

"You have a keen sense of taste." Kit took a mouthful before he spoke again. "I believe the witches in the Southern Witchland invented a charm to dry and powder coconut to export. It's quite clever really."

"I wonder if I could use that in tea?" she mumbled into her bowl, focused on the soft potato she'd discovered.

Fenn was already helping himself to more. "Before I forget, the woman you mentioned in that letter. I found her."

Elsie's spoon clattered into her bowl. "In the prison?"

Kit watched her, unsure how she would react. She didn't seem like one to have outbursts, though she was highly driven by her emotions and not so much by logic. At least, that's what he had observed. Hopefully, she wouldn't run off to the prison in the night and try to see her mother.

"Ay, she's in the prison at Snowspire Palace. I'm sorry to bring such ill tidings." Fenn scooped up a flatbread from the center of the table and dunked it into his bowl.

Elsie's face drained of color, and Kit moved the edge of his seat in case he needed to catch her should she fall.

"Did you see her yourself?" Kit asked.

"No, just the prisoners' list. The name Tia Fielding, just as your letter said."

Elsie gripped the edge of the table. "What will happen to her? Will there be a trial?"

Fenn shook his head, his face serious, and he even stopped eating. "If there was one, I'm afraid it's been and done."

"And what of her sentence?" Kit asked.

Fenn shuffled in his seat. "She is in the executioner's wing."

Elsie gasped and held her hands to her mouth, blinking and staring down at the table.

Kit was worried she would burst out crying or faint as mortal women were so often said to do. But she did neither, just sat there, still like an ice sculpture of Azure Sister, goddess of healing, life, and emotions, frozen in a moment of grief.

A silent sob hitched her chest, jolting Kit from his trance as he realized he had been staring at her.

"It will be alright, Elsie. We will get to her," Kit said confidently. If there was a way, he would find it.

Elsie bit her lip and looked up, her eyes foggy. "I will go to her tomorrow," she said with utter confidence.

"No," Kit and Fenn said in unison.

Kit leaned closer to her, keeping his voice low. "You cannot go there. The palace is far too dangerous for mortals."

"They can't arrest me. I have done nothing wrong."

"My—the king needs no reason. He can arrest people for buttering his toast wrong if he pleases," Kit said. "Your mother's wrongdoing is reason enough to arrest you."

"That is ridiculous. Is there no law? Perhaps I could employ a barrister here in Midwinter."

Kit needed her to understand but didn't know what to say to make her listen. He could not let her go into that place without a plan and risk never coming out again.

Fenn leaned closer to Elsie, his great forearms taking up half the table. "I advise against it, miss. Laws of the mortal lands, or even Midwinter, don't apply in the Winterfae Kingdom. Nothing good will come of it."

"Surely you can help us, Fenn, being a guard and all. Can you get me in with no one knowing?" Elsie pleaded.

Finn exchanged a look with Kit and raised an eyebrow. It didn't go unnoticed by Elsie.

Fenn shook his head. "If anyone can get you in, it's your man Kit here."

Kit glared at Fenn. In his letter, he'd explicitly stated not to give any indication of his identity.

"Kit? Because he worked in the palace too?" Elsie asked.

"If that's how you wish to put it, yes." Fenn wouldn't look at Kit.

The last thing Kit needed was her asking too many questions. Best to preempt with extra information and divert the question. "Fenn worked for me in the palace. I was in an important role and needed a suitable bodyguard. We became friends and have since drifted into different work."

Hopefully, that would satisfy.

Elsie leaned in. "So, what you are saying, but not saying, is that you have better contacts than Fenn in the palace?"

She was far too astute. Though his expectations of mortals had always been rather low. "In a way, but I am afraid they would not aid our cause."

Elsie's shoulders slumped. She glared at her bowl, her lip trembling, but she did not cry. Since he was fae, she had to at least know he wasn't lying.

"I best be off." Fenn got up awkwardly. "Thank you for the dinner, and if you think of a way I can be of assistance in the palace, please send me a message right away. I wish I could be of more help."

Elsie stood up and unexpectedly went around the table and hugged Fenn. He wrapped his bearlike arms around her tiny frame, his wings folded flat down his back. Kit felt a rise of jealousy burn in his chest.

"Kit will find a way, love, you'll see," Fenn said as he unwrapped himself from Elsie and patted her shoulder the way a parent would.

"Thank you," she mumbled before Fenn left.

Elsie didn't sit back down, just stood there patting Pepper, who had shuffled over to sit next to her. "I might go to bed."

"Let me walk you up," Kit said, feeling foolish for being jealous. Elsie didn't have anyone she knew around her. She was in a foreign land dealing with an impossible situation, and he had no idea how to comfort someone like that.

He paid for dinner and ordered some hot water for his next batch of medicine tea, then walked Elsie up to her room, just two doors down from his. They stopped outside her door, and she fumbled in her pockets for her key.

"I'm going there with your help or not," she said.

"Just wait." He stopped her before she lifted the key to the lock. His hand wrapped gently around her wrist as he lowered it. "I want to help you. Just give me time, and I can come up with a plan."

He meant it. If there was a way he could get in safely without putting her or her mother in danger, he would do it. If he was extra careful, he could do it without his father knowing.

She shook her head, refusing to look at him, but she didn't pull away as his fingers slid down her wrist, and her palm slipped into his, entwining his fingers with hers.

"I don't have time. By the sound of it, my mother might not either." Elsie wouldn't look at him but didn't pull away.

He knew what the king was doing, making an example of her.

"You might not want to hear this, but they won't execute any prisoners until after Midwinter. We have at least until then. Give me two days, and I will find a way in."

Elsie stepped in and threw her arms around his waist, burying her face in his chest. He froze, then realized he should do something and encircled his arms around her. Kit relaxed as her warmth seeped into his skin. The sweet scent of pine and lavender from her hair enveloped his senses.

"You'd really do that?" Her voice muffled in his shirt.

"Of course." Clearly, she hadn't thought much of him up until that point if she was that surprised he wanted to help. Had he not shown that already?

She pulled away, and Kit suddenly disapproved of the gap between them. Perhaps so did she, because she looked up at him and ran her tongue over her lip as if she were thinking the exact same thing. He wanted to know what she tasted like, to run his hands through her hair, to feel the softness of those lips.

He dared step forward, hardly breathing, and sure she would pull away, but she didn't. She gazed up at him, a hungry look burning in her eyes. Challenging him. He leaned toward her as she lifted her chin, her lips slightly parted.

A cough sounded behind him, and Elsie gasped, pulling away. Her gaze darted to the key in the door as if she'd realized what nearly happened.

"Excuse me, sorry about that. Your hot water, Your Highness," Liri interrupted.

He suppressed the urge to growl but didn't react. He knew Liri was trying to wind him up for not telling Elsie the whole truth like she had suggested from the start.

Elsie's hands were already on her door, pushing it open. "I better get to bed. Goodnight." She slipped inside before he could say anything further.

Kit spun around. Liri was smiling sweetly with a teapot on a tray. "Did I interrupt something?"

"Yes," he growled, fished his key out of his pocket, and let Liri into his room.

She set down the teapot on the small table and headed back to the door but stopped and leaned on the frame.

"Kit, do you know what you're doing with her? I rather like her. Hate to see her get hurt."

He shook his head, wondering the same thing. "Not a clue."

CHAPTER 22

ELSIE

Elsie started the day eating her porridge in a sunny window in The Fae's Folly pub dining area, hoping to spot Kit. Waiting was the worst part. He'd been out the whole day before and hadn't returned until late in the night and must have left early again that morning since he hadn't answered when she'd knocked on his door. She wondered if he was avoiding her after their near kiss. She couldn't stop thinking about it and wondered what would have happened if they hadn't been interrupted.

Was he thinking the same? Or was he avoiding her in the hope she would forget?

Angels, she had wanted to kiss him at that moment. But perhaps it was for the best. He was fae after all; it could never work. Though part of her really wanted to find out.

To put her time to good use, Elsie had ventured into Midwinter Haven the day before to see if she could gather any extra information about the palace.

She had learned nothing useful and had come back empty-handed but was getting to know her way around and was keen to do the same today to discover more of the town.

She finished breakfast without spotting Kit, so set off into the chilly morning air lit with bright sunlight without a cloud in the sky. Pepper trotted at her side, having joined her as soon as she stepped out the front door.

Elsie was more than happy to admit her preconceived notions of the town were quite wrong. After her explorations yesterday, she found everyone was friendly, save for a few folks who must have been having a bad day, but most were happy to have a chin wag and welcome a newcomer.

She explored several new streets and found some quaint cobbled alleyways with an eclectic range of bookshops, grocers, cafes, a blacksmith, and even a vampire cafe that was far too intimidating to enter. She had to draw the line on her curiosity somewhere.

Elsie rubbed her gloved hands together to try to warm them. As much as she enjoyed the sunshine, it did little to provide warmth. She glanced up at a golden cauldron sign outside an all-black shopfront. Did she dare go in? It wasn't as bad as a vampire cafe. She shrugged.

The door opened with the ring of a bell, and she jumped.

"Morning," a cheery woman with dark skin and a halo of bright purple and black hair sang out as she stepped onto the street and started sweeping the footpath while humming a tune.

Pepper, who was not shy, went right up to the woman for some attention.

"Sorry, she is very friendly, I assure you," Elsie said, hoping the woman liked dogs.

"She's darling." The woman scratched Pepper behind the ears, and Elsie had a chance to glance at the badge of the arm of her black leather coat, the Great Northern Citadel.

"Would you both like to come in? You're looking a mite frozen."

Her mother always said never to pass up hospitality on the road, and Elsie's curiosity was winning out about taking a peek in the shop.

"Thank you, that would be lovely. I'm Elsie, and this is Pepper."

"Zika." The witch smiled and opened the door for them, and Elsie followed her into the shop.

She wasn't sure what she had been expecting, perhaps bottles of bugs, newt eyes, and stacks of cauldrons, but what she was met with was a classy boutique with curated shelves full of beautiful items: gilded-edged books, brass instruments, candles with delightful labels, and exotic scents with wonderful sounding names like Celestial Meadow, Midnight Lily, Arcane Oak, and Enchanted Moonstone.

Pepper stuck close to her side, which she was glad of. Elsie's eyes drifted up past the many shelves of crystals and up to the ceiling, where she stood there gaping like a fish. Was the ceiling under a charm, or was it more fae magic or witch magic? It was midnight blue and lit with sparkling stars, and at the center hung a chandelier with what looked like fae lights in the shape of candles, but they did not need to be lit, just glowed on their own.

Perhaps she could bring back some strings of fae lights. They would look wonderful lighting up the tea house stall and the wagon, though it would put her at risk of being accused of witchcraft...

"You're not from around here, are you?" Zika asked, and Elsie took her gaze away from the ceiling. Zika probably thought she was some sort of simpleton.

Elsie picked up a candle to smell Mystic Midwinter. "Is it that obvious?"

"Not at all. I just have a sense for these things." Zika dusted around some breakable-looking glass flasks.

"Like a magical sense?" Elsie asked, trying to hold back her awe.

"No, just a normal sense." She grinned. "I haven't seen you around here before."

"Oh, right." Elsie placed down the candle. She might have to buy that for the tea house also. It smelled of cinnamon, vanilla, and fig and had a definite Midwinter cozy ambiance to it. "Perhaps you could tell me a little about the Winterfae Kingdom? I don't know much about it." Any information could be helpful, and she planned on buying a few items to make it worth Zika's while to deal with Elsie's interrogation.

Zika's eyes lit up. "Well, this might shock you. One of the fae princes hasn't been seen in more than a year, and people are bursting with gossip about where he might be. He was on a quest for his father, so the fae say," Zika told her excitedly as she crouched down and fawned over Pepper.

Elsie's skull prickled. That sounded awfully similar to Kit, but he couldn't lie, and that was something rather difficult to conceal from conversation. Still...

"What are the princes named?" Elsie asked, just to be sure. She picked up a snow globe, a white and red finch of some sort holding a red berry in its tiny beak. Kit's favorite bird was a finch, she recalled. Her thoughts turned to Kit giving her the bracelet; she ought to get him a Midwinter gift.

"Prince Andriel and Christarel Whitewood. Andriel is the one to be married. Christarel was on the quest."

Elsie let her shoulders drop in relief. He could not lie about his name. She placed the snow globe down and continued looking around.

Zika stood up and, with an elegant turn of her hand, sent a jar flying toward her from a high shelf.

Elsie gasped. "Was that witch's magic?" She realized it was a silly question after asking.

Zika giggled. "I'm only learning still. I hope to join the Midwinter Coven once I graduate. Now the other prince—" Zika paused, struggling to undo the jar. "Andriel, is next in line for the throne. He is the most eligible bachelor in all the lands and is being very fussy in choosing a suitable partner. The king keeps throwing balls to no avail, and we are all waiting with bated breath to see who he will select."

Zika pulled something out of the jar, and Elsie tensed. Was she going to put a spell on them?

"Can I give her a treat? It's just dried rabbit."

Elsie relaxed. "I'm sure she would love that." She told herself to stop being paranoid and listened politely to all Zika's theories on potential suitors for the prince from a range of noble fae families from all the fae kingdoms, but it was not particularly interesting to her.

After half an hour chatting and looking at every item in the shop, Elsie purchased two Midwinter candles, the snow globe, a teacup with a peony on it for her mother, some string lights, and left with a very happy and treat-filled Pepper. She wasn't sure anything she'd learned from Zika was useful, but you never knew when random gossip and local knowledge would be of use, and it had taken her mind off her mum and Kit for a short while.

Pepper trotted at Elsie's side, and on the next street over, Elsie spotted the most spectacular cupcake in the window of a bakery. "You've had your treats, Peps, maybe it's time for mine." The cupcake called to her with its white icing and something glittery within the perfect swirls.

She could use a break. She'd covered many new streets already, and it had been a while since she ate that porridge.

The bell tinkled as she entered the shop and signaled to Pepper to wait outside. Elsie ordered her special cupcake and a cup of tea, plus a special bone-shaped dog treat for Pepper. They sat outside the bakery cafe beside a roaring brazier that kept the open air nice and toasty.

"Let's hope your master returns soon enough. I don't know how much more waiting I can take." Elsie stroked Pepper's head, but Pepper was wholly focused on her treat.

Elsie sighed and sipped her tea. It wasn't nearly as good as theirs from the tea house, over-brewed for sure, and it left an ache in her chest that made her miss Marie. She hoped her sister was faring well without her.

"There you are." Kit appeared, his dark hair tousled like he had been in the wind. "I've been looking everywhere for you."

Elsie nearly dropped her teacup, and Pepper jumped up to her full height and licked Kit on the cheek.

Composing herself, Elsie remembered how to speak. "Good afternoon, Kit." *I missed you.* She kept that last bit to herself; that would have made her sound like a madwoman. But what a relief it was to see him. All her anxiety washed away like lukewarm tea down the drain.

"Fenn found a safe way to get us into the palace." His brow creased into serious lines; he didn't approve. Yet he had followed through.

They had a way in. "Let's get planning then." She grinned at him and resisted the urge to jump up and hug him. She was certain he would not like that. "Want some cupcake?"

CHAPTER 23

ELSIE

Elsie twisted the thin band of gold around her wrist to distract her from her numb feet as she crouched in the bushes next to Kit. Snowspire Palace was right in front of them, well, across the road and behind a massive stone wall, but it felt close. She had to tilt her neck upward to take in the towering points that appeared to pierce the clouds themselves. Points that looked just like ice, though she supposed they were made of something more sturdy, or it was magic. Not something she was going to ask about when they were supposed to be quiet as they waited for the signal at the gate from Fenn.

She twisted the band once more that would mark them as palace staff, as would the uniforms they both wore: Elsie in a thin light blue dress with mother-of-pearl buttons and a high collar of silvery lace and a white apron. A garment that might be warm enough in the palace, but outside the icy wind cut right through it.

As if he could read her mind, Kit took off the jacket of his silver and blue guard's uniform and draped it over her shoulders.

"You'll have to give it back when we leave," he whispered.

"Thanks," she whispered back, breathing in the smell of Kit all around her. Woodsmoke and mint enveloped her along with the warmth of Kit's residual body heat, causing a pleasant shiver to run through her.

"He'll be here soon." Kit glanced at her with deep concern on his face—a new face. A glamour, she kept telling herself, but it was highly unsettling that he looked like a very unapproachable guard. At least that would stop her fantasizing about what it would be like to kiss him, something she couldn't help thinking about, despite the fact that he was still fae, and that wasn't going to change.

Too cold to answer, she licked her lips, hoping it would warm them. But it just made them colder as the wind stole away the moisture and replaced it with ice.

Neither of them had mentioned the near kiss yet. Once Kit found her the day before, their evening was all about planning and preparing. She hadn't been able to think beyond that. Then Kit was out all day again, this time securing them palace disguises, him a guard's uniform, and her horrible uniform, because apparently that's all humans were good for in the palace, well that and being courtesans.

Fenn's note told them to wait until sunset outside the palace grounds, and he would escort them in.

Elsie tucked the note into her pocket, sure it was the right place. They had a clear view of the side gate that was manned by two guards.

"There's a lot of people going in and out," Elsie whispered, as a group of around fifteen fae and humans bustled out the gate, all chatting away. Some piled into carriages, and others continued walking up the road towards the town of Snowspire, its sharp-peaked roofs visible on a hill above the trees of the vast forest, not too far from the palace.

"It's the changing shift. There's Fenn." Kit took her numb hand and helped her up. "You're still freezing."

"You can tell through my glove?" Elsie swallowed, wishing the glove wasn't a barrier between their skin. She bit her lip, ignoring thoughts of his touch on her skin, and tried to stretch her fingers, but they were stiff and painful once again. She really must find a way to get used to this cold if she was going to live in Winterfrost.

Fenn tipped his fox-fur guard hat to a group leaving.

"That's the signal." Elsie slipped off the jacket, and Kit dressed. She grasped Kit's hand and pulled him along as if it were perfectly normal to walk out of the bushes, and together, they marched toward the gate with great purpose, still holding hands as Fenn instructed them to. She did a double take as she caught a glimpse of Kit's wings, still not used to the fact that he'd had them all along. Seeing them made the fae thing so much more real.

Elsie pushed her shoulders back, acutely aware of Kit's tight grip and the warmth of his hand pouring into hers. If she didn't know better, she might have said he was nervous.

Fenn said something to the other guard, and he took a bag from an elderly woman in a servant's uniform and helped her to one of the silver carriages with snowflake crests on the sides that were all lined up.

Kit walked faster.

"Oi, you two! Get in here now. You're late for the shift," Fenn bellowed.

Elsie kept her head down and didn't make eye contact as they flowed past Fenn and the stream of workers leaving the palace.

"You can let go now," Kit mumbled, and Elsie dared to look up as she let his hand fall away, her heart racing.

"We made it in." She tried not to beam and couldn't help her eyes grow wide as she marveled at the pure white walls of the palace that sprouted right from the ground into glimmering ice spires.

"You work here, remember? Try not to look so astonished by everything."

Fae lights lined the paths, and the white marble was cleaner than anything she'd ever seen indoors, let alone leading to an outdoor servant's entrance. "By the angels, I've never seen anything like it."

"Surely you've been to Middlemarch Castle?"

"Well, yes. But it's nothing like this. This is a true fairytale castle, like in the books." Middlemarch Castle was like an extension of the city of Middlemarch, all gray stone and blocks where everything was square and straight, and nowhere near this clean.

Her boots clicked across the marble path that was perfectly free of ice. Beyond the path were rows of clear crystal buildings in the shapes of hexagons all filled with plants and flowers.

"They're the kitchen gardens. To supplement the produce we import from the Elven Kingdom." Kit kept his head forward as he spoke. The perfect guard. She supposed he had trained as a guard, so it was fitting.

To have all this fresh food in winter while people in the south went without. If only humans were more open-minded to magic, they could all benefit. She realized how strange it was to think of her people as 'humans,' before they were simply just 'people,' though Kit always referred to them as *mortals*. She wasn't sure what to call anyone anymore.

How her eyes had been opened this past week.

Elsie was almost sad to leave the winter wonderland courtyard as they entered the palace through the large wooden doors. She tried not to stare at the shimmering wings of fae that passed by, or the gilded tapestries that adorned the white walls, or the orbs that lit the wide hallways with warm light as bright as daylight. And this was just the servants' level? What must the rest of the palace look like? It was a shame she wouldn't find out. But her heart fluttered at the thought of being so close to her mother.

The previous night, Kit had drawn her plans, so she knew exactly where they were to go, and she tried to follow them in her mind. The kitchens were off to the left, confirmed by clanging pots and the mouth-watering scent of something roasting in garlic and butter.

She hadn't eaten before they left Midwinter Haven, being too nervous and knowing the carriage ride to the border would likely make her ill along with the anxiety of actually making it down to the prison to see her mother.

Following Kit's lead, she walked with purpose and confidence, ignoring the many servants and guards who passed by, feeling the warmth returned to all her limbs. The castle was a perfect temperature. Even in these huge stone hallways, she supposed the uniform wasn't so bad now.

They descended two levels of stairs, and the hallways became narrower. The white stone was replaced with generic castle-gray, and the flagstones beneath their feet were uneven and easy to trip upon in the dimness due to fewer wall lights.

They passed another set of guards on patrol, and Elsie tensed.

The footsteps faded away, but her heartbeat remained like a drum in her chest. "Why has no one stopped us yet?" It felt the deeper down they went, the more risk they were taking with so many people around.

"The bands, and the fact that the staff turnover is so high here. You could never recognize every face, even the guards."

"Why the high turnover?" she asked to keep her mind off what they might discover when they found her mother.

"The king does not treat people well." Kit's voice was neutral, maintaining his guard persona extremely professionally.

Elsie swallowed. If he was that horrible to the staff, what was he like to prisoners? How had they treated her mother? A sickening feeling trickled through her. Had her father been here? Was he all alone, captured, tortured, killed? Her mind raced with horrendous images. It was better she didn't know.

A door to the side opened ahead of them, and a figure stepped out but remained in the shadows.

Kit threw his arm across Elsie, so she stopped abruptly, having to grab it to stabilize herself, his muscles firm beneath her hand.

A voice chuckled. "You've resorted to sneaking into your own home like a coward?"

"You have mistaken me for someone else. Please let us pass," Kit said politely.

Elsie tried to look past Kit to see who was speaking.

"Give me a little credit, Kit. I recognize those skulking footsteps, not to mention your voice."

"Piss off, Anders. I have somewhere to be. Please let us pass," Kit demanded.

This was not a friend. Elsie tried to make out a face in the shadows.

"That's not much of a greeting, now, is it?"

"You got to Fenn, didn't you?" Kit said rather rudely.

Elsie gasped as the man stepped from the shadows. He was no servant. He was stunning and dressed head to foot in fine fabrics of silver and blue that matched his glorious silver wings, he had to be a noble or royalty. It wasn't just the clothes, but the look of privilege—the arrogance and entitlement wrapped up in one beautiful, though dangerous, fae package.

Elsie remained still, standing just back from Kit, but was unable to judge if the handsome stranger was being playful or threatening. Despite him being fae and noble, she wasn't drawn to him like she was to Kit.

"Don't worry about your favorite bodyguard." The fae man studied his nails and frowned as if he might have touched something dirty on this level. "I simply had Fenn followed. I knew if you returned, you would reveal yourself to him before anyone else."

"What in the name of Astriel is going on? You know this man?" Elsie couldn't keep quiet any longer. They had little time to get in and out while Fenn was at his station. If this man could help, she was going to take it.

"You allow her to speak to you like that?" Disgust spread across the stranger's face, rendering his handsome features warped and detestable.

Elsie decided right then she didn't like him.

"Shut it, Anders. Elsie, I can explain." Kit's unfamiliar face faltered, revealing a glimmer of his true face, then flickered back.

"The rumors are true. You are in hiding because your magic has weakened. I see why you would delay your return."

"I am not hiding." Kit's fists clenched at his sides. "I am here to help Elsie find her mother."

"Ah." Anders tapped his chin, and a sly smile crept to his lips. "I see. This charade was for a girl, a mortal girl." He wrinkled his nose.

Elsie narrowed her eyes. She liked this man even less than the first time she'd met Kit.

"Excuse me. I am right here. There is no need to be so rude."

"My apologies." He gave a mock bow. "Kit, would you be so kind as to introduce me to your lady?"

"No, I would not. Get out of our way and stop wasting my time."

Elsie took in a breath, surprised Kit would risk speaking to a noble in such a way. The only explanation was, as she suspected, he was one of them. She knew where her mother was, just a few hallways and another level down. Perhaps she could run past them.

Anders shook his head and chuckled. "She doesn't even know who you are, does she?"

Kit stepped forward and shoved Anders hard in the chest. "Don't press me. Just leave us be, and I won't hurt you."

Elsie kept her ground, not daring to take her eyes off the two men as she eyed her escape route. Kit's glamour flickered once more and disappeared altogether. That couldn't be good. Could she really leave him with this horrible man?

"It seems for once I might beat you, brother." Anders grinned.

"Brother?" The word escaped Elsie's lips, and she turned to Kit.

Kit's face paled, his fae features on full show. His cheekbones appeared sharper, his face less friendly in the harshness of the shadows. His pointed ears and blue-black eyes portrayed the truth. This was a man she knew nothing about.

"This isn't how I wanted you to find out. I was going to tell you." Kit reached for her hand, but she pulled away.

Elsie fought the bile rising in her throat. How could she be so stupid? So trusting.

"While Kit continues to be so rude, allow me to introduce myself. You may address me as Your Royal Highness, Prince Andriel Whitewood, heir to the Winterfae Kingdom." He twirled his hand in a more authentic bow this time, but as he rose, he grinned at Kit.

Elsie didn't move. Couldn't move, or even process what was happening.

"Prince. He is your brother, and you are a prince?" She turned to Kit, as anger roared through her blood, knowing that if she didn't let it, she would break.

"Yes." Kit shot a glare at his brother, then turned to Elsie. He didn't even mask the fear in his eyes.

"This whole time we could have walked into the palace and asked about my mother?"

"Well, he could have. Not you." Anders looked her up and down in disgust. "Why would your mother be in the palace? Is she a courtesan? I know a few nobles like the odd human, though I can't see—"

"For the last time, shut it, Anders," Kit barked as he took a tentative step toward Elsie. "I couldn't risk just walking into the palace. Without these bands to conceal us, my father would have known I was here and summoned me right away. Then I could do nothing to help you."

"You could get my mother freed from prison." Elsie kept her voice low and controlled, fighting the urge to scream at him.

"No, he couldn't," Anders chimed in. "Not if she's in prison. Our father would never allow it."

Kit rubbed his forehead.

"You could try to explain. You are his son." Elsie heard the waver in her voice and detested that it gave away how afraid she was. How could she have been so wrong about someone?

Anders blocked the hallway and any hope of her making a run for the stairs. "You will go no farther today, and I regret to inform you, you will not be seeing your mother." He grinned with a true wickedness that made Elsie sick to her stomach. She fought back tears.

"But in my graciousness, I will allow you both to leave, despite your treasonous deception and scheme to infiltrate our secure prison." This Anders thought everything was one big joke.

Kit took a step closer to Anders. "Move aside."

Elsie took two strides to stand next to him, not trusting him to make any decisions anymore. It was clear she was on her own. "You have to let me in. I need to see my mother. She doesn't have much time!" Elsie heard the desperation in her voice, but she was so close she no longer cared.

Anders shot a blast of ice from his hand and pinned Elsie to the wall. Her breath escaped her chest, and she gasped as a burning collar of ice that chained her throat to the wall. Her hands and feet snapped into ice shackles.

CHAPTER 24

KIT

Rage surged in Kit's chest as he blasted Anders without a second thought. Despite the stone hallway of the palace being so narrow, his brother sidestepped Kit's ice dagger and sent his own straight back. With a rapid snap of his wings, Kit dodged left as the rush of wind breezed by his cheek, showing just how close he was to the deadly blade. He shouldn't be fighting. He was too weak for this and no match for Anders.

"Let her go," Kit growled as he took his eyes off Anders to make sure Elsie was breathing. Her neck was red where the collar of ice held her against the wall. She glared at him with pure hatred. If she had powers, he had no doubt that fiery glare would burn right through that ice.

"You started it. I have no wish to fight you." Anders dodged once more.

Kit held up his hands, despite it going against everything in his body telling him not to let Anders get off that easy. "Fine." He couldn't leave Elsie hanging there any longer.

"Very well." Anders sighed, and with a wave of his hand the ice shackles melted, Elsie tumbled to the ground, gripping her throat as she took deep gasps of air.

Kit rushed to her side. She made a feeble attempt to push him away, but her eyes locked with this. Silent tears trailed down her cheeks, and guilt crashed over him. He had done this. He could hardly be surprised.

To her credit, once she caught her breath, she accepted his hand and straightened up. She faced Anders as if she might attack him herself. Hopefully, she was far too sensible for that.

"Please let me pass so I may see my mother. I just wish to speak with her." Her voice cracked.

Kit knew nothing he could say right now would help the situation.

"No." Anders reached into his pocket. "But if you two are done attacking me, I have something for you."

Anders handed two envelopes to Elsie, and she took them automatically in the confusion. "What is it?" she asked.

"Open it," Anders said sweetly as if he were giving her a Midwinter gift.

Kit refrained from snatching the letters from her to check they weren't full of poison. Anything he did right now would only make her hate him more, and Anders had never been one for poisoning.

"An invitation to a ball?" Elsie glanced at Kit, perhaps forgetting she was mad in the surprise of it.

He'd take it as a way in and took one step closer to her. "What does it say?"

"It has my name on it." She furrowed her brow. "And it is in three days' time."

Kit felt the blood drain from his face. "Elsie, this is a trap. We can't go."

"Well, I certainly don't want to go with you."

Anders laughed aloud. "Turbulence in these waters."

Kit shot Anders a dark glare. He would be lucky if Elsie talked to him after this; he did not need Anders making the situation worse.

She wouldn't want to go with him, but he wasn't going to leave her to go alone, or at all for that matter. But he could see her mind ticking over. It was clear Anders would not let them go farther today, and this was her shot at getting back into the palace. If it got her away from here for now, it was a small win.

"Why would Father do this?" Kit asked.

"I'm sure he wants to meet the human who has kept you away from your duties for so long."

"Elsie has nothing to do with this. I will speak with Father alone."

"No. You are not welcome at the palace until the ball. You will be formally reintroduced to court, and you will bring your plaything along with you."

"Like hell I will."

"I'm not his plaything," Elsie spoke at the same time.

"Either way, neither of you will be entering the prison today." Anders pressed a button on the wall, and footsteps sounded from every direction.

"Now, if you would be so kind as to let me and my friends escort you out."

———— ❄❄❄ ————

Kit knew when a fight was over, and they had no chance of making it to the prison floors with Anders' army of guards in their way. Their only choice was to be escorted through the narrow hallways and back up into the bright light of the palace to the contrasting darkness of the night and the waiting carriage. Thank the Ancient Mother it was a plain black one without any royal insignias or colors.

The air was still and silent but for the sound of marching feet on stone and a lone owl, a northern scops owl if he wasn't mistaken, which he never was with owls.

He offered his hand to Elsie at the steps. She didn't take it. He followed her in. Someone threw in his bag from the bushes behind him, and the door slammed shut as the carriage jerked into motion right away. Elsie shuffled to the window, the invitations tight in her hand.

Kit sat on the opposite red velvet bench seat.

She turned to him; her eyes wild with anger. "I trusted you, and all this time you have lied to me."

"I—"

"Do not say you didn't lie. I know very well you can bend and hide the truth as well as any true lie."

What could he say to make her understand without sounding like a privileged prince trying to defend himself? Despite that being exactly what he was.

"You could have done something," she said in a near whisper.

His heart almost cracked at the weight of despair in her words. "I wish I could. But trust me, Elsie, I couldn't have. Once I am back in that palace, I am gone. I am useless to you and back to being a pawn for my father."

"So you say. But you must have all this power, you probably don't even know it. People will listen to you, the king..."

"You don't know him like I do, and I don't want you anywhere near him." That came out more forceful than he meant, and Elsie frowned.

She shifted to face him. "Why? Give me the honest truth, no talking around things, an honest to angels' reason."

He swallowed. He didn't want her to know the truth. He enjoyed being with her as Kit and liked her treating him like any other person, scolding him for being an idiot, showing him how to make tea properly, playing with Pepper. If he was being honest with himself, he just enjoyed being with her—her spark for life, her generosity, her loyalty.

That was all over, and it would only get worse once she learned of his true nature, proving everything she thought about the fae to be true.

"You'll hate me more."

She crossed her arms. "I'm not exactly a fan of yours right now."

"Fair point." He couldn't blame her.

"Just tell me what happened with your father."

"Fine. Before I left, I was in love." There he said it. There was no going back now.

"Oh." She hadn't expected that, he bet.

Kit wrung his hands on his lap. "But my father did not approve of her."

"Well, he doesn't need to approve of me." That fire shot through her eyes once more. There was that spark he loved.

She continued, "It's not like we are together, and I have my wits about me enough to know I will never be good enough for a prince."

"That isn't it—"

She set her jaw firm and continued to glare.

Had she wanted him before? He figured the near kiss had been a fleeting moment, that she would not feel the same way as he did, after all, she had never mentioned it. Now she would think he just wanted her as a conquest, another woman good enough to bed, but not good enough for a prince to marry.

"I just want to find my mother, and if I have to go to this ball to get inside once more, then so be it." She smoothed out the invite across her knee.

"He cut off her wings," Kit blurted out.

"Who?"

"My love, Marella, was her name. She did nothing wrong except be herself, and he made an example of her and cut off her wings in front of the entire court." Kit wrung his hands tighter. Was that too shocking, too harsh? He hadn't meant it to sound that way, but there it was, the bitter, disgusting truth that still ate away at him. He hadn't been able to protect Marella, but it wasn't too late for Elsie.

She sucked in a breath.

"I'm sorry." Elsie's eyes widened as she covered her mouth with her palm. "But why would he do such a thing? Why did he not approve?"

"She came with a delegation of the Springfae Court. Marella was a lady's maid to a countess my father wanted Anders to marry."

Elsie didn't speak, just listened as her hand moved to her heart.

Kit continued, "I met her at the inn. She'd escaped the palace to explore and 'get some proper ale,' her words." He smiled, remembering the first time he'd seen her. Her green wings and golden hair glowing as she argued with a barman about the difference in hops varieties, something he knew nothing of, nor cared about until that very moment.

"And you fell in love?"

"At the time I thought so." He'd tried so hard to push her from his mind he could no longer be sure what he'd felt. It was certainly passion. She lit a fire in his life he had never experienced before. "She was here only a month, yet we got close. Every chance to meet up, we were together."

"Then your father found out?"

"He invited her to one of Anders' 'matchmaking' balls without me knowing. She thought it was me." A sickening guilt made his stomach turn as if it were yesterday, not that well over a year had passed.

"When she walked in, my father dragged her out in front of the entire court, like a game."

Elsie stared at him, eyes wide with understanding. "And you couldn't save her?"

He nodded. "He placed a silencing charm upon me and had the guards hold me at the edge of a balcony above so I could witness his cruelty but do nothing to stop it."

Elsie shook her head in disbelief. "That is vile."

He shifted in his seat and clenched his fists, pressing them into the velvet at his sides. The last thing he wanted was Elsie's pity. That was not the point of this painful story; it was supposed to be a warning.

"He sliced off her wings himself, and he laughed. No one stopped him. No one stood up for Marella. There was no one who could." He sat rigid, feeling her inch closer with sympathy, damn her gregariousness. He wanted nothing more than to push her way. All the way back to Winterfrost where she'd be safe.

Hopefully, that was enough of the tale to shock her. She didn't need any more detail. She didn't need to know that Marella was discarded by the countess instantly, that she was left mutilated and marked never to be able to accept any role at court again. That she had no choice but to return in shame to her father's hops plantation.

Of course, he made sure she was looked after. But he never tried to see her, and she made it clear she would never speak to him again. He took solace in the fact that she never wanted a life at court anyway. It had been her father's ambition that drove her there in the first place, and he knew she would be happy in the fields she had missed so dearly.

It could never make up for the horror Marella endured, and Elsie didn't need to know that Kit was a coward and didn't see Marella ever again.

"This is why you should not attend this ball." He fought the urge to rip the invitations from her hand, to forbid her to go, just to make her understand.

"Kit." The force in her voice caused him to turn. "I am very sorry this happened to you and your lady. I know you have no love for your father, and I have never heard you mention your mother, but my mother is the most important thing right now, and I have come all this way. I am not going home without her."

"You will attend the ball, knowing what my father is capable of? That this is a clear message of how he wishes to control me and how he will treat you?"

"Yes, I will attend knowing that I did everything I could to save my mother."

"We still have time. I can come up with a new plan," Kit said out of desperation, though nothing came to mind.

"Your brother made it clear you aren't welcome before the ball, you won't make it in undetected. This is my best shot."

She was right. There was no other way he could think of right at this moment.

"Tell me you will think about it? At least give me a chance to think of something else." He knew he was pleading, but at this point, he was considering locking her in the inn and going to the ball alone to keep her out of harm's way.

Once he was back in there, his father would not let him leave a second time, not until he had the Bloodgate Ruby, and Kit had made a blood vow as part of his quest. He had very few options and had not yet worked out a loophole to keep the stone from his father. What he needed was more time and for his magic to be stronger.

"I promise I will think about it. But only if you promise the same." Elsie held his gaze with a fierceness that terrified him. She crossed her arms and turned to face the window.

CHAPTER 25

KIT

Kit made no attempt to stop Elsie as she marched straight up the stairs to her room as soon as they arrived back at The Fae's Folly. Even Pepper's exuberant greetings didn't keep her from storming away.

Kit, not wanting to face sitting alone in his room with his thoughts, ordered a tumbler of Elvish brandy and slunk into the darkest corner booth he could find. He dumped the bag with the guard's uniform next to him, glad to be back in his familiar traveling cloak. Though the room was almost too warm to keep it on.

He held out his hand, concentrating all his magic into his palm, and drew moisture from the air as his other hand made rounding motions above and formed the growing ball into a smooth circle of ice. He dropped it in his glass and breathed a sigh of relief. With his glamour failing back at the palace, he couldn't be sure of even the most basic magic anymore.

"Thought I might find you here." Liri slid onto the bench across from him and around the side against the back wall. "Rough day?"

"It could not have gone more wrong." Kit refused to let his shoulders slump in defeat. He sat upright and filled Liri in on everything that happened, taking generous gulps of brandy between each horrible recalling of events.

"I told her what happened to Marella, and she still wasn't deterred. That woman has a spirit of fire."

"Oh, Kit." She reached over and squeezed his hand. "I best get us more brandy."

Liri always knew the right thing to say. Releasing his hand, she jumped up, her coppery wings sprung open behind her, and she sent a stream of sparkling metallic magic toward the bar, then twisted her fingers in a graceful spiral as the bottle of brandy made its way through the air and into Liri's waiting hand.

Kit made another ball of ice for Liri.

"Your magic has returned, I see. He won't catch you off guard twice. All you need to do is stay with Elsie at all times." Liri was serious.

"You are siding with Elsie. You believe we should attend the ball?"

"It is very clear that you care for her, Kit. I've seen the way you look at her, and she at you."

His thoughts flicked back to the other day. If only he had kissed Elsie then. He'd missed his chance.

"This is why I am a fool. I should not have allowed myself to get close to her. Now she knows who I am, she will never..." He shook his head. It wasn't even worth saying aloud.

Liri rapped her knuckles on the table. "I will not hear of such talk. What happened to Marella will not happen again. You can't just lock your heart away because you are scared."

"That is not the issue here, Liri, and you know it."

"If you say so." She raised an eyebrow as she sipped her drink.

Kit stared into his glass, the effects of the brandy already dulling his magic and his judgment. He could just hand over the ruby. Then when his father took the surveillance off him, he could find a way to break out Elsie's mother. But then Midwinter Haven would be at the mercy of the king. It would come down to a fight with his father, a real fight, and in his current state, he was sure to lose.

"I need to enhance my magic." Why hadn't he thought of that sooner?

Liri looked appropriately stunned. "You mean an amplifier crystal?"

"They aren't just for thieves and lowlifes. I've seen plenty of guards use them to ensure they pass their basic training."

"I know who uses them. I just didn't think it would ever be you."

"A lot more is at stake now. It doesn't matter if I lose my position at court or my magic. I cannot let my father win, and I need to protect Elsie." That and he seemed to have lost many of his morals over the last year since his eyes had been opened to the wider world. The truth was, with every bad decision he made, he became more like his father. He kept telling himself if he was doing it for the right reasons, it was acceptable.

"So that's what this is all about. You're finally standing up to him."

"Message for Prince Christarel!" A fae with blue wings in a meticulous silver and blue uniform bellowed across the room.

Kit pulled up the hood of his coat and suppressed a groan, but it was too late. They might not be able to see his face, but if one person knew he was here, the whole blasted town would.

He exchanged a look with Liri, who shrugged unsympathetically. "It was good while it lasted, mate."

Sitting up straight, as a prince would, Kit raised his hand. All eyes turned on him as the ruckus of the tavern lowered to a murmur.

"You never seen a man receive a letter," Liri yelled, breaking the tension and chuckling as everyone turned back to their drinks, keeping watch from the corners of their eyes.

The guard marched across the room, handed the letter to Kit, and left without another word when Kit placed a few coppers in his palm.

"What does it say?" Liri leaned in.

Kit broke the royal seal from the parchment and unfolded the note, still feeling the eyes of the entire room on him; a feeling he had not missed at all.

Prince Christarel,

You have received the invitation to Andriel's ball. I expect you and your human whore to be in attendance.

I have it on good authority that you obtained the Bloodgate Ruby. Do not attempt to deceive me.

Present the gem to me in front of the court before the midnight bell at the ball and the human girl will remain unharmed.

King Valendor, High Ruler of the Winterfae Kingdom

Classic Father.

With a tightening in his chest, Kit handed the note to Liri and sat in silence as she read. There was no way he could take Elsie there after that threat. The message must have been following right behind their carriage, thanks to Anders, no doubt.

"Kit, listen to me. You can't stop Elsie from going. Not short of locking her up or poisoning her, and we both know you won't do that."

He was certainly considering those options. "I hardly have a choice. He's forcing my hand."

Pepper whined under the table and licked his hand.

Liri locked eyes with Kit. She was just like Elsie, stubborn and determined. "You will wither if you break the oath and don't present him with the stone, and Elsie will find a way in whatever you do to stop her. Be smart."

He downed the rest of his brandy. "Whatever I do, someone gets hurt, Elsie, her mother, the people of Midwinter Haven. My father has me cornered."

"I'm sure you will think of something," Liri said. "How about that amplifier crystal?"

"I'd have to give up something in exchange." Kit tried to think of something he could use. Gold wasn't enough, it had to be something he valued enough to charge an amplifier crystal.

Liri lowered her voice to a whisper and leaned in. "If you have something to exchange, I know a fine fellow in the Narrows who deals in crystals of all types."

"I see you've been making new friends in my absence." She never used to have any witch friends, nor seek company in the dodgier areas of Midwinter Haven such as the Narrows.

"I have many friends other than you, Kit." She smirked.

Kit tapped a finger to his lips. If he was going to a crystal dealer he could also get a fake ruby... "I might not have to give up the ruby. I could swap it out after I present it to my father..."

Liri poured them another drink. "Now you're thinking."

A fae woman in a bright yellow gown swished by, sparking another idea. "And what do you know of protective cloth?" Kit asked.

"I might know a very cute witch who *happens* to have the ability to imbue protection magic into cloth."

"Do you now? That is rare indeed, and expensive." They were on the same page, and he'd seen that look in her eyes before. He supposed that meant she'd moved on from the intimidating elf she'd been courting before he left.

"For a ball gown. I could take her there tomorrow to get fitted for a dress."

Kit tucked his hand into the inner pocket of his coat, pulled out his coin purse, and handed it to Liri. "Take as much as you need. You could get it so fast?"

"If I sent a note now, I hope so." Liri fished around in the purse and took out a few gold pieces.

"Thank you, Liri." Money was not the issue. Liri had taken enough to buy a horse, but it would be worth it. Getting access to witches as skilled as that was never an option for the royal family since his father had made his hatred for witches clear by taking away all fae funding from the Great Northern Citadel, the university that was open to all.

Liri grinned and handed back the purse. "Better get you an outfit too. Any requests?"

He put his drink down. He better switch to his medicine tea if he was going to recover his magic in just two days' time. "A court suit that matches whatever Elsie chooses."

"No royal colors?"
"Not this time."

CHAPTER 26

ELSIE

Elsie ran her hand over the smooth pottery of the teapot. When in doubt, make tea. That's what her mother always said, and it had never let her down yet. Pacing might help too.

She had spent a great deal of time thinking about the ball, and Kit. She simply didn't have another option, and Kit hadn't come to her with a better plan. Ideally, he would accompany her to the ball, but she didn't see that happening.

She would have to go alone.

Sitting still was unbearable, and it was too early to go out shopping for a dress. She would leave as soon as the shops opened.

She had been up half the night, either being tormented by horrible nightmares or lying there awake worrying about her mum, about Kit, about Marie.

She walked across the room several times before she set the teapot down and picked out a small linen bag, but her hand brushed another—the spiced tea mix. Elsie pulled it out, guilt clutching at her stomach. She could hardly believe the lengths her mother went to get the secret powder, though she was sure there was more to it. If something had happened to her father as well, she wasn't sure she wanted to know. It might be too much.

She shoved the spiced tea deep into the bottom of the tea collection. No tea was worth losing a life over.

The feeling of missing her mother suddenly struck her. She swallowed back horrible thoughts of what her mother must be enduring in the prison. The two of them had always clashed in opinions, but when they were together in the tea house, their movements flowed like water, each knowing what the other would do and working in perfect unison, and with Marie, a perfect team. She attempted to push the memories to the dark corner of her mind.

Opening the drawstring of another pouch, she was greeted by the familiar scent: bergamot and black tea, the perfect morning wake-up.

With a cloth, she carefully pulled the small kettle from the fire, poured a little hot water into the teapot, and swirled it around with practiced ease. Today she would find a ball gown. She had the rent money saved for the shop. Perhaps she could resell the dress after using it once.

She poured the water into the spare cup to reuse later and scooped the tea blend into the warmed pot. Tea *was* the solution to everything,

Yes, that's what she would do. Step one: get a dress, step two: write to Fenn to ask if he would assist her, step three: attend the ball, and step four: with Fenn's help, poison the guards' tea, slip into the prison, and get her mum.

She felt good about this.

Steam rose from the pot as she poured the water over the tea leaves, and as she breathed in the misty tendrils, her head cleared with new focus.

A knock sounded at the door, and her stomach clenched. She wasn't ready to talk to Kit yet.

She stood up but couldn't bring her feet to move. It hurt her heart to think about it, but she should have known better. Should have listened to herself at the start. She knew he was wrong for her, knew he was hiding something, but she allowed herself to be pulled in by his willingness to help, his pretty face, and, of course, Pepper.

She smoothed out her green dress, taking her time in case he decided to leave, but he knocked again. Getting attached always meant getting hurt.

She marched over and swung open the door. *Please don't be Kit.*

"Good morning," a servant said, holding a basket of firewood, and nodded toward the fire. "May I?"

Elsie's heart dropped. *It wasn't Kit.* She masked her disappointment with a polite smile. "Thank you."

She shook her head to herself. Had she really wanted it to be him? The servant was quick about unloading the new wood, and once he was done, she shut the door and leaned against it letting out a heavy breath.

A knock sounded behind her, and she jumped forward.

She smoothed down her hair, then opened the door. It was him. Her chest squeezed, and she nearly forgot how to speak.

"Good morrow, Kit," she said as if nothing were amiss between them.

His face was a sorry sight. His eyes were dark like he hadn't slept, though he still had on the human glamour which must be draining his magic. As if a glamour would make her forget what he truly was. A prince and a liar. Even if he technically couldn't lie.

"I am sorry about the way I acted yesterday and would like a chance to speak with you civilly," he said in an overly polite manner. His jaw was lined with stubble, and his hair was even more unkempt than usual, yet she was still drawn to him. She still wanted to be close to him...it was infuriating. But he was being polite, so she swallowed it down.

"Very well. Where is Pepper?" she asked, wishing the dog was there to help break this tension.

Kit cleared his throat. "Liri took her on an errand."

"Oh." An awkward silence, but for the crackle of the fire, filled the space.

"Will you take a walk with me?" Kit said abruptly. "I know of a park you may enjoy."

Angels, yes, anything to get out of this room. Tea could wait. She could find a dress shop as they walked. "A walk would be lovely."

Downstairs, Liri and Kit were deep in whispers near the back door but stopped speaking when Pepper barked and dashed over to Elsie.

"Good day, sweet Peppermint." Elsie braced herself as Pepper licked her hand and leaned hard on her leg as if trying to get as close as possible for some loving pats. Elsie was more than happy to oblige and so glad Pepper was there as a buffer once more.

"Have a pleasant walk." Liri grinned as she walked past, making Elsie wonder what she and Kit had been discussing.

"Shall we go?" Kit asked.

———❄❅❄———

The morning was crisp and quiet in the small park Kit had taken them to. They walked side by side, their arms almost touching leaving a charged static tension in the air.

Elsie craned her head to the ancient larches towering overhead, their branches hosting an orchestra of morning songbirds. Kit's gaze followed birds that Elsie couldn't even see in the high branches, no doubt he could pick out each type by their song alone, but she didn't ask. It felt wrong to break their silence.

Elsie was glad of a distraction as Pepper ran after a squirrel that was far up a tree close to the edge of a small pond. Should she say something to Kit? Maybe she should tell him her plan, even if he didn't want to go to the ball, he deserved to know.

Her hand went to the coin pouch in her inner coat pocket, just checking it was there. She would go to the dressmaker she'd spotted on her way to the park.

They stopped near the frozen pond. Kit cleared his throat, the sound bringing Elsie back to the present. "So...you like it here?"

She felt like that wasn't what he had wanted to say. He'd opened up to her yesterday, something she suspected he did not do too often. Even if it had to be to scare her, her heart ached for him. His father truly sounded like a monster.

"It's lovely." She wanted to hear what Kit had to say, but she really needed to get going soon. The shops would be opening any minute.

Pepper barked at the squirrel who had stopped halfway back down the tree, taunting the poor dog on purpose.

"I want to ask you something, Elsie." Kit's voice was smooth and steady, the voice of a practiced deceiver.

Her hands grew sweaty in her gloves. This was it; he was going to tell her to give up on her mum, that it was too dangerous, or perhaps he had a new plan. Perhaps he had changed his mind to help. Still, her belly fluttered with hope.

She pulled off her gloves, tucked them in her pocket, and wiped her damp hands on her dress. "Very well." She held still in expectation, hardly daring to breathe.

Kit stopped and turned to face her, his eyes as light blue as lake ice and so sincere that they made her stop in her tracks.

Her heart raced in her chest, despite her telling it not to, her body urging her to step closer to him, but she would not listen. She still wanted the Kit she had known before yesterday, wanted to feel the touch of his hand once more, wanted to kiss him, to become one with him, perhaps something more...but he was gone... he had never even been.

Kit reached into his oilskin coat and pulled out a perfect rose made entirely of ice. "Elsie, will you do me the honor of attending the ball with me?"

Her mouth fell open. She forced herself to close it again and swallowed. She had dared to hope it was true. He wanted to go to the ball with her! To do things her way. Had Liri said something to change his mind?

"Well?" He shuffled between his feet, holding out the rose.

She took the flower and turned it so its petals sparkled like diamonds in the sunlight. She held it to her nose; the sweet floral scent brought her back to reality with a sharp breath, surprised it had a scent at all. "It's beautiful." Yet again, stunned by the wonders of magic. "You truly mean it; you want to go to the ball?"

"Yes, that is why I asked you." Kit rubbed the top of his ear.

She twirled the rose on her fingertips. She had to be sure. "Why? You were so set on not going. On finding another way."

"Because I know I cannot stop you." He shook his head as if he didn't believe he was doing it himself. "Liri helped me come up with some ideas on how to protect both of us, so if you would still like to attend, I would be honored to accompany you and ensure you make it out alive."

Her chest tightened. He could not lie, and his eyes said it all, he wanted to help. "Of course, I will go with you!" She threw herself at him in a heartfelt hug. She couldn't help herself. As much as she told herself she would go alone, having Kit at her side made the whole process a lot less daunting.

Kit was rigid at first but melted as she clung to his waist. Her face pressed into his chest, and his arms folded around her. A day ago, this would have been so different. They worked so well together. Her mind flickered to when they hid in the bushes waiting to get into the palace, his legs pressed up against hers. He'd given her his jacket, not because he was a prince, but because he was a good man.

She swallowed hard, not wanting to let him go. This was what she wanted, she wanted him, but Kit the bird tracker and traveler, not Kit the prince with a despicable father. But now she knew he was a prince and that this could never be.

She forced herself to pull away, to have a little pride. But he didn't step back.

She couldn't bring herself to let go of his arms, and they stood there facing each other, tension burning between them.

Kit tucked a strand of hair behind her ear, and a shiver ran through her.

Oh, no. There it was again, the allure of the unattainable. She knew what this was, she was a duty to him. He was trying to protect her the way he couldn't Marella. But none of that mattered right now, not in this moment.

She wanted to know what it felt like, wanted to feel his lips on hers. Heat coiled in her belly.

Kit's eyes moved to her lips, like he knew what she was thinking. Elsie went with her gut and moved her hand to his cheek, guiding his face toward her. Reaching on tiptoes, Elsie's lips parted as she pressed them softly against his. A thank you, a challenge, a last chance.

He kissed her back.

Everything was forgotten. The world was silent around them, frozen in a moment. A familiar warmth spread through her, but this felt like something new, something she wanted more of. His mouth moved against hers in such a perfect fit she didn't want it to end.

His hand brushed against her lower back, pulled her closer, and sent a fluttering through her heart. But her thoughts were determined to destroy her happiness. This was not real; it could never be.

He was the one to pull away.

"You're so perfect," he whispered as his hand fell away from her back.

Her cheeks heated. "Hardly. You're the last person I should be kissing." She probably shouldn't have done that—kiss a prince.

"I'm glad you did." Kit smiled.

"We should make a convincing couple at the ball, at least." Her pulse hadn't slowed one bit. A frivolous moment of weakness and she should have known better, yet she couldn't bring herself to regret it.

"That may be our problem." He brushed his fingers across her cheek.

A shiver danced through her. "I'm aware of how dangerous and potentially foolish this quest is, but I have no choice but to try, for my mother's sake." She smiled softly, hopefully hiding how shaken she was by the kiss.

His face fell, cold, a prince, back to being the man she'd ordered herself not to get attached to.

"I understand. But before you commit, you need to know what you're walking into." Kit reached into his pocket and handed her a note.

CHAPTER 27

ELSIE

E lsie reread the note from Kit's father several times as she waited for Liri on a surprisingly comfy wooden bench next to a roaring brazier outside of the dressmaker's. *I expect you and your new whore to be in attendance.* That line particularly stuck out.

Kit had once again said they could find another way, but the truth was she was out of time, and she couldn't risk her mother's life any further. This was the perfect opportunity to get into the palace, and there wouldn't be another chance.

They would be well protected if what he said about the dress and the magic amplifier was true. It was hard to think about anything so serious after kissing Kit. Yes, he was a prince who she would never see again after next week, or perhaps she would be in prison alongside her mother. Or dead. But whatever the outcome, there was no future with him, and she knew this, yet she couldn't bring herself to regret kissing him.

If they were putting their lives at risk, she might as well try to enjoy herself while doing it. Pretend she was in a fairytale going to the ball with a prince and they would dance the night away and fall in love by the end of it. Marie would call her as nutty as a fruitcake, or something much ruder, but she would be sure to agree after Elsie rescued their mother and proved hypothetical Marie wrong.

"Elsie, are you alright?" Liri was standing right in front of her, dressed in all leather, with many buckles like a pirate might wear.

"Liri!" Elsie realized she was being rude and stood up and hugged Liri, hardly noticing the strangeness of the wings that settled over the top of her arms. "So sorry, I was captured by a daydream."

Liri laughed. "Was it a dream about a handsome prince?" she teased.

"Partly." Elsie let a smile slip across her lips.

"The two of you made up, then?" She quirked an eyebrow.

"Yes, well, sort of. He agreed to go to the ball with me, so for now nothing else matters."

"I'm glad you found out who he is. I told him not to keep it from you." Liri sank onto the bench, and Elsie sat back down.

"Clearly he can't listen." Elsie sighed.

Liri leaned back. "Don't be too hard on him."

"Why not?" Elsie focused on a dress in the window, trying to turn her mind from the anger that came and went. It did not work. She tried to turn her thoughts to the blissful morning, but she couldn't so easily forget everything that came before, as much as she wanted to.

"He has a hard time trusting people. He grew up in a snake pit. His father is a monster, and his mother might as well have turned to ice when she became queen."

"I'm not sure that's an excuse."

"Not to mention his brother is a prat who loves to wind Kit up."

"We met."

"Oh, right. But Anders isn't all bad. He just knows exactly how to push Kit's buttons."

"He seemed pretty bad. He's supposed to be the next king?"

"I know. Let's hope he never gets married. But going back to Kit, he's lived in Anders' shadow his whole life. All he wants is to be free."

"I don't see how that will work out for him." She couldn't bring herself to feel pity for Kit.

She had grown up without a father, dealt with a mother who fell apart from grief, then coped by dragging her children on endless travels across the lands searching for what were apparently illegal mushroom powders. Yet no one felt pity for Elsie, no one cared she didn't have a dad or that she had raised her sister and run a shop when her mother could barely get out of bed. It just proved she could only rely on herself, and it did not do well to trust others.

"You're more similar than you know." Liri gave a sly smile. "He's never opened up to anyone about Marella, not even me."

"Oh," Elsie said, realizing what a big deal it was for him.

"His father really messed him up you know, but he's finally being himself. It's nice to see him happy." Liri nudged Elsie. "That's all you."

"I don't know about that." Elsie's cheeks heated. She wasn't sure she had that sort of influence over anyone, let alone Kit. She couldn't think about this now. "How about we find me a dress?"

"Oh, yes! We better get a move on." Liri pulled Elsie off the bench and pushed open the door. The tinkling of bells announced their arrival into the room which looked like a rainbow had exploded all over the walls.

Elsie marveled at colors she had never seen in her life, fabrics that appeared to glow from their own light, and material so sparkly she was sure it had to be made entirely of gemstones.

"I'm not sure I can afford this," Elsie whispered to Liri.

Liri grinned. "No need to worry about that, it's on Kit."

"Really?" He didn't even want to go to the ball, yet he was offering to pay. No one had ever been so generous to her before.

"If you are accompanying a prince, unfortunately, you have to dress to royal standards, so let Kit pay."

"Very well." Her heart sank. He was a prince. Money was probably nothing to him. It only proved how very different their lives were.

"You like this one?" A woman appeared next to her. She had elegantly styled curly black hair piled atop her head and eyes outlined in kohl, her lips were deep red, and she was as tall as Liri, despite being human, or perhaps a witch judging from the amulets and rings adorning her wrists, neck, and all her fingers.

"It is lovely." Elsie pulled her hand away. Intimidated by the woman's style and confidence. She couldn't be much older than Elsie's twenty-two years, but she seemed so much more put together than Elsie had ever felt in her life.

"Elsie, this is Runa. She's going to take your measurements and whip you up a dress overnight."

Runa bowed slightly. "It is an honor to serve you, Miss Elsie. I have made many gowns for balls, but this is the first a royal has honored me with their patronage."

Elsie laughed nervously. "I'm not sure what Liri has been telling you, but I'm hardly worthy of this treatment. Truth be told, I kind of blackmailed the prince into taking me."

"I like you even more." Runa laughed. "And you, missy." She ran a finger down Liri's forehead and tapped her affectionately on the nose. "Holding out on me that you were friends with the prince."

Liri grinned back. "Slipped my mind. Promise I'll make it up to you later."

"Oh, you better." Runa planted a soft kiss on Liri's cheek so close to the edge of her lip it sent butterflies through Elsie's stomach just watching.

Elsie didn't know where to look. No one in the shop seemed to care. A fae kissing a witch was something she never would have imagined seeing in a thousand years. So, if a witch and a fae could be together, that must be okay for humans too...

"Now, Miss Elsie. Please take your time and take a turn about the shop. Listen to which fabrics speak to you, which colors scream your name, which open your soul." Runa's low voice made the process seem so romantic, seductive even. She could see why Liri was drawn to this woman.

The witch winked at Liri, then spun away and disappeared out the back.

"Thanks, Ru," Liri called after her and took Elsie's arm in hers. "Ooo, what about this one!" She spun Elsie around.

Elsie glanced at the fabric Liri was pointing to. "You and Runa are together?"

"Only for about a month. Isn't she great?"

"She's wonderful." Elsie's heart grew light, and something, perhaps a worry, detached like a dandelion seed caught in a summer breeze. It felt like Liri was giving her the permission she had been wanting to hear from herself. She just didn't know it.

"You're thinking about you and Kit, aren't you?" Liri grinned.

"Is it so obvious?" A flush crept across Elsie's cheeks as she moved to another table with folds of blue and green silky materials.

"In Midwinter, people are on the whole very open-minded, but in the Winterfae Kingdom it is a different story," Liri said. "Kit taking a human to the ball is a scandal, so you must be prepared for that." Liri picked up a silver and blue bolt that reminded Elsie of ice on a lake, and she held it next to Elsie and scrunched up her nose.

Elsie moved on to a black and red fabric that glowed like simmering embers. A heat of guilt crept over her. Kit was doing this for her, she hadn't thought about the repercussions with his father, and there was no benefit to him. She ought to be more grateful. "Will there be other humans there?"

"Perhaps, there will most certainly be diplomats and representatives from the other kingdoms: witches, werewolves, vampires, fae from down south. The king always likes to make a spectacle, so people speak of the opulence and wealth of the Winterfae Kingdom."

"What color is Kit wearing to the ball?" She'd choose whichever color he wanted to match, probably royal colors.

"He said he'd match whatever colors you select. I have all his measurements to give to Runa."

"Should he not wear royal colors?" Elsie assumed that meant silver, light blue, and black judging by the flags she saw at the palace and the guard's uniform.

"He probably should, but I believe he is proving a point to his father."

"To do with the stone?" Elsie hoped it was about the stone, not her.

Liri looked around and lowered her voice. A fae couple and two human women in the shop were engrossed in fabrics on the other side of the store. "Be careful what you say, but one reason, yes, I believe so."

"He means to give it to his father, then?" Elsie whispered. She knew little about it, only that Kit guarded it closely, and she'd put two and two together that it was the item he'd mentioned that had something to do with Midwinter Haven's wards.

"He didn't say, but he hinted he has a plan. There is no way he will just hand it over."

Elsie doubted he would let her in on his plans. She moved to the next stack of fabric and when her hand brushed over the next bolt, a fuzzy sensation spread into her fingers and up her arm.

She pulled her hand away. The most exquisite material shone back at her. The deep green reminded her of the heart of a forest. It reminded her of the walk to Midwinter Haven. It reminded her of nature and calmness, not to mention that it matched Kit's emerald green wings. It was perfect.

"This is the one." She let the cool material trickle over her arm.

"Wonderful!" Liri clapped her hands and rushed off to find Runa.

CHAPTER 28

KIT

Kit paced the hallway outside Elsie's room while Pepper watched him from the floor by Elsie's door. He pulled at the high collar of the coat of his new court suit, its buttons so close to his throat, it felt like a leash his father had set from afar.

Though the deep emerald green and silver ensemble was perfectly tailored, he had gotten used to dressing in comfortable traveling clothes, and the stiff, new material felt unfamiliar, like he was stepping back into a version of himself that no longer existed.

At least Elsie hadn't chosen royal colors. He had secretly hoped she wouldn't. Instead, she had opted for a dress of deep forest green he had yet to see, but if his jacket was anything to go by, it would be exquisite, and it matched his wings. Liri's friend, the dress witch, had done an exemplary job. His coat fit snugly across his wide shoulders, cinched in at the waist with elaborate silver buttons, and the tails flared out behind his knees with fabric that caught the light with his every movement. It was crafted from the finest silk and adorned with silver embroidery in the shape of vines and leaves, winding their way down the front, around the cuffs, and along the hem.

He confirmed that the Bloodgate Ruby, along with its counterfeit version and the clear amplifier crystal, were securely tucked away in his pocket. The outfit was complete with new black boots and a waistcoat of silver and green brocade.

"You be good for Liri and look after Elsie." Kit kissed Pepper's head, unsure when he would see her again since he couldn't risk Pepper going anywhere near the palace.

Finally, the door opened. His breath caught in his chest as Elsie stepped beyond the threshold of her room.

"Isn't this dress amazing?" She beamed and spun around; her eyes fixed on the shimmering skirts that billowed around her as Pepper barked in approval.

She is amazing. Kit couldn't help but grin. His pulse spiked as she twirled in the narrow hallway like they were already at the ball. Her skirts of deep forest green swished against the walls and shimmered like moonlight where the fae light caught the swirls and vines of silver embroidery. The molded corset top, elaborately decorated, hugged her slim figure perfectly. At the ball, only he and Elsie would know the true magical properties that made it far more valuable than any mere ball gown.

"You are the vision of beauty." He caught her hand mid-twirl. Her eyes locked with his, and she stopped. Her face fell.

The settling of her dress sent the hallway into stark silence. Should he not have spoken?

"Your face, it's so different. Again." She looked at the floor. Her eyes lined in kohl surrounded by green shimmers; her skin as smooth as porcelain.

His heart sank. "I'm sorry. I should have prepared you."

"No, I understand. You just don't look like you."

His royal glamour was a lot, and it certainly wasn't him anymore, however, it was how everyone recognized him at court. He was an idiot. He should have warned Elsie.

"It's only temporary, for tonight, then I'll be back to myself." Though he doubted he would ever see her again once he was under his father's thumb. He wasn't going to tell her and ruin the evening, which was stressful enough as it was. All that mattered was she made it out with her mother. He would make sure of that, even if she hated him even more by the end of it.

An uncomfortable tension filled the air as she nervously nodded and locked eyes with him, a feeling of unease settling in. Suddenly her hand was on his cheek. Her fingers trailed his cheekbones with a softness that sent electricity down his spine. She was studying him, and he let her.

He swallowed as she followed the shape of his jawline, his nose, even his eyebrows, then she pulled her hand away, looking into his eyes with such intensity.

"Your eyes are the same. Midnight blue tonight. You are still you." She bit her lip and nodded as if trying to convince herself it was true.

"I'm glad to hear it."

"But a scary version of you," she added.

Scary, that did not seem at all like a good thing. "Once again, you do not find my face pleasing?" he teased, hoping it would put her at ease.

"It is very pleasing, beautiful, the face of a prince."

"But?"

"But not *my* Kit." She looked down and twisted her mouth to the side. Even under the dusting of rouge on her cheeks, there was a noticeable increase in color.

My Kit. It sent a warmth through his chest. He might never see her again after this night, but at least they could pretend. They could have this one night.

"I am still your Kit." He took her gloved hand and placed a kiss on it. He wanted to say he would prove it to her, that he wanted to be hers for longer than tonight. But he could make no such promises.

"Good. Then let us pretend this night will not end in a prison break or me as a potential new prisoner. It is simply Kit and Elsie attending a ball at the grandest court in all the Celestial Isles." She forced a smile that nearly made it all the way to her eyes.

"Well said. Would my lady care to accompany me to the carriage?" He gave a practiced bow and held out his hand.

"I would like that." She smiled nervously.

Footsteps thundered up the stairs, and an out of breath Liri appeared and stopped in front of them.

"Well, aren't you two a sight?" She grinned.

"In a good way?" Elsie asked.

She stood there, still grinning. "In a very fine way. You make a handsome couple."

"You're still able to take the bags?" Kit asked.

"I said I'd do it, didn't I?" Liri put her hands on her hips. "Behind the old stone wall just off the start of the track, I'm not a simpleton."

"Thank you for everything, Liri. Mine and my mother's bags are on the bed." Elsie rushed forward and hugged Liri.

"Not a problem. You are welcome back anytime," Liri said as Elsie pulled away.

Kit narrowed his eyes at Liri. "Was there something else you wanted to say?"

"Oh, yes. There is a heard of reporters and townsfolk waiting outside by your carriage." She gave a mocking bow. "Your Highness."

"Blast it. A messenger the other day gave away my identity." He updated Elsie.

"Oh." Elsie stroked Pepper's ears. That dog was going to miss her, and he suspected Elsie might miss Pepper even more than him.

"You can't be surprised. News spreads like pixie pox around here." Liri leaned against the doorframe of Elsie's room.

"Blasted parasites is what they are." Kit clenched his jaw.

Liri snorted. "You can hardly be surprised."

"What do they want?" Elsie asked.

Liri crossed her arms. "They want to know what the king is planning. There are rumors. There'll be a riot to claim Kit's first interview."

He shook his head. "There will be no interview. Liri, please make sure Pepper is inside and safe." He turned to Elsie. "We will go straight to the carriage. Do not speak to anyone, just walk, look ahead like everyone is beneath you, and smile."

She nodded. "I can do that."

"You're sure you still want to do this?" Kit asked, hardly believing they were going through with this.

She nodded again. "Of course I do. A few reporters and an angry mob won't scare me off." She leaned down and kissed Pepper on the head. "Be good, Peps."

Kit hugged Liri, bent down, and gave Pepper a treat he had been saving. "Be good for Liri. Remember what we talked about." He hugged the giant wolf hound, not caring if he got fur on his suit.

This was it.

Elsie shut her bedroom door and led the way down the hall, flashing Liri a nervous smile as they passed. An ache twinged in Kit's heart. He wished there was another way.

At the bottom of the stairs, two of the bar staff propped open the main door and blocked it to keep the mob out. Kit offered his arm to Elsie once more, and she slid her arm into his.

"Make way." Kit stopped at the door's threshold and announced in his trained princely voice.

The crowd went silent—for a second. Then the questions began: Where have you been this past year? Prince Christarel, what was the task your father asked of you? Why do you not wear the royal colors? Why are you staying in Midwinter Haven? Who is this woman? Who is this mortal? Is it true the king wishes to take back Midwinter Haven? Does Prince Andriel have anyone in mind as his partner?

"Silence!" Kit bellowed. "I will not be answering questions. Please stand aside." He did not wait for a response but acted as they would expect a prince to. He drew from the power of the amplifier in his pocket, a crystal he had exchanged not only for too much gold but also his rare elven watercolor set that he loved so dearly.

Pulling water from the snow in the doorway, he raised a solid spear of ice in his hand and slammed the base into the ground.

The crowd parted. Elsie's grip grew tighter on his arm, but she didn't say a word. Just smiled past the crowd and followed his lead as he walked toward the silver and blue carriage.

The spear was merely a warning, a show of power. Everyone believed the royal family to have superior magic. That was the illusion his father had spun since the beginning of his reign. All it took was some flashy ice magic to maintain. The truth was, even when Kit's power was strongest, he could do little to hold back a crowd like that.

Elsie continued to smile as they reached the footman at the steps of the carriage who opened the door.

Kit turned the spear to snow, and it flurried around them dramatically as they climbed into the carriage. The door slammed, and Kit took his seat next to Elsie on the plush blue velvet bench. The soft glow of fae lights made her black hair twisted up on her head appear an ethereal blue.

Elsie let out a breath as she arranged the folds of her dress around her.

"Are you well?

"I'm fine. That was rather exciting, and just the start I suppose." Her eyes dropped to his lips, but she quickly looked down as if catching herself.

Had he imagined that? He remembered the way her lips had felt against his. "I wish I could promise that would be the end of it, but I suspect you will not find the palace any better."

"I expected as much. Do not worry yourself, Kit. I will do my best not to make a fool of myself and embarrass you."

"That's the last thing I'm worried about." He reached for her hand and placed a chaste kiss on it. Their eyes locked, and a lump caught in his throat. He didn't want to let her go.

The carriage jerked into life.

She kept hold of his hand and lowered it to the space between them, taken up by her dress. "It will be fine, Kit. You'll see."

It might be if all went well. He had his amplifier crystal, she had the tea for Fenn to poison the guards, and he had the stone to present to his father as a distraction. This could work. He just hoped he wouldn't have to resort to Plan B, something Elsie would not approve of.

For most of the carriage ride, they sat in silence, a simmering tension building as they got closer to the palace. Should he kiss her now, before it was too late? Is that what she wanted?

They crossed the border into the Winterfae Kingdom, barely minutes from Snowspire Palace. It was nearly time.

He turned to Elsie. "I'll be with you the whole time, just try to look like you're having fun."

"I trust you, Kit, and we will have fun." She smiled at him, a warm genuine smile that went right to her eyes.

He swallowed. Gods he wanted to kiss her, and this might be his last chance. "You are quite remarkable, Elsie Fielding."

"So are you, Prince Christarel." She shuffled in her seat, and suddenly her lips were on his.

He was stunned for a second, then remembered to kiss her back. Energy raced between them, frantic, desperate, like they were stealing time they should never have had. It was a goodbye kiss, and they both knew it. It hung unsaid between them like a storm cloud ready to break.

He hated that his hands trembled, and the way her fingers twisted in the fabric of his coat, pulling him closer, made him want to stop the carriage and refuse to let her out. Hang her mother. At least Elsie would be safe.

But he would not do that.

Instead, he savored the softness of her skin, trying to commit the curve of her jawline to memory with his lips. Her breath danced across his skin, and for a brief moment, the world outside the carriage melted away. Just the two of them. Elsie and Kit. A fleeting fairytale.

He found her lips once more. Their kisses became softer, slower, like they were savoring what was about to be lost.

At last, when their lips parted, he opened his mouth to speak, but the words caught on his tongue. Nothing he said could make their situation any better. If anything, he was certain to render it worse.

"Don't," she whispered and pulled away, leaving him with a sinking in his stomach, making him want to tell her everything, to beg her not to go in there to warn her he would break her heart.

But he didn't. He was still a coward, and this journey was nearing its end.

As they pulled into the palace gates, she smiled at him, a genuine Elsie smile, not the one she had put on for the crowd, this one was all for him.

"That was—" She shook her head, lost for words.

"Intense?" he offered.

"Indeed." Her chest heaved with quick breaths. "Do I look presentable?"

"Perfect." Not a hair was out of place, nor any makeup smudged. "May I escort you to the palace, my lady?"

The carriage jerked to a stop. "Take me to the ball, my prince." She giggled as she leaned in and kissed him softly on the lips.

He was going to make sure she made it out of this gilded snake pit, even if it cost him everything.

CHAPTER 29

ELSIE

Light poured into the carriage, and for a second Elsie considered telling the driver to turn around and head right back to Midwinter Haven. Instead, she gathered the folds of green fabric of her dress and stepped carefully after Kit, hoping her black boots wouldn't show. She had to be ready to run when the time came.

Elsie squinted into the brightness of the scene she could hardly believe to be real. Snowspire Palace rose before her, its pinnacles like gleaming icicles, its white facade lit with waves of mystical rippling blue ice.

Don't look like the ignorant human. She forged a smile of indifference and did her best not to stare.

She took Kit's arm, barely noticing that they were already walking. Roaring braziers were interspersed with candlelit Midwinter trees along the blue-carpeted walkway, and the guards stationed on either side were perfectly still, their uniforms shimmering silver in the flickering lights.

Keeping her head high and her shoulders back, Elsie focused on walking straight. She would not let Kit down and embarrass him. She would blend in, smile, dance, make small talk, and creep away when it was time.

Then Anders walked toward them.

She squeezed Kit's arm in warning, and a low growl rumbled through him.

She glanced around, looking for a distraction to mask her fear. *Oh, wow, a lady with horns. Man with a lizard on his shoulder. Why? An elven couple, or was it elvish?* They walked like they were floating across air. *A vampire lord judging from the insignia on his jacket, wow, he was an intimidating fellow dressed in all black, but what pretty gold detailing on his court suit jacket.*

"Welcome, brother." Anders bowed stiffly, and Kit did the same in return.

Elsie curtsied, as it was the thing to do and did not want to make a scene, but Anders was the last person she wished to be polite to.

Anders fell into step with Kit as they continued their procession to the grand entrance at the same slow pace as the other guests.

"I thought I would have scared you both off," Anders said lightly, but there was something more behind his words.

Kit kept his gaze straight ahead. "I did not wish to be here, but it seemed I had no choice."

"The other choice was to run the other way," Anders hissed so low Elsie couldn't be sure she'd heard right.

"What do you want, Andriel?"

"To warn you not to do anything stupid." Anders poked his head past Kit's broad shoulders and looked into Elsie's eyes.

She glanced away. Not wanting him to see just how scared of him she was.

"We thank you for the warning, but I assure you, we neither require advice nor assistance," Kit said.

Elsie had been so distracted by Anders she hadn't realized they were at the doors. Servants bowed low as the two princes passed through the great doors and into a grand reception hall. Elsie's pulse began to race. There was no going back now. She was stepping into the realm of the enemy, the fae, and the only path forward was the opulent white staircase that lay before her. She could do this.

Garlands of winter greenery dotted with red berries adorned the banisters and outlined the windows of the largest sheets of glass Elsie had ever seen, yet the vast room was not cold.

At the top of the stairs, the crowd parted way revealing yet another set of doors. They were made of some sort of metal and carved with detailed patterns of falling snowflakes.

Elsie swallowed as they walked through the parted crowd and the heralds at the door bowed low. Behind the doors was the faint sound of unfamiliar music, not at all like the Midwinter hymns she was used to.

The guards at the door bowed deeply. She didn't let go of Kit's arm.

By the angels, this was so much more than she'd expected. Kit was a prince, and this was not a game.

The doors were suddenly open; the music slammed into her: violins, flutes, even drums, all woven together in a majestic melody, exotic and unfamiliar. Then it stopped.

"Announcing Prince Andriel of the Winterfae Kingdom, Prince Christarel of the Winterfae Kingdom, and accompanying them, Elspeth Fielding of Middlemarch."

How did they know her name? Spies, she supposed.

Elsie walked forward as if the angels themselves were controlling her legs. She was glad to have Kit's arm to grip. The silence was filled with the sound of an entire ballroom of ball gowns and suits folding over and crumpling in a sea of bows and curtsies.

Gripped with nerves, Elsie didn't need any help in keeping her face neutral as Kit had instructed. This was not a smiling matter, and the daunting prospect of her task crashed over her like an unstoppable avalanche.

CHAPTER 30

KIT

The familiar feeling of power rushed over Kit as the entire ballroom bowed before him, his brother, and Elsie. Using his practiced expression of regal indifference, he looked out over the sea of noble fae adorned in all their glitter and gold like Midwinter ornaments themselves. He hated himself for reveling in it, even just for that split second before he remembered himself.

It wasn't the same tingling of pleasure one got using magic. No, this power was a sick addictiveness of control over others, something his father taught him to value above all else. And why shouldn't he? He'd believed his family to be gods. Fae worshiped his father with the same reverence as the true gods, and he'd had no reason to believe otherwise.

Now he knew better.

This was not the way, but tonight he had to maintain appearances.

Elsie gripped his arm with the strength of a harpy eagle's talons, though no one else would ever know it from her serene, uninterested expression.

With a dramatic introduction of violins, the music started up again. Kit gently tugged on Elsie's arm, and they descended the stairs into the crowded ballroom.

He wished he could have witnessed Elsie's genuine reaction to the forest of live pine trees that surrounded the massive room, their branches weighed heavily with gold baubles.

Delight danced in her eyes, but she hid her excitement behind a stoic expression.

He purposefully didn't look to the left where, if his father was already there, he would be sitting on his blue velvet and silver throne on the raised dais at the end of the room. Perhaps with Kit's mother at his side, perhaps not. She must be sick of throwing these matchmaking balls for Anders by now. Kit had no desire to catch up with her, they had barely spoken in years even though they lived under the same roof. She had no interest in her children.

"Father plans to call you to present the ruby much earlier than midnight," Anders whispered.

Kit kept his gaze ahead. "Why are you telling me this?"

"So you might be prepared. You're awfully thick sometimes, Kitty. I'm just trying to help."

Gritting his teeth, Kit did his best not to rise to Anders' goading. "Do not call me that, and if you wanted to help, your chance was the other day when we needed it." He didn't for a second think Anders was on their side. There was always another motive with him.

"I don't know what you're planning, but whatever it is, you must give him the stone. For everyone's sake." Anders looked past Kit at Elsie.

"I know what I'm doing. Goodbye, Anders." Kit led Elsie in the opposite direction of Anders as soon as they stepped from the last stair. Kit couldn't shake his unease, something that Anders had said burrowed beneath Kit's skin.

"What did he say?" Elsie spoke low, clearly aware of the many eyes that had settled on them.

Nosy bastards, the lot of them.

Kit ignored her comment. They needed to get away from these prying eyes and ears. "Would you care for a refreshment, Miss Fielding?"

"Indeed, thank you." She smiled politely but not warmly enough to get the gossips speculating.

He took two glasses of sparkling mead in one hand from a passing servant and guided Elsie to an area on the outskirts of the room next to a tree covered in gilded pears and an oversized portrait of his parents. Two guards stuck very close by to them. He suspected his father might have something to do with that, at least they would keep a gap between them and anyone who wanted to speak with him.

"Do not drink this, just pretend to sip." He handed Elsie the glass and took a fake sip of his own. "Fae spirits do not end well for mortals."

"Nor for your magic, I imagine." She pretended to sip and smiled. "Mmmm, lovely."

"My magic is strong for now. We are in this particular spot because it is warded to conceal any speech, a secret among my father's close circle. There are several around the room."

"That's rather handy. I take it these are your parents?" Elsie tilted her head back to take in the full image.

"Indeed, that is them. I intend to avoid them as long as possible."

Elsie nodded. "That is fine with me."

Kit pretended to take another sip of his drink, then casually tossed the glass at the base of the pear tree. Elsie was doing so well, but as she held the glass to her lips, he couldn't mistake the tremble in her hands. "We will have to dance soon before the grace period of my entrance wears off and people begin to seek me out to speak."

"Very well. I am an excellent dancer." Elsie's lips spread into a wide grin. "But tell me, what did Anders say?"

Kit didn't doubt she was an excellent dancer. "He appeared to be trying to help. Gave me a warning my father will summon me to present the stone much earlier than midnight."

"And you trust his motives?"

"Of course not. But I can't work out what he wants. Stick to the plan for the eleventh bell to meet Fenn." Time was tight, but Fenn couldn't meet them any earlier, and Kit trusted no one else. Guilt churned in his gut at the thought of how the end of this night could turn out. If his father didn't call on him, all would be well. If he did, he would be forced to resort to Plan B.

"Very well, though I don't know how I shall wait that long."

He turned to her, gave a shallow bow, and held out a hand. It would only cause more scandal and questions if he bowed low for a human. "Would you honor me with this dance, Miss Fielding?"

She dipped into a perfect curtsy and accepted his hand gracefully. "I would be delighted."

The blush that tinged her cheeks a warm pink didn't escape his notice. Perhaps time would pass faster if they were dancing.

Of course, Elsie was right; she was an excellent dancer. No one outright objected to a human joining the dance. No one would dare challenge him in front of the court, but the looks toward Elsie were not kind, though a few were simply curious. She did well to keep her expression to a look of indifference as Kit ignored all the courtiers, trying to catch his eye to spark up conversation.

They danced a minuet, Elsie in perfect time with Kit's bows, steps, and turns as her dress swayed around her, catching the glow of the chandeliers with each move.

Between dances, Kit had no choice but to speak with two of the wives of his father's advisers, who cornered them right away. Gossiping busy-bodies, but it could be worse.

"Miss Elspeth Fielding, please meet Lady Hallows and Lady Willowwild."

Elsie's arms curved and held the sides of her gown as she dipped to a delicate curtsy. "Pleased to make your acquaintance."

She did well to remain polite, despite the ladies' absurd appearances. Lady Hallows had the look of a tropical fish, complete with colorful scales covering her face and gills on her neck. It must be a fashion thing because he had it on good authority that her true form was a fox, something that would have been much more appealing.

Lady Willowwild had gone all in with the royal colors, with a glamour of sleek ice over her skin and elaborate crystal shards in her hair. In any other setting, it might have been impressive, but here it was a blatant show to gain favor with the king. Embarrassing.

Thankfully, before they could get too far into conversation, the next dance began. Kit excused them, and Elsie shot him a brief look of gratitude.

They danced the next four dances. Each time making a little polite conversation between performances. Elsie's cheeks were pink with the exercise. She appeared to be enjoying herself, but occasionally, he caught a flash of worry as her smile dropped, as if remembering why they were there.

Kit filled a glass with clean water from a fountain he knew to be direct from a spring beneath the palace. He turned back to hand it to Elsie, only to find Anders.

"I hear you have been keeping Miss Fielding to yourself all evening." Anders took a sip of champagne, though he did not appear drunk—yet.

"And I would prefer to keep it that way." Kit stepped around Anders and handed Elsie the glass.

"Is that what you wish, Miss Fielding, or would you care for a new dance partner, a better one if I do say so myself?"

"I am quite content with Kit's dancing. Thank you, Prince Andriel."

Kit couldn't help but smirk at Anders, who was not used to rejection. He took satisfaction in turning away and offered his arm to Elsie, but Anders stepped in and pulled Kit in closer, so they were right next to her. "I am here to offer one last warning. Father plans to announce you much sooner. I fear you need a new plan."

"What do you know of our plans?" Kit hissed.

"You ought to stop placing so much trust in your friend Fenn. I can read him like a book."

"Why do you have to meddle? This is not a game, Anders. This is Elsie's mother."

Elsie's face paled. "How much time do we have?"

"I am well aware it is not a game, Kit," Anders said, all serious-ness. "And you are out of time. But I am here to help. If you trust me, I can get Elsie to her mother."

"I am not trusting you with anything." Kit struggled to keep his voice low. Anders had done nothing to help Marella that dreadful night. Kit would not risk putting Elsie in the same position.

"It seems you don't have a choice, brother, and there is only one way this ends." Anders let go of Kit's arm and turned to the front of the room as the king stepped up to his throne.

The music slowed and then stopped. The room fell to silence but for the click of a few shoes on marble.

Blast it. He was out of time. Better he was proactive now and in control than let his father mess up their plans.

Kit stepped closer to Elsie, resisting the urge to brush a fallen lock of silky black hair from her cheek. "Everything will be fine, just trust me."

"What are you going to do?" she said in a panicked whisper.

"Get you to your mother." A weight sunk in his stomach as he said those words. She would hate him for what came next, but it was the only way. If he presented the stone to his father now, she would be left alone, alone—with Anders and at the mercy of the court. It would give her little chance to meet Fenn to give him the tea. Their plan would not work.

"Would my son, Prince Christarel, present himself?" The king's voice boomed across the room.

This was it. He met Elsie's warm brown eyes one last time. He wanted to tell her he loved her, to whisper that things would be okay. But he could make no such assurances.

"Trust me," he whispered as he stepped away, feeling like a great chasm opened between them.

Setting his jaw firm, Kit walked through the crowd to the front. He kneeled before his father and waited for his father's permission to rise. The seconds went on for an eternity as anger flushed through Kit's blood, knowing his father's despicable intentions for the ruby Kit had worked so hard to obtain. He swallowed it down. Now was not the time to lose his head.

"Rise, my son. I welcome you back into the fold of the Winterfae Court."

Kit held in a scoff. He made the court sound like a family. It was anything but. "I thank you, Father. I am pleased to return."

"Tell the court of your quest."

Kit rose to face his father. Their eyes locked. Kit could not seek out a challenge, not yet. He averted his gaze to the floor like a good subject.

"I am pleased to announce my quest was one of great fortune." Kit reached into his pocket, and the smooth wood box brushed his fingertips. He grasped it, not wanting to share it with anyone, let alone this viperous court, yet he held it up so all could see. They always liked a spectacle, and this was as close as they would get with him.

"I present to you the Bloodgate Ruby of Stonehelm," Kit said in his best dramatic voice. He bowed and held out the box, open, so his father could see the real stone. The fake weighed heavily in his pocket. His father needed the real thing for the blood oath to be broken. Kit prayed an opportunity would arise so he could switch them later.

Gasps of awe rustled through the crowd. Idiots. They'd never even heard of the stone before.

With his arms still out, Kit held the box steady as his father descended the stairs of the dais.

"Rise my son."

Kit stood to his full height, which was still half a head shorter than his father. "Does it please you, Father?" he asked, hoping to sound like the weak-willed prince he was when he left.

The king took the stone from the box and held it to the light of a chandelier above, peering into the tiny windows of the crystal. Crimson shards of light danced around the room, his father using magic to enhance the effect.

A sickness rose in Kit's throat at the thought of what his father would do with the stone. That Kit was the one handing over the fates of every resident of Midwinter Haven. That he was the one to blame if this all went wrong.

"It pleases me greatly. A successful quest," the king announced to the room.

A thunderous cheer erupted from the crowd, but it did nothing to ease Kit's guilt. In fact, it increased it a great deal. He gave his best princely smile, which was actually a well-practiced smirk, and raised a hand acknowledging the audience.

"I, too, would like to make an announcement," Anders called from the side of the room, where he remained next to Elsie.

Kit was not about to let him do whatever it was he wanted to do to mess up their plans. "Actually, I had not finished."

His father frowned. Old Kit would not have interrupted or spoken over the number one Prince Andriel.

"I brought with me another gift to the court." He paused, allowing the silence to add tension for the crowd. The pretty fae, caught up in their fantastic world of parties and gold and games, stared hungrily at him, always wanting more, more wine, more gifts, more creatures to toy with. This is what drove the court, and he would give them what they wanted.

"I present to the Winterfae court—a criminal." Wicked smiles curled onto the faces of the courtly fae, always hungry for the pain of others. He once more waited for the still of silence.

He turned in the direction of Elsie and Anders, ignoring the taste of bile in his throat, the agony of his heart, the voice in his head telling him to abandon this plan—his body's attempt to keep the poison of these words spilling from his lips. He ignored it all.

"Guards, seize that human." Kit pointed right at Elsie.

She didn't move, didn't even blink or fight as the guards locked onto each of her arms. It was clear she had not seen this coming. He did his best not to look at her, but her dark eyes drilled into him, and if she had possessed magic, he was sure her fire would have burned him alive in that moment.

"What is this woman's crime?" the king asked, not showing any outright surprise, but Kit knew he was thrown off, able to tell by the speed of his question.

Kit smirked internally. He had outwitted him for the first time. "She planned to break her mother from the prison this very night." Kit forced his gaze from Elsie and to the crowd. "Her mother stole from the sacred forest, a crime punishable by death."

"Then her vile daughter shall join her. Take her away." The king clapped, and it felt like a vice clamped over Kit's heart.

It happened so quickly.

He didn't know what to do when his father rested a hand on his shoulder. "I must say, son. You have impressed me beyond expectation."

Kit forced himself to answer, despite wanting to take back everything he had just done. "I thank you, Father. But I only followed your training and guidance."

"You are far too humble for a prince. Join me at my table. We have much to speak of." His father tucked the box into his pocket.

Kit kept his face blank as he followed his father up the steps. For the first time, he had everything he thought he wanted: to be accepted at court, a successful quest, and his father's approval. But he no longer cared.

As he sank into the plush velvet chair at his father's side, he couldn't help but stare at Elsie's back as she was hauled away. His thoughts flashed to Marella as her wings were ripped from her back, the helplessness he felt, but this would not be a repeat. Elsie would be safe; he would make sure of that.

She did not fight. She did not scream or cry, and as she turned the corner out of view, he was certain his heart ripped in two.

CHAPTER 31

ELSIE

lsie did not cry; she didn't even react as the hands clamped
around her arms. Her mind was feverish with anger, like a
great hornet was buzzing around, desperate for a way out. But she
did not speak. She did not fight the grip of the guards, knowing
it would not do her any good.

She sent one last death glare toward Kit, sitting up there by his
father, a pair of deceivers. Marie had been right about the fae after
all.

He didn't so much as spare her a glance as the guards swiveled
her toward the door. Though her eyes caught Prince Anders' as
she left, and his look was that of confusion. Was this not exactly
what he'd wanted?

No matter.

Floors of white marble turned to gray stone as they went down and
down. The music and warmth and Midwinter magic trickled away,

already like a distant memory being replaced with a new reality of cold stone walls and no hope.

She had failed her mother and failed Marie. Poor Marie would sit there alone on Midwinter's Eve awaiting Elsie's arrival, and she would never again step through those doors, nor would their mother. He told her to trust him, but how could she after this? A sob caught in her chest, but she would not allow herself to break now.

The walls blurred by, all looking the same. Her chest felt like it might explode from fear.

This was her fault for trusting a fae. She had gone against her better judgment and her own beliefs in the blink of an eye. Why did she not listen to herself? Getting attached always meant getting hurt. This was something she was all too familiar with, yet it got her every time. She should have found a way to get her mother out, not lead herself straight into a trap.

Everyone always leaves me. This is no different.

But it *was* supposed to be different this time. She was supposed to stay in Winterfrost and find a nice man and a cottage and a dog.

Her thoughts snapped back to reality with the creak of an iron door, likely made for fae prisoners. They threw her into a room before she could even blink. She stumbled, unable to catch her footing. The door slammed, and she crashed to the floor, her dress padding her fall. Fortunately, they hadn't thought to check her for weapons. Her knife was still in her dress pocket.

"What's this then?" A guard's voice echoed in the hallway of cells.

"The prince's whore. She planned to break out the other prisoner. Looks like the rumors about him were all wrong."

"You mean Prince Christarel? Don't believe you." The voices trailed off down the hall and a door slammed.

Elsie took a slow deep breath. She was on her own, but this was exactly where she had wanted to be this evening, not on this side of the bars, obviously, but she had to make the most of it before she accepted utter despair.

"Mother, are you in here?" she called between the bars of her door. The only view she had of the hallway as the rest of the cell was solid stone. She could see no other prisoners in the other bare rooms.

"Mum!" No one answered back, though the sound of hay rustling with slow dragging footsteps in a neighboring cell told her she was not alone down here.

She released her hands from the bars, and they came away with an orange coating and flecks of rust all over them. She crouched to wipe her hands with hay to try to remove the strong metallic scent that reminded her far too much of blood.

"Mother, are you in here? It is me, Elsie!" she called again, hating the shake she couldn't keep from her voice.

"Elsie?" a croaky voice came from the neighboring cell.

"Mum?" Elsie pressed her hands to the wall and shouted to the small gap high above between the two cells.

Hay rustled. "Tell me you are not real."

"I am real. I am real!" Elsie jumped at the wall, trying to grip the high window, but slipped.

"No." A mournful groan followed.

"No, do not despair, Mum. I came here to rescue you."

"Oh, my love. How I wished to hear your voice. But not like this."

"We can get out of here."

"This is a trick of the fae. Tormenting me in my last days to break me. I will not break," she said stubbornly.

Yes, that was her. That was the woman Elsie knew, and she allowed relief to rush over her. It was not too late; she had not lost her wits at least. They could get out somehow. She had a knife, her protective dress, and the poisoned tea still.

"I assure you; it is me, Elsie. Marie is safe in Winterfrost. You needn't worry for her or the tea house."

"My Elsie would not be so foolish to come to the fae lands. I taught her better than that."

"You did, Mum. But you know how I never listen. Do you recall our last conversation?" Perhaps winning her trust was a good first step. She was right to be skeptical.

"You wanted to stay in Winterfrost, start your own tea house. Abandon me."

Maybe that wasn't the best topic to start with. "And I said I wanted to call it *The Tea Cozy,* and you said, 'That's a daft name for a tea house'."

"True enough, I did say that. But you could have taken that information from my Elsie. What have you done to her?" she yelled and let out a wail that curdled Elsie's gut.

Elsie pressed herself to the wall as if she could merge through it somehow. "Mum, please don't get upset. I assure you it is me. Fae can't lie. Remember, it was you who taught me that."

"But they could trick someone into pretending to be my Elsie. Either way, I will take solace in the fact that you are taunting me, and my Elsie is safe at home."

Elsie's throat grew thick. If only that were true. She had made this situation a lot worse for her mother. But if they were to find a way out, she needed to believe her.

"I have something for you." Elsie reached into the pocket of her dress. Alongside the healing crystal and folding knife Kit had insisted she carry, her fingers wrapped around her mother's heart-shaped locket. She looked to the window, hoping it would make it through and not get caught. "Look up at the window between our cells."

Elsie tossed the locket and chain in a tight ball, and it slipped over the stones of the window and fell to the other side.

A sob followed. "Oh, my Elsie. No..."

The sound of her mother's near-silent weeping broke the floodgates for Elsie. Tears made hot trails down her cheeks, and she couldn't stop the heavy sobs in her chest as her palms slid down the rough stone wall. She sank into a heap of green fabric and scratchy hay.

"I'm so sorry, Mum. I tried."

CHAPTER 32

KIT

The night had passed too slowly. It took everything in Kit's willpower not to go down to the prison. But he knew he could not, not if his plan was to work.

He'd met with Fenn late in the night once he could safely slip from the festivities. They formulated a new plan to get Elsie out with her mother. He trusted Fenn to see it through, and he had to pray Elsie would forgive him for the deception.

He stared into the expansive wardrobe of his old room. Why had he needed this many clothes? Such an extravagance. Elsie had made such a deal about her dress, and at the time, he thought she was showing gratitude. She had a generous nature after all. But he now realized how overindulged he was.

He dug around, right at the back, for a set of forest green breeches and a natural linen shirt, something easy to hike in that also wouldn't be out of place in Midwinter Haven.

Slipping on his boots, he stood for a moment, listening for the guards. They lingered outside his room, no way he could shake them inside the palace, which meant getting to Elsie himself was still not an option. It would only put her and her mother in more danger if he showed interest, precisely what his father was waiting for.

It went against every bone in his body not to do anything, not to tell her everything, but he had to trust it would go accordingly. Right now, he needed to recover the ruby from his father and prevent the attack on Midwinter Haven.

Kit swung open the door, his royal glamour upon his face and his amplifier crystal and fake crystal safe in his pocket. As expected, the two guards were at the ready.

"Good morrow, gentleman," he said as if he hadn't a care in the world.

"Your Highness," they greeted him. Both held ceremonial spears tall at their side. They might be ceremonial, but they were also lethal, and he knew they would have orders to restrain him with force if he tried to do anything suspicious.

"I wish to attend the library if you would care to accompany me. I have missed my books."

They said nothing, just fell into step behind him.

As he descended the stairs from his tower room, he did his best not to think of Elsie. It did not work. She had the dress to protect her, she had her knife, and Fenn was going to get her and her mother out.

It was just as he planned, yet he felt sick at the thought that she now hated him. He had done what he had to. That's what he told himself, anyway. Perhaps there had been another way to protect her and Midwinter Haven, but he could not think of it.

His only spark of hope was that she would read the note he left in her bag and forgive him for the deception when she was safely away from this place. He suspected it would not sway her. She would be safe with her mother. Why would she come back to him? But still, he held onto a tiny spark of hope.

He turned the corner and made his way up the familiar hallway of tapestries and portraits, one of the few interesting walls in the stark palace that had a splash of color. This used to be his daily routine, walking to the library after breakfast to begin his studies for the day.

His boots clacked out of time with the guards. His heart raced more than it should for this simple walk. It was nerves or the magic from the crystal, both he suspected.

"Kit! Good to see you back skulking these halls."

"Good morrow, Anders." Kit forced politeness and did not stop walking, not having time for a word battle or any other kind. "I am headed for the library." He marched past.

"Not off rescuing your girl? Surprising, though it was a rather convincing display."

"It was no display."

"Come now, Kitty. I saw how concerned you were when I had her up against the wall the other day. You can't say I didn't warn you." A hand wrapped around Kit's arm. "Not so fast."

"Bugger off, Anders." Kit had no choice but to stop. "I don't have time for this." He peeled his brother's fingers from his arm, doing his best not to let the anger lash out. It would only spur Anders on.

Anders leaned in close. "You've got Fenn on the case, don't you?" Anders whispered quietly enough the guards would not hear.

Kit froze. Anders' voice was serious.

"It is under control. Do not mess this up," Kit mumbled under his breath, his heart drumming in his chest. He didn't have time for Anders' meddling.

"I have not and have no intention to. I'm not your enemy, Kit, and I can help," Anders whispered and stepped back and brushed his velvet jacket as if Kit had dirtied it.

Kit couldn't risk believing he was sincere and stepped in so his face was close to Anders, so he could see the seriousness of the situation. "This is no game, Anders. This is a life, two lives. Please, for once, do the right thing."

Anders rested his hand on Kit's shoulder. "I won't let you down." He grinned, turned on his heel, and clicked off down the hallway.

Why did he feel that Anders hadn't gotten the message? He had to trust that Fenn had things under control.

Kit kept to his plan, went into the library, set up a stack of books, and got to work researching for his book, just as he used to. Once Kit convinced the guards that he was settled in, he dismissed them to go outside and stand in the hall. They were more than happy to do so.

He only needed five minutes. They would not check on him right away for fear of angering him being disturbed.

Kit slipped down the aisle of cookery books—the one place no one in the palace ever went. At the end was a panel in the bookshelf. He stacked the books to the side and removed it, then crawled into the secret tunnel behind.

He ran lightly, using his wings to take his weight and make his footsteps nearly silent as he hovered along. He had to admit it felt good to use his wings again.

In a few brief minutes, he was at the panel that led to his father's study. There was no chance his father would come in. It was breakfast time, and he always took breakfast with his advisers in the west wing of the palace in the room overlooking the training yard.

Kit went straight to the safe behind the painting of his father at his coronation. Taking the knife from his pocket, he made a small prick in his thumb and let two drops of blood fall into the tiny vial in the door of the black safe.

Please let this work. He had never attempted to gain access to his father's safe, but he knew it was blood-warded and hoped it would recognize his royal blood.

Several seconds passed and nothing happened. Kit glanced over his shoulder.

The safe door swung open, and there it was. The wooden box.

He plucked it from the safe and opened the lid. The intense crimson of the ruby sent dazzling flashes dancing across the walls in the morning light. It was nearly impossible to look away, its facets like tiny windows to another world.

Kit reached into his pocket and pulled out the replica he'd had made. It looked similar, but it was only red glass and very obvious if you looked closely. His father would know instantly if he picked it up. One reason he couldn't use it last night, the other being the blood oath, which was now fulfilled.

Kit tucked the ruby in the velvet pouch in his pocket and shut the fake stone in the box in the safe.

Retreating through the wall, he made it all the way back to the library without incident.

His heart was ready to explode out of his chest by the time he sat back down at his books. Sweat soaked his forehead, and his breathing was heavy from the dash.

The door opened, and a guard poked his head in.

Kit didn't look up from his books, and the door closed again. Step one complete. Step two, make the stone disappear.

CHAPTER 33

ELSIE

E lsie awoke to the sound of her mother's voice.

"Elsie, wake up." Her voice was urgent. Was something wrong at the tea house? Oh, sugar. Clara must have burned something again.

Her eyes shot open, and a pain in her hip came with it. "Ow," she said aloud. The hardness of her bed had left a bruise. Where was she? The wall right in front of her was dark, and her head was cloudy like she hadn't slept at all. She rolled over and nearly fell off the wooden bench. Right, she was in prison.

Panic turned her skin cold with sweat. How could she have slept when they needed to get out?

Stay calm, Elsie. All was not lost—not yet. She had examined every inch of the walls during the night. All solid stone. The door was unmovable iron, presumably because most of the prisoners would have been fae. She had found no weaknesses but for the crisp, rusty coating lining the surface of the bars.

Her mother's voice trembled with concern from the cell next door. "Elsie, please let me know you're still there."

"I'm here, Mum." She stumbled up and yelled toward the tiny window between them, wishing the wall wasn't there. It was a cruel torture being this close to her mother but not being able to see her, to hug her, to know she was well. "What time is it?"

"It nears the noon hour. They left food, but you did not wake. I was worried."

Angels, she had slept that long? She had stayed up the whole night filling her mother in on her adventures at Midwinter Haven tracking her down. She told her mother all about Kit, the tracker, leaving out the fact that she had fallen for the fae who tricked her into this prison or that he was a prince.

She picked up the pitcher and sniffed it. Water. But she didn't dare drink from it. She couldn't be sure it came from the safe spring that Kit had mentioned.

Kit—she had to stop thinking about him. She considered asking the guard to fetch him, but that was just silly. He could come down himself if he wished to. He had told her to trust him, and there was still the slim chance Fenn was on her side and might come. But she couldn't count on it. She needed a backup plan of her own.

Elsie set the pitcher down. "How long until the guards come back around?"

She could picture her mother's brow creasing with worry as she spoke. "About two hours. They will collect the trays."

Elsie pressed her face up to the bars and peered out. There were no guards and no other prisoners in this section. She slipped the poisoned tea from her pocket. "Collect as much rust off the bars as you can."

Waiting felt like an eternity. But Elsie did as best she could, which involved pacing around the tiny cell. She was glad of her solid boots that kept the chill away from her feet.

She let the poisoned tea steep in water for the past few hours. Hoping that mixed with rust, it would have some effect on the fae guards.

She jumped when a figure appeared right in front of her, silent as an owl in flight. He was a fae guard, not tall, about the same height as Kit. He wore white gloves, same as all the other guards, and she eyed the keys dangling from his belt.

Finally, the door swung open, and Elsie was prepared.

She stepped forward, her heart racing like it might explode. The guard went to draw a dagger. But she was faster.

She threw the cup of poisoned, rusty water right at the guard's face, hoping it would get in his eyes and mouth. Kicking the door wide open, she wasn't prepared for the horrific moan he made as he clawed at his face. Blisters bubbled across his skin, turning his flesh a painful pink.

Maybe it had worked too well...

But he squinted through his pain and lunged at her.

Elsie almost didn't react because she felt sorry for him, but she pulled her knife in time. She faltered as something hard hit her in the ribs, but she sucked in a breath and instinctively drove the small blade into the guard. Her focus was clear as hot blood coated her hand, and the fae dropped to the ground.

Gasping for breath, she pulled away and stepped back, clutching at her rib. She dared take her hand away for a second, but there was no blood.

The guard twitched on the floor, a silvery dagger fallen from his hand as a vermilion pool spread around him, trickling along the cracks in stones like tiny rivers ending in clumps of hay.

"What is happening? Speak to me, Elsie!" her mother cried.

"It's fine, Mum. I got him." Elsie pulled the keys from the man's belt; a wave of nausea rose in her throat when she bent down, then she threw up on the hay.

She had killed him. Wiping the blood off the knife on his jacket, Elsie calmly folded the blade and placed it in her pocket.

Her hands shook as she fumbled with the keys. She was finally going to see her mother. All the searching and the moment was finally here. Her chest tightened.

She stumbled up and went straight to her mother's cell.

Elsie gripped the cold bars, and her mother clutched her hand, her warmth, her realness flooding into Elsie like a soothing tea as their eyes met.

"My love, you did so well." Tia raised her hand and stroked Elsie's cheek.

She pressed her face into the warmth of her mother's hand between the bars for a second longer. "Let's get you out of here."

Elsie forced herself away from her mother's touch and shoved the key into the lock. She yanked open the door and fell straight into her mother's arms. They nearly tumbled through the door as Elsie pivoted them out of the cell.

Hot tears crept from her eyes, seeping into the scratchy wool of her mother's stained traveling dress as she hugged her mum tight. She didn't want to let go, but at the same time was acutely aware of the boniness of her mum's shoulders and how urgent it was that they got out of there.

Her mum pulled away, but her gaze dropped to the blood coating Elsie's arms and part of her dress. "I had not expected you to come dressed as a princess," she teased, though her voice was weak. "You look beautiful."

"I'm a mess." Elsie looked down at her skirts, feeling like she should apologize to Runa but glad her mum seemed like herself, though her cheeks were hollow and her usually straight black hair was frayed with bits of hay sticking out in all directions.

She was still her mum, the fae hadn't broken her.

"Mum, are you okay?" Elsie realized it was a silly question after she asked. Of course, she wasn't.

"I am now that you're here." Tia smiled.

Footsteps in the next hallway clicked against stone. They were coming closer.

Elsie's eyes darted to the door. "Do you have your water?"

"I do." Tia ambled into the cell but went to the back wall and hesitated, lingering for a moment, her hand pressed against the stone almost as if she didn't want to leave.

"Mum, we need to move."

Tia turned and grabbed her cup from the floor. "Hold out your arms." She poured the contents onto Elsie's hands, washing off some of the blood, replacing it with the thin orange sludge of rust.

The footsteps drew closer. Elsie glanced down the hall, no one there yet. She took the cup and used the remaining rust mixture to coat her mother's arms. She didn't know if it was much of a barrier against fae grabbing them, but it was worth a try.

They walked silently toward the exit, past Elsie's cell. Elsie glanced down at the guard, who had turned an unsightly gray.

"Don't look at him, Tea Leaf. You did what was necessary."

Elsie looked away and pulled the knife from her pocket once more as the footsteps drew near their hallway. She wasn't sure what the plan was here, but she knew she would fight for her life. She pressed against the wall and waited, her heart thundering in her chest like a drum.

She angled herself in front of her mum, both backed against the wall near the door.

A shadow rounded the corner. She tensed, not daring to look at her mother, but she could feel the same tension coming from her. Like two bent bowers waiting to snap.

The figure stepped around the corner. Elsie lunged, but a hand gripped her wrist mid-air. A coldness spread into her flesh as her hand lowered.

"I see you didn't need my help after all." Anders released her hand, and she stepped back, her arms out trying to shield her mother behind her.

Elsie risked a glance at her hand, no ice. Anders wiped his hand on his jacket, a long brown merchant's coat, not something a prince would wear, and frowned at his hand then shrugged.

At least it had made him let go, though it hadn't seemed to cause harm.

"I suppose that's what you've come down here to do, rescue us?" *How considerate.* Elsie didn't take her eyes off Anders, trying to figure out the best way to get close enough to drive her blade into him. The best thing was to keep him talking.

"I thought so." Anders leaned against the stone wall.

"I take it you are Kit?" Tia said from behind Elsie.

"He's not Kit, Mum. It's his brother. We can't trust him."

Anders' lips pressed into a tight line.

She didn't bother with introductions. There had to be a way to get past him.

"Pleased to meet your acquaintance, madame. I take it you are Elsie's mother I have heard so much about."

"Indeed I am. Did you mean what you said? You are here to help us?" Tia asked, her voice raspy and weak.

Anders smiled. "I did, and I do intend to help you escape."

"Did Kit send you?" Elsie demanded.

Anders feigned a sigh. "In a manner of speaking."

A flicker of hope fluttered through her. She knew she shouldn't let it.

"You are fae. How can we trust you?" Tia's voice trembled.

Elsie gripped the knife tighter. She would have to make a move soon.

"Because I say so. I am an honorable member of the Winterfae Court at your service." He gave a bow with a fanciful wave of his hand as he did so.

"He is one of the fae. He cannot lie," her mother stated.

"That doesn't mean I trust him." Elsie shot Anders a look to let him know she was serious.

"Nor do I, but we have few options, and this is the best one," Tia said.

Good point. But what was his angle, then? Rescue them, then let a hunt come after them? Perhaps the best option was to take their chances. One step at a time. If he got them out, they could deal with his trickery later.

"Listen to your mother, Elsie. She is not wrong." Anders stood up straight. It was odd to see him dressed so plainly, though his features were still princely, almost too perfect, too beautiful to be real.

"Allow me to introduce myself to begin building trust. Prince Andriel Whitewood, at your service." He bowed respectfully.

Tia let out a tiny gasp. "Prince?" she stammered.

Anders stepped back, grinning. Tia stepped to Elsie's side and pulled her hand to her chest.

"Oh, Elsie failed to mention that detail, I suppose?" Anders smirked.

"I failed to mention you at all." Elsie gritted her teeth. If they were going to get moving, they better be doing it soon, unless this was part of his game.

"You wound me. But never mind. We shall become acquainted on the carriage ride."

Who was this, and what had he done with Prince Anders?

"Do we have any choice?" Tia whispered.

"No." Elsie didn't trust him as far as she could throw him, but this was worth the risk. He was their only way out of here right now. "Very well, lead the way, Prince Anders."

CHAPTER 34

KIT

Kit reentered his bedroom with an armful of books. Once he'd returned to the library, he waited a torturous half hour to make his research ruse believable.

The guards were at his door, waiting like well-trained dogs.

"I'll just be a moment, then we shall go to the forest," Kit called from his vast closet.

"The forest, your highness?" the blond guard asked.

"Yes." *Why should they sound so surprised?* This new batch of guards certainly enjoyed asking questions.

"Should we not be here for the Midwinter's Eve court?" said the even blonder guard, whom Kit had come to recognize, had a deeper voice.

Kit found an old satchel and two canteens, to one of which he added two vials of strong sleeping powder he used to use for insomnia. Should be exactly enough for two of them.

"I will be back in time, I assure you." *You will not be so lucky.* He planned to lose the guards as soon as he got into the forest. Sleep, not kill, Elsie would approve of this plan.

He found a spare oilskin traveling coat, much nicer than the one he had left with Liri, and slipped it on, then selected a sword from his rack of old swords that were still sharp and had nothing wrong with them. He had just enjoyed replacing them because he could.

Slinging the bag over his shoulder, he went to the bathroom and filled both canteens with water, putting the dark one containing the powder in the front of his bag. He turned and marched out of his room. "Come along."

Kit chose the main palace doors for his exit. The more people who saw him leaving for his hike, the better. A weak alibi for Elsie's escape that he hoped would be happening anytime soon but better than none. The guilt clutched at him once again. He should be the one rescuing her, not delegating the most important job to someone else. But he also had to be the only one to know the location of the stone, and he had to be the one to face his father.

He told himself it was to give her the best chance. Fenn was far more qualified to get her out, not to mention he wasn't being trailed by guards reporting to the king like Kit was.

Setting his face to a princely frown, he marched through the reception hall of the palace. Servants scuttled out of his way, bowing as they went.

Even more Midwinter decorations adorned the grand room than the night before. A few more trees had sprung up, rising into the high ceiling and glistening with lights and strings of sparkling gems. The smell of cinnamon and incense almost made him want to stay, awakening memories of his childhood at the palace during Midwinter when he and Anders used to race around the trees, pretending they were hunting pixies in the forest.

He kept walking toward the door.

"Christarel!" His father's voice boomed behind him, and Kit turned around.

Oh, blast it.

"Father." He dipped his head respectfully. "A blessing to you on this Midwinter's Eve."

"I thought you were done with all this bird nonsense." He stopped in front of Kit and rested his hand on the sword pommel at his side.

"I nearly am, Father. Just some minute details to finish and my book will be complete."

"Thought that quest might have shown you what is important in life, so you would forget this."

Oh, it did, Father. "I will be back for the Midwinter's Eve court."

"Very well, see that you are." He slapped a hand on Kit's shoulder, then marched off with an army of advisers in tow.

Kit blinked for a moment. That was the most affectionate his father had ever been to him since he was a child. A shame he was going to ruin it all. The man might have a soft side under all those layers of hatred. But risking the lives of the Midwinter Haven residents to indulge his past self was not worth it.

Kit hurried out the door and walked straight up to a royal carriage that was on hand. He couldn't trust himself not to go to Elsie if he was here any longer. He took a deep breath, reminding himself of his confidence in Fenn.

Clouds were amassing overhead, but no new snow had fallen overnight.

"To the Veiled Waters' southwest shore," he ordered the driver and stepped inside.

The carriage ride was brief. He would have opted for walking if it had been possible, but he was trying to keep up appearances.

He stepped out of the carriage and took in the fresh lakeside air. He pictured Elsie seeing this view for the first time. Her face would light up and she'd say how glorious it was with a wide smile across her face. She was always so open with her joy. He wished he could be more like her.

The lake was still and silent, the ice keeping its secrets locked below. The trees had no movement, except for a lone squirrel swiftly descending a trunk headfirst.

Kit flexed his hand. He'd remembered to take his vial of potion that morning. His arm felt fine for now, just a dull pain.

He told the carriage driver not to wait after his guards stepped down from the back.

The two fae fell into step behind him without complaint. He led them a good twenty minutes along the lakeside path before stopping to watch a pair of robins.

"Care for a drink?" He handed the dark leather canteen to the closest guard.

Kit kept a wary eye on the guards as he pretended to watch the robins and drank from his own flask. Both men took large swigs.

It happened quickly. One guard leaned against the tree and slid down it, the other blinked, then crumpled to the ground in a heap.

Kit appreciated the uneventfulness of the task. He'd estimated the dose perfectly. Working quickly, he dragged them off the track, hid them well behind a rock, and sent a fresh dusting of snow across the whole area.

Kit spread his wings behind him and took to the sky. The icy breeze rushed against his face in a refreshing jolt of sweet winter air, like he was a bulb awakening in spring after being dormant all winter. He knew it was the amplifier crystal giving him this much strength, but it felt glorious. He had missed flying.

Keeping above the path, his eyes narrowed, seeking the wooden marker that indicated the border between the Winterfae Kingdom and Midwinter Haven.

The frozen lake resembled a cracked blue mirror, creating an eerie and beautiful spectacle from above. In the distance, he heard bells from Midwinter Haven starting the Midwinter's Eve celebrations on the lake shore.

He spotted the border from a great distance. There were guards there—Winterfae guards.

His thoughts turned to Elsie. Soon she would be free, he just hoped she would talk to him again after the change in plans.

He flew lower and landed at a run on the lakeside path, his footsteps leaving no prints. He walked to the guards so as not to drop in and alarm them and switched from his royal glamour to his true fae face they would not recognize.

"Good day, gentleman."

The guards straightened and unsheathed their swords. They must have been warned to prepare for trouble, which could only mean his father had something planned.

"I bring no ill tidings, just out for a stroll." Kit held his hands up and did his best to force a smile.

"No one is to go between the borders. Turn back."

Kit lowered his hand to his pocket, his fingers wrapped around the amplifier crystal. There were four of them. He could take them.

"I wasn't aware there were restrictions." Kit called to the roots of the trees below their feet, his power guiding them up, aiming to burst through at the same time.

"What are you doing?" A guard stepped forward; his sword raised.

Kit didn't speak while focusing his energy. He held his breath. Just a little more...

"Arrest him. He's using magic against the crown," a guard ordered.

Power surged in his blood, and with one push, Kit thrust the roots straight up through the earth. He let out his breath. Thick roots snapped around ankles. A few missed, and one guard stepped forward, but Kit was on it. He sent another root up and twisted it around the guard's legs, slamming him into the snow.

One down.

Despite being locked to the earth, the other guards remained standing. Sweat beaded across Kit's forehead. He wiped it away with his forearm, but growing the roots higher on all four of them was slow.

Air shot past his head with a whoosh. *Too close.* A single ice dagger, he suspected. He raised a wall of solid ice just in time as a swarm of frozen daggers stabbed into it right in front of him. He pulled the sword from the scabbard at his side.

Sending his power through the ice wall, he urged the roots of the trees to grow faster as the guards cut through them. One guard broke free and darted around the wall. Kit raised his sword to block it just in time. The reverberation rattled his good arm.

Pushing forward, Kit forced the guard to defend and didn't stop attacking. He might be out of practice, but the instinct and years of training were still there at heart.

He focused part of his mind on constricting the other guards with tree roots. The heat of battle seemed to spur his magic on. Power surged in his chest as he lunged and parried, keeping up the fight for several minutes with the guard, who already appeared to be tiring.

Kit's muscles burned, his blade calling for blood. The guard stumbled, and Kit saw his opening. His steel bit flesh, and he fought the urge to sink the metal right through the heart.

He paused, his blade hovering above the man's chest.

There was no denying the rush of it, the feeling of having another's life in his hands. He was a monster of his father's making…but he didn't have to be. Here he had a choice, and he knew what Elsie would want him to do. She would not want him to be a murderer.

His hand shook, but he leaned back and retracted his blade.

The guard lunged forward. Kit slammed the sword hilt into the guard's temple and knocked him out cold.

Kit stepped back, he had done it, restrained himself against killing. He was not his father.

He swung around at a shout. One guard was nearly free. He forced his magic to the other guards. The roots shot up around them, tight around their necks, compressing their chests. Kit relished the power once more, it would be so easy to take their lives. But now he knew he didn't have to kill.

One by one, the guards passed out and fell to the ground.

He had done it and without killing anyone. His lungs expanded with a deep, satisfying breath.

He quickly hauled the unconscious bodies off the path and leaned them all against a tree. Then he sent a flurry of snow over the area, covering any evidence.

He stopped for a quick breath, and the pain in his arm hit. Kit peeled back his sleeve to see the wound had reopened, and his shirt was thick with slow, seeping blood. He quickly bound the wound with the ripped sleeve from his shirt, then eased on his oilskin coat.

Setting off at a run, it didn't take too long to cross into Midwinter Haven land, and he plodded along for as long as his breath would allow, not having the energy to fly.

He stopped and took his bearings. This would have to do.

Turning off the lakeside path into the forest, Kit dodged between the trees, running at a shameful pace until he reached an area of thick growth about ten minutes off the trail.

Using magic, he dug a small hole, and without ceremony, he reached into his pocket and dropped the Bloodgate Ruby in, mourning the fact that such a beautiful gem would never be seen again.

"Protect us," he whispered as he covered it with earth and stood up. He snapped a small twig from a nearby pine tree, stuck it in the ground above the ruby, and stepped back.

Gripping the amplifier, he forced all his will into this tiny twig. He felt as its new roots gripped into the solid earth, when its first leaf sprouted, and the stretch as it shot up into the air, rising to join its fellows in the thick canopy.

Only Kit would know that the stone was entwined deeply in the hidden roots of a tree that looked like every other pine in the forest.

Elsie should be free now if all went according to plan. He pictured her smiling as she was reunited with her mother. Her mother didn't know how lucky she was to have a daughter like Elsie go to such lengths to find her.

He stumbled back and leaned on another pine to gather his breath and stabilize his footing. He had to get back to find out if she had made it out. The dizziness subsided, and he began the walk out, sending puffs of snow behind him, covering his tracks.

CHAPTER 35

ELSIE

With golden palace bracelets upon their wrists, Anders led Elsie and her mother through the underbelly of the palace and up into the bright halls with no one so much as blinking an eye.

Elsie followed like she was in a waking dream with thoughts of sleep and calmness flooding her mind.

Before she knew it, they were in a nondescript carriage, so nondescript in fact, that Elsie could not have recounted the color, nor design, if someone had asked her.

She leaned back in the velvet seat letting the softness envelope her, sleep calling, but she could not heed its call, not when they had come this far. Getting her mother home was too important. Her mother, who sat next to her, fell asleep straight away, her head resting on the cushioned velvet wall.

"What have you done to me?" Elsie slurred her words.

Anders, who sat opposite Elsie, leaned forward so their knees were touching. "Oh, right." Anders took her hand. She tried to pull away, but her limbs were like noodles floating in broth. His hands were icy but soft as silk. It reminded her of Kit, and a shiver ran through her, wishing she could push all thoughts of him from her mind and keep her heart locked in ice. She was sure he would not be thinking of her. Why should she allow him the space in her precious thoughts?

The bracelet slid from her wrist, and her thoughts sharpened. The memory of Kit's betrayal hit her as fresh as before, and she held back a choke at the rush of clear emotions.

"Sorry, it was the only way to get you out." Anders lowered her hand gently to the folds of her gown, blanketing her lap.

Elsie rubbed her wrist. "I thought the bracelets were supposed to stop anyone from becoming enchanted or controlled," she grumbled, though her heart wasn't in it. She was actually starting to tolerate Anders, though the journey wasn't over yet. He still had time to go back to being himself and reveal whatever game he was playing.

Anders leaned back in his seat, though he still managed to look regal in his merchant clothes. "I was not controlling you; I was concealing you and added a little of my own enchantment. It was not malicious, therefore the bracelets allowed it."

"And the palace servants and guards?"

"I was controlling them just a little." He held his fingers up and pinched them apart a tiny amount. "It was for their own good not to see you. It will keep them alive if questioned."

The carriage clattered over some bumps she believed were the gates out of the palace grounds, though she couldn't see due to thick black shades covering the windows. She eyed the door handle, visualizing how she could both grab her mum and roll out the door when they were far enough, should she need to.

"Thank you. If this is not some cruel trick, I am grateful for your help," Elsie said sincerely.

"I should remove your mother's one too."

Elsie grabbed his hand in midair. "No, let her rest for now." She released his hand, and he complied with her request. Her mum had been through enough. She needed the rest and to regain her strength for the walk back. "Where are you taking us?"

"Back to Midwinter Haven. Is that not where you wish to go?" he asked as if it were so obvious.

"Yes. Could you drop us just out of town by the forest at the southern gate?"

"Of course, anywhere you ask. This carriage even has discreetness charms upon it, so no one will blink an eye."

That would be helpful since she was still wearing her full ball gown. They could easily slip from the carriage to the forest and find their waiting bags. She tensed, eyeing the door handle as she waited for the catch to appear at any moment, an ambush, a roadblock—whatever Anders had concocted.

"Why are you doing this, Anders?"

"Can it not simply be from the goodness of my heart?"

"No." From Kit's tales about his brother, she was certain there was more to it.

"Very well. If you must know, I wish to reconcile with my brother, and this is how I will prove myself to him."

"Why didn't you just help us the first time we tried to get in?"

"Because my father already knew you were coming. There was no way you or Kit could have made it out. I attempted to scare you off, but for some reason, you took my threats as an invitation to the ball."

She stared at him blankly. "You *gave* me an invitation to the ball."

He brushed some invisible dust from his coat. "Yes, but the code behind it was *do not* come to the ball."

"And you just thought I would forget my mother?" Elsie raised an eyebrow.

"I had hoped so. I was going to rescue her myself and send her to you and Kit as a peace offering."

Elsie wasn't even sure he saw her mother as a person, just a means to an end. Which was still rather unclear what exactly that was. "But why do all this to win Kit over?"

"Because I must wed soon, and every suitor is more ridiculous than the last. I have accepted that the king or queen at my side will be as incompetent as I. Hence the need for Kit."

Did he just admit he would be an incompetent king? This was not the man Kit had described to her, and he couldn't be lying.

"What do you need Kit for?" She had seen how protective, caring, and loyal Kit was, how he fought for what was right. How he cared so much about what happened to the people of Midwinter Haven. But she suspected Anders didn't know that side of Kit at all.

"To advise me on how to not become my father. He seems to be doing well at that."

Oh, so maybe he had noticed. She wondered if Anders had ever said that to Kit. Kit believed his brother hated him, but this was clearly not the case. He was not lying. Even if he was twisting the words, the sincerity was authentic.

"You couldn't have just asked him?"

"Of course not."

Elsie was unable to relax for fear of an ambush or Anders turning on them, though he seemed genuine in his reasoning. But she was done being tricked by the fae and wanted this carriage ride over as soon as possible.

Her thoughts turned to Kit. She remembered the coldness in his eyes as he walked away from her; it had felt so real. He had said to trust him, but it was difficult after being thrown in a cold prison.

She should be happier. Against all odds, she rescued her mother, yet she couldn't bring herself to celebrate. The guilt crept over her.

She had only been partly responsible for rescuing her mother and with help from Anders, of all people. Maybe once they returned to Winterfrost, reality would settle in, and she could celebrate with her mother and Marie.

Noises of the town grew louder, and the carriage slowed as they made a series of turns in what she assumed were the streets of Midwinter Haven.

"We are nearly there. I should remove your mother's bracelet and my enchantment." Anders nodded toward her mother.

"Mum, we're nearly there." Elsie shook her mother's shoulder gently, and she sat up, blinking in confusion.

Anders took her hand and removed the bracelet. Tia sat upright. "Where are we?"

"Midwinter Haven. Nearly free. But we've got a big walk ahead of us, Mum."

Anders peeked out the window. "Do you know the way back? It will be nightfall in a few hours."

"I know how to find the path Kit led me here on. We have lights in our bags. I'm sure we can find the way," Elsie said with false confidence.

Anders reached into his pocket. "In case you do not, take this." He handed Elsie a compass.

She turned it over. It was the fanciest compass she had ever seen. The casing was painted deep blue, and the edges lined with gold filigree borders. There were even tiny gemstones inlaid in the face. "Thank you."

"Do you even know what that is?" Anders rolled his eyes.

"A compass?" Elsie turned it over again. Yes, it was still a compass. "An expensive compass?"

Anders shook his head like she was a simpleton. "It is not a compass, it is a wayfind." He watched her, waiting for a follow-up question. He was like a puppy needing to be fed attention.

"What is a wayfind?"

"I'll have you know this is a most rare object."

"What is its function?" Tia leaned in with genuine interest.

"It is a device that will keep the user on their desired path."

"It will lead us home to Marie?" Elsie asked, still skeptical.

"Indeed, it will. But I'm only lending it to you. You must return it to me."

"Very well, thank you, Anders." Elsie had been worried about finding the path home, but figured being lost in a forest at Midwinter would still be better than being next in line for an executioner's block. With any luck, they would be home in time for Midwinter the next day.

The carriage stopped.

"End of the road," Anders said cheerily and didn't make any move to exit the carriage.

"Thank you for your help, Your Majesty," Tia said.

Elsie was glad she had been the one to say it. It seemed more authentic coming from her.

"What is your price for rescuing us?" Elsie asked, better to know now than as an unwelcome surprise later.

"I'm glad you asked. All I ask of you, dear Elspeth, is when I call upon you, you will ask Kit to be my adviser. I know he will listen to you."

Anders obviously hadn't gotten the news that she and Kit were not a couple and never had been. Still, it was something she could easily agree to and hold up her end of the bargain if she had to. It was worth their freedom, after all.

"That is all?"

"That is all."

"Very well. I agree to your terms, and I will return the wayfind to you." She wasn't sure how she'd do that, but if that was the hardest thing she had to work out, then it was hardly a problem.

"Good, now get out of my carriage. I have tomorrow's Midwinter celebrations to prepare for."

CHAPTER 36

ELSIE

E lsie and her mother stepped into the chilly afternoon air, and before they could turn around, the carriage was gone.

"This way." Elsie gathered the fabric of her dress in one hand and took her mother's hand with the other, then dashed toward the trees, not taking any chances of being sighted. They got to the edge of the forest and didn't stop until Elsie spotted the old stone wall and turned off the small path next to it, as Liri had instructed.

Elsie breathed a sigh of relief and took in the scent of pine needles and snow, relishing the freedom as she spotted their bags tucked away.

Silently, Elsie handed her mother her bag and realized there were only two there. Kit had never planned to go with her, even going through with the ruse of packing his bag for Liri. Angels, she was so foolish to be sucked in by his charms and magic.

"Are you alright, love?" her mother asked.

Elsie brushed the tears from her eyes with the back of her hand. She should be worrying about her mother, not feeling sorry for herself.

"I'm fine," she lied. "Let's change into traveling clothes. I think I have all your things here."

Elsie untied the stays of her dress and gasped as pain ripped through her side at the sudden release. She clutched her ribs, trying to dull the pain.

"You're injured!" Her mother was there in a flash.

Elsie shivered against the stillness in the air; it had an odd feel about it, like everything was too quiet. She let her mother take away her hand along with the bodice of her dress.

She looked down to see a line of black bruising across her ribs matching a slash in the dress she hadn't noticed before. So, the guard had got her with his blade.

"How in the heavens did that not slice you open?" Tia frowned at the bruise.

Elsie clutched the dress to her chest and silently thanked Runa once more. It was a shame she couldn't fit it in her bag, but Liri had promised to return to this spot to take it.

"Luck, I suppose." Elsie bent down and winced. It was likely a broken rib. "There is a bandage in my bag I can bind it with for now." Her hand slid over something soft. She pulled out a leather drawstring pouch. Kit's crystals. Why had he put them in her bag? She pulled one out, recognizing it as a healing crystal.

"What are you doing?" her mother asked, a mirror of Elsie's own ignorance toward magic before she had come to Midwinter Haven.

"Healing it." Elsie pressed the crystal to her side without hesitation. She realized how she had changed in just a short time. Despite Kit's betrayal, she didn't fear magic, rather, saw its purpose as a tool.

Her skin glowed a soft pink, and the blackness of the bruise turned a sickly yellow and instantly felt better.

"Well, I never. I think the fae might have used one of those on me," her mum exclaimed.

Elsie didn't offer her mother an explanation or apology. There would be time for that later.

A rustling in the bushes alerted Elsie, and she froze. Had they sent guards already?

Then Pepper burst from a bush. Elsie's heart nearly exploded in her chest from the fright of it. Pepper leaped up, bowling her over, and she had never been so glad to see a dog in her life.

"Oh, Pepper. It's lovely to see you, but you must return home to the inn." Elsie managed to hold her dress to her chest as she hugged the giant dog, then stood up and pointed. "Go home, Pepper."

Pepper sat.

Tia stepped to Elsie's side. "It is safe?"

"Very." Elsie nodded. "But I don't want her to follow us and get lost. Go home, Pepper," she said in her best commanding voice.

Pepper did not budge.

"Perhaps she wishes to accompany you?" Tia suggested.

It seemed that way. "We don't have time for this. If you want to come, Pepper, I will make sure you get back to Kit, but we must make haste."

They dressed in traveling clothes and donned warm coats and traveling cloaks before they were on their way along with Pepper. She hoped Kit wouldn't think she was stealing his dog again. It could certainly appear that way.

Once she was sure no one was on the main path, they started south. Elsie held the wayfind in her gloved palm and opened it as she walked.

A faint rope of gold coiled out of it, and she jumped, but it moved as she did and followed the curvature of the path with a mesmerizing liquidity that she found enjoyable to follow. She thought of Winterfrost and Marie, and it seemed to know what she wanted.

They didn't come across any other travelers, and the afternoon stayed unusually calm, without any trees rustling above and only occasional birdsong.

Elsie knew she was pushing it, but her mother would never complain. She kept up, and after about an hour, when it felt safe to stop, Elsie stepped off the path behind a rocky outcrop to give her mother a break.

"We do not need to stop. I can keep going." Tia's face was pale, and a sheen of sweat coated her brow.

"We will have to walk all night. It is best we eat while there is still light, so you have some strength." Elsie tried to hide her concern. Her mother needed a rest if they were to walk all night.

Her mother didn't protest.

Elsie wished they could make a fire to have tea to revive them, but they would have to do with water for now. They were a good distance from Midwinter Haven already, and she hoped Anders would prevent any guards from coming after them.

Her mother was very quiet. Elsie handed her small amounts of cheese, dried venison, and some figs, and they sat there nibbling away. Pepper drank water from a puddle on a rock and Elsie shared her venison.

She finally built up the courage to speak. "Did you find what you were looking for?"

Her mother stared off into the distance. Elsie wasn't even sure she heard her.

It was several moments before Tia turned to her, and Elsie's stomach dropped. Silent tears tracked her mother's cheeks, and she shook her head slowly. Elsie already knew what she was going to say. She wanted to block her ears or run into the forest so she didn't have to hear. So it didn't have to be real. Deep down, she suspected she already knew what happened to her father.

"I found him." Tia's voice was barely a whisper.

Elsie's throat tightened. She couldn't speak. She swallowed hard and waited.

Her mum faced her with a sad smile. "I'm sorry it wasn't better news, my love. I found it in my cell. His name was carved into the wall, and I just knew."

"Do you know what happened?" Elsie's voice cracked. Her skin grew hot and prickly, every muscle tensed waiting for the finality of the truth but dreading it, still a sliver of hope remaining that none of it was real.

"He was executed," Tia said the words without faltering. Like she had already accepted it.

Elsie's blood flushed with ice. She couldn't breathe, couldn't swallow. Her chest grew tight at hearing the words spoken aloud. It was not a surprise, not unexpected, but it somehow still hit her like a horse at full gallop.

Elsie twisted the wish bracelet on her wrist, and her lip quivered. She had done her best to be strong, but there was only so much she could take, and she burst out crying.

Her mother's arms were around her in seconds.

Elsie sobbed into her mother's shoulder. "I'm sorry. I shouldn't be the one crying. You've been through hell."

"There, there, Tea Leaf. Let it out. I've already done my crying."

Elsie cried, knowing it was wasting valuable daylight. Her mum told her how she found out the truth from a guard who used the information to torture her. But if anything, Tia seemed relieved by the news. Perhaps since she had been searching for so long, this was the closure she needed.

In return, Elsie told her mother everything about Kit when she asked. Perhaps she needed the distraction. Elsie told her how she had met him in Winterfrost, how she trusted him, how he hated his father, how he loved birds, and how she fell for him.

Her mother stroked her hair and didn't speak; she was just there when Elsie needed her. Pepper came and rested her head on Elsie's knee.

Perhaps she was being too harsh on Kit. He had gotten her to her mother, and they had made it out, whether it was according to plan or not didn't matter.

But then again, he hadn't come for her himself or sent Fenn. It was Anders of all people. Was she being selfish? Kit had more than her to worry about. He had to get the stone away from his father. After all, saving the entire town of Midwinter Haven was more important than her.

She shook her head. There was no time for such thoughts. They needed to get back to Marie and as far from the Winterfae Kingdom as possible.

"Let us be on our way if you're up to it." Elsie stood and dusted crumbs off her dress. The sun would be setting soon. Pepper was already on the path.

A hand wrapped around her wrist. Her mum looked up at her. "Elsie, I don't want you to think I planned to leave you and your sister. You know I never would."

Elsie nodded, swallowing as she didn't trust herself to speak. The thought had been eating away at the back of her mind since her discussion with Marie.

"Good, good." Tia patted the back of Elsie's hand and smiled a genuine smile. "I am feeling much better, thank you." She took Elsie's hand to help her up.

It felt like a great burden had been eased from her mind, and she suspected her mum felt the same way. Elsie was glad her mum finally had the closure she had been seeking for so many years.

Elsie slung her bag on her back and set the wayfind in her palm, the golden thread even brighter in the dimming light, and she realized the compass made her heart light while walking. When she set it down was when her despair had returned.

"I think you should hold the wayfind, Mum." Elsie handed it to her, watching her mother's face carefully.

A serene smile curved her mother's lips as her fingers wrapped around the device. Her shoulders relaxed, and she stood with an ease in her bones that had not been there before.

"That food revived me quite nicely." Tia adjusted her bag.

"Let us make haste to surprise Marie for Midwinter morning." Elsie grinned as they set off. If they walked all night, they could make it in time to arrive by sunrise.

Without the wayfind, walking was more of a chore, and the sun had set, throwing dark shadows across the forest floor.

Elsie swallowed. This would be a long night. She tried to distract herself, following her mum's rhythmic footsteps and Pepper's happy lolling tongue swaying, but her thoughts returned to Kit. How could she ever trust him again?

CHAPTER 37

KIT

K it arrived at the palace just in time to join the flock of adorned fae entering the palace between the rows of sparkling Midwinter trees bordering the blue carpet.

His thick oilskin coat masked the blood trickling down his arm. The hard part was done. He'd hidden the ruby. Now he needed to stand up to his father. He wanted to make sure his father knew it was his own son who stopped him from taking Midwinter Haven.

But first, he needed to find out if Elsie's escape had been a success. He needed to find Fenn who should be around there somewhere.

Onlookers cast a few sideway glances his way, no doubt due to his less-than-courtly appearance. His true face was on full display, no glamour whatsoever, and they didn't recognize him as the prince.

He needed to conserve his magic for when he needed it, but he also wanted to save his princely face for when the time was right. One last time he would be the Prince Christarel Whitewood they all recognized, after this day he could just be Kit.

"Did you hear two prisoners escaped this very day?" a woman with blue horns and a silver gown said to a man in an over-the-top gold-decorated navy court suit.

Kit halted. His breath caught in his chest at the news. Perhaps he didn't need to find Fenn. Kit sidled up to the woman. "What more do you know of this?"

"Oh, my." The woman's hand went to her chest, and she looked at Kit in horror.

The overdressed man, who had a glamour of a lot of makeup, stepped between them. "Step away from the lady, sir."

Kit's vagrant appearance was not helping his situation. "Just tell me," he snapped.

The man put his arm around the woman and guided her away, looking very proud of himself.

Kit fought the urge to yell after the woman in frustration. A man appeared next to him, dressed similarly to Kit's level in a merchant's cloak and plain breeches but with extremely shiny boots.

"Hello, brother. I thought I recognized that voice."

"Anders?" Kit did a double take.

"Taking a page out of your book, Kitty. It looked fun to dress up."

There was no doubt it was Anders's voice, but in a glamour and a merchant's cloak? "What do you want?"

They stepped through the open palace doors. "Did you hear of your lady's escape?"

"It's true then?" Thank the Ancient Mother. He had been right to put his faith in Fenn.

"A little gratitude would be nice."

His heart clenched. No. Was Elsie okay? The last thing he needed was Anders' involvement. He pulled his brother out of the crowd and shoved him between two overdecorated trees. "What did you do?"

"Don't you want to know where I sent her?" Anders picked up a bauble on the tree, looking at himself in the reflection.

"I don't have time for this, Anders," Kit said through gritted teeth.

"Don't worry that plain head of yours. I set her and her mother free in the woods to tottle back to their quaint mortal town."

"You tricked them!" Kit hissed under his breath. "What did you ask for?"

Anders held up his hands. "No trick, honest to the Ancient Mother herself."

Anders was being honest. He could always tell when his brother was dodging the truth. "And she is safe?"

"Yes, she is safe." Anders plucked a twig from Kit's shoulder, then his gaze went to Kit's arm. "What have you been up to?"

Kit had to believe she was safe, but even if she made it to the forest, she'd have to walk through the night to make it back to Winterfrost, and who knew what state her mother would be in? Every bone in his body told him to race after her, but he had to be smart, finish what he started, and he needed to get his arm seen to or he wouldn't make it past Midwinter Haven. "Where is Fenn? Why isn't he the one telling me this?"

"He had a rather urgent royal order to relay a message to the vampire watch at Frosthaven Keep. No need to worry about him."

Kit rubbed his forehead. Fenn could not disobey a royal order directly from Anders, and Kit had not given a royal order himself. He would never force Fenn to help him.

It was fine, not according to plan, but the Bloodgate Ruby was away from his father, and Elsie was safe.

Kit took a calming breath and turned back to Anders. "Then I owe you my thanks. I don't agree with your methods, but perhaps I have underestimated you."

"I'm certain you have. I only wish for there to be peace between us."

"Truly? That is why you did this?"

"I don't know why no one believes anything I say." Anders shook his head. "I honestly wanted to help."

Kit knew better than to believe Anders outright. But these words were no lie, even if there was another motivation behind his actions. For now, Kit would give him the benefit of the doubt.

A bell chimed, indicating the court session was about to begin.

"Come, brother." Anders grabbed Kit's sleeve and dragged him into the crowd once more. Caught up in a sea of perfume, frills, and elaborate headdresses, Kit and Anders were herded into the grand ballroom along with everyone else.

Somehow Anders pushed his way to the front, apparently enjoying his new disguise and the looks of disgust as they passed.

The king took to the dais at the front and held the box with the fake stone high above his head.

Kit's chest grew tight.

"I need to stop this," Kit whispered to Anders.

Anders rubbed his hands together with a grin. "I suspected you might say that."

The king called for silence, and the noise of the audience fell instantly.

"What are you going to do?" Anders whispered.

Kit turned to his brother, a last attempt to judge which side he was on. He looked sincere in that unfamiliar face, perhaps that's what made him more believable.

"I'm going to do what I should have done a long time ago. Stand up to him."

Kit had been naïve taking up his father's quest; he'd thought it was a way to make his father proud, to be seen. But the more time he'd spent away, the more he realized he could make decisions in his own life. He didn't need his father.

Kit's palms grew sweaty as the king's gaze fell across his audience of brainwashed fae, all of which listened to the king wholeheartedly. His father was convincing when he told them they were better than everyone beyond their borders; the Winterfae were more elite, smarter, stronger, and true descendants of the gods.

The king's voice boomed across the room. "Once we claim what is rightfully ours, we will control the trade in the north."

Anders nudged his side. "You better do it soon before he has the crowd worked up."

"Soon." Kit wasn't sure what he was waiting for, but he needed the right timing.

It had taken him the better part of a year to find the Bloodstone Ruby, and several weeks of unsuccessful negotiation before he knew he would have to take it. The dwarves knew what the stone could do, and they were right to refuse. Only then did Kit realize what his father had planned for it.

Kit had to be the one to take it, so no one else could. He made sure it was the only one of its kind and stole it in the dead of night.

His father held the replica stone, still in the box, to the crowd. The audience thrummed around Kit. Hanging on every word the king spoke. "I will restore what King Therdril took from us! Make our army even greater! We will defeat Frosthaven Keep!"

The crowd roared in response.

Kit's blood turned to ice. He had known his father wanted the tax from Midwinter Haven trade to build his army, now he knew why. He planned to attack the neighboring vampire realm.

He had to move soon.

"Tonight, we will make our stand." The king paused, and Kit took that as his cue.

He snapped out his wings and launched himself onto the stage. His face morphed into his recognizable royal glamour as he set his feet down gracefully beside his father.

The guards closed rank around him, spears aimed at his chest.

"Set down your arms!" the king shouted at the guards. "That is my son, you halfwits!"

Kit smirked at them as only a young, untouchable prince would.

"I wish to contribute to your announcement, Father."

The king looked Kit's attire up and down and frowned. "Make it quick."

"Hear me, citizens of the Winterfae Kingdom!" Kit held up his hands, commanding the full attention of the audience with his voice as demanding as his father's.

Despite the confidence in his voice, Kit's hands were sweating, and his heart raced, his wings pressed flat against his back. He had a clear line of sight for the exit and was acutely aware of the presence of the crystal in his pocket should he need to grab it at a second's notice.

"I know many of you have not ventured beyond the borders of these fae lands, but if you had been to Midwinter Haven, you would know it is just that—a haven." Kit paused, testing his father. He did not stop him, but his eyes grew dark. "My grandfather, King Thedril, gifted these lands as part of a crucial peace treaty to unite the people of all the lands of the North. It is a place of trade, unity, and learning. We have no right to destroy this, to bring fear to such a place, to take the taxes for ourselves."

The crowd remained silent. All eyes were on the king for guidance. It was becoming increasingly clear that this attempt might be futile.

"Enough!" his father boomed.

Kit had known there would be little hope of convincing the courtly fae otherwise in a few sentences. That task required months or years.

His eyes locked with Anders' for a split second, and he prayed that his brother was on his side.

The king's nostrils flared, and his fists shook at his side as he contained his anger. "You will take back your treasonous words. Or they will be the last you speak," the king snarled.

"No, Father. Not this time." Kit turned to face the king, making certain the audience had a clear view of both of them.

The king's hand rested on the pommel of his sword as his blue eyes turned to smokey darkness. "I should have known you hadn't changed. Still too soft, weak-minded, not willing to do what it takes for this kingdom, for these people," the king bellowed as he gestured to the crowd. They clapped and roared in response.

Kit gripped the crystal in his pocket and held his father's gaze. He had always been a disappointment in his father's eyes. But his father was wrong. He had changed. He knew what was right now, and he knew what love felt like. And his father held no love for his sons, not even Anders. They had always just been pawns in his game.

Turning the amplifier crystal in his palm, Kit took it from his pocket on the side the audience couldn't see, regaining the power he had expended earlier.

"You have no right to destroy peoples' lives, Father," Kit said so only his father would hear.

"I'll make their lives better," the king hissed.

Kit knew his father fully believed this. But the fae way was not right for everyone, and his father would destroy that town within days. Force people out of their homes, back to kingdoms they didn't want to live in.

Kit turned to the crowd. "You are all fools for following my father. Midwinter Haven deserves better." Kit spread his wings with a snap.

His father drew his sword. "You will regret your words, boy."

Kit held his stare. "The stone is gone."

The king's lips pulled back, baring his teeth. "What did you say?"

"That one is a fake," Kit said defiantly, keeping an eye on the guards as he planned how to take them down.

The king hesitated, then took out the stone, and held it up. He shot beams of light through the stone, but unlike last night, it did not light up reflecting the magic within but sent shards of ordinary red light around the room like glass.

The king placed the stone in the box, shook his head, and stepped closer. "It is my fault."

Kit drew a trickle of power from the crystal, the smooth surface warming against his palm in response.

The king drew his sword. "I listened to your mother, and this is what I get. A thankless, disobedient, wastrel of a son." His face grew red as his voice reverberated around the room.

Kit blasted vines straight at his father. The power released from his fingers before he even had time to think, the crystal pushing him to act. So, he pushed harder. The vines writhed around the man like hungry snakes, snatching his limbs and strapping them to his body before hurtling him into the guards behind him.

"Duck!" a voice called. Anders.

Kit ducked to the side, avoiding a barrage of ice aimed at his chest from the row of guards. He sent more vines to envelop them in a living net, determined to press them into the ground.

With the crystal fueling his power, Kit manipulated the net expertly. The king would have everyone use amplifier crystals if it weren't for the deteriorating effect over time.

A guard came at him from the left. Kit blocked the sword with an ice shield just in time. The impact shattered his shield into a million glittering shards of ice but protected him as intended.

He had to get away. There were too many of them.

Just off the stage, Anders shuffled the panicking crowd out of the room playing the hero of the day. No one had noticed him helping Kit.

Despite the courtly fae possessing powerful magic, none would risk using it in the king's court against his son, even if he was committing treason. They all had their pretty lives to preserve, and they let the king dictate their morals. They could be of no use to either side.

Kit tested his wings with one large sweep, then launched above the crowd. He didn't wait around for the guards to untangle themselves, or for his father to find some way to keep him there. Something sharp bit into his calf as he flew over the panicking crowd.

A water whip sealed around his leg and slammed him back to the floor.

Landing hard on his bad arm, Kit sucked in a breath as pain blackened his vision. He forced his eyes open as the water from the whip melted away.

He got to his feet just in time and drew his sword as his father lunged. A clang of metal reverberated through Kit's torso as he blocked. There was no way he could beat his father in a direct fight. He had to get airborne again. He dodged and parried and even got in a few blows his sword master would have been rather proud of. But it wasn't enough.

"Yield to me," his father yelled, his eyes blazing. Kit had no chance of winning or his father relenting.

"You don't deserve to be king." Kit blocked another blow. He couldn't keep this up much longer.

The king backed Kit toward the wall. "And I suppose you do?"

"I don't want to be king; I want to protect Midwinter Haven as Grandfather wanted."

"He was a fool, just like you." In three swift sword strokes, the king backed Kit right up to the wall through the border of Midwinter trees. Kit stumbled, and his father's blade was at his throat.

"He was no fool." Kit dropped his sword in surrender but slipped his hand into his pocket. He closed his eyes and forced the trees to yield to his magic. Instead of asking them as he usually would, he took their will and demanded they change. Branches shot out, knocking the king back.

"You are no son of mine! I exile you." The trees muffled the king's voice as they pulled him in, covering him in more and more branches.

He didn't bother to answer his father. He could have the last word, as he always did.

But Kit was free.

A smile twinged at his lip as the trickle of hot blood ran down his neck. But it wasn't bad. The trees continued to grow into a bushy mass that engulfed his father. Kit snapped his wings out once more and took off into the open air of the vast room.

Kit had a free line of sight to the exit, where a stream of bodies continued to pour out.

The rush of cold air outside the palace was a welcome relief. He flew straight for one of the nondescript black carriages closest to the gates but overjudged his landing and slammed into the side.

He sat up as the driver stood over him.

"To Midwinter Haven, The Fae's Folly, and with discretion," Kit begged and held out a purse of coins. The driver snatched them away, his eyes widening at the weight of the pouch, and helped Kit up without even counting the coin.

"Right this way." He bustled Kit into the carriage.

It was a lot of coin, enough for the driver to keep his mouth shut and worth it to get away from here. Kit didn't protest the rough handling as he was shoved in. They needed to hurry to beat the rush of traffic out of the palace gates.

He let out a shaky breath as he fell into the plush seat, not caring if his blood stained it. The gold would cover any damage. He could barely believe he made it out and that he had stood up to his father.

His eyes closed, and darkness swam at the edge of his vision. His arm pulsed. He may have overdone it.

CHAPTER 38

ELSIE

Elsie and Tia emerged from the darkness of the forest into the soft glow of the morning sky, a haze of warm yellow tinting the edge of the horizon. Smoke drifted in lazy coils from the chimneys of cottages on the outskirts of town, and Elsie let herself breathe a sigh of relief.

They had made it to Winterfrost.

Pepper stayed right next to Tia as she trudged with heavy footsteps in front, the wayfind still guiding her steps as Elsie caught up to her.

"May the first Midwinter light bring you a blessed year, my love." Tia smiled wearily, wrapped her arm around Elsie's shoulder, and kissed her head.

"I am just glad I found you in time." Elsie relished the warmth as she wrapped her arms around her mother's waist, and they stopped before the forest edge.

"And I am grateful to be safe. All thanks to you, my dear." Tia kissed her head once more. "Now, let us make haste for home to our Marie."

Pepper barked in agreement, and Elsie ruffled the dog's head. She was sure Pepper had kept them safe through the night; no night creatures or anything else had bothered them.

Pepper trotted ahead, and Elsie pulled her traveling cloak close around her, keeping out the worst of the morning chill as they stepped out of the wilderness and onto the road into town. Even through the weight of tiredness, the relief propelled her forward like a horse, knowing it was nearing home.

They walked through town in silence, Pepper sniffing at doorways as they went but never straying far. Bells already chimed in the air as the early risers bustled about ready to get on with their Midwinter morning.

It hadn't snowed overnight, and the roads were clear. After fifteen minutes, they neared Riverview Cottages. The smell of baking bread drifted on the light breeze, and the frosted dewdrops on the shrubbery out in front of the cottages glistened like tiny fae lights in welcome.

Tia stumbled at the gate, but Elsie caught her arm and held onto her as they made their way up the neatly swept path to Peony Cottage.

Elsie almost collapsed in exhaustion when they got to the door. But she kept herself together and knocked quietly so as to not give Marie a fright, though Pepper gave a few helpful barks to announce their arrival.

The door flew open.

"You found her!" Marie sobbed and threw herself at their mother. Tia wrapped her arms around Marie and stroked her sleek black hair.

"My baby, I'm so sorry I left you both. I'm here now."

Marie peeled herself off her mother and wiped her eyes. She shook her head at Elsie, then threw her arms around her. Elsie folded into the warmth of her sister, who smelled of tea and home.

"I knew you would come back," Marie whispered into Elsie's neck.

"Sorry, it took so long. We had a few complications." Pepper was nudging the back of Elsie's legs.

Marie pulled away. "You must be exhausted. Come in by the fire. Warm yourselves." She pulled their mother inside, and Pepper bounded in, taking that as an invitation for all of them.

Elsie shut the door and noticed another person standing there. It was Kit's friend from the pub, and he had a wide smile on his face. Pepper dashed up to Elsie, looked at her for approval, then rushed to the man. Thomas was his name, she recalled, and Pepper wagged her tail furiously. Thomas bent down and hugged the dog, letting her lick his face all over.

"Midwinter's blessings to you, Elsie. Apologies for my intrusion." He stood up, twisting his cap in his hand as Pepper head-butted his leg, and he continued to pat her. "I didn't like that Marie was here all alone. I stopped in early to bring her some spiced bread and mulled cider. I hope that's okay."

"Glad tidings to you, Thomas. That is very kind. Please stay." Elsie smiled, glad that Marie had someone looking out for her so well. "Pepper is very glad to see you."

A crooked smile spread across Thomas' face. "Where might her owner be?" he asked cautiously.

Elsie kept an eye on her mother as Marie wrapped her in a blanket and guided her into the chair by the fire. "That is a long story. But I assure you he is well."

"Are you well, Mum? Can I get you anything?" Marie asked as she took in their mother's weary form. A deep frown formed across her brow.

In the light of the fire, even with the blanket, it was obvious how thin their mum had gotten.

"I am well enough, Marie. Something hot to warm my bones would be lovely, but please don't fuss."

"Thomas, how about you warm that cider now? It seems we are in great need of it," Marie ordered, bossy as ever, though Thomas seemed more than happy to oblige as he raced to the bench, set out a glass flagon, and searched for a pot.

"Mother, this is my friend Thomas." Marie waved a hand toward Thomas.

"A pleasure to meet you, Thomas. I take it you are staying near here," Tia said, her way of asking if he had stayed the night.

"Ay, I've been lodging at the White Fox. Not far from here." Thomas set the pot hanging over the embers of the fire. "Just stopped in to bring some Midwinter cheer."

"Leave Thomas be. He has been nothing but a gentleman, I assure you." Marie selected a wool blanket from the back of the armchair.

Elsie didn't protest as Marie wrapped the soft wool around her and set her in the chair by the fire across from her mother. The sweet smell of cider drifted from the pot as it simmered, and Thomas added some dried orange and cinnamon quills.

Elsie's strength was quickly being sapped away by the coziness of the blanket and the mesmerizing lull of the dancing flames. Pepper lay sprawled out across the flagstones in front of the hearth, her job well done.

"You must tell me what happened. I've been worrying myself sick," Marie said a little harshly.

Elsie didn't begrudge the biting tone. She knew Marie would have been out of her mind with worry for them.

"It was my fault, Sweet Pea." Tia shook her head, staring into the flames. "If it wasn't for Elsie and her friends, I would not have made it out alive."

"Out of where?" Marie's brow creased with concern.

Tia wouldn't meet Marie's gaze. "Out of Snowspire Palace. I did not understand the seriousness of taking the mushrooms for our special tea. I'm sorry I was so foolish."

"What is she talking about, Elsie?"

"It is a very long story, Marie." Elsie shivered uncontrollably. If her mother would rather make herself look the fool and protect Marie from the horrible truth about their father, then Elsie would respect that. They could tell Marie when the time was right.

Marie darted to the kitchen. "Then we best get some food and drink in you both so you can tell us all about it."

Thomas was at the cider pot, and before she knew it, Elsie had a steaming mug in her hand, and Marie had placed a plate of spiced bread with jam and cut-up dried figs right next to her.

Elsie sipped the hot brew and savored the sweet, tangy, appley flavor before letting the warmth slide down her throat into her hollow stomach.

Marie pulled up two wooden dining chairs close to the fire for her and Thomas and didn't press the matter while Elsie and her mother revived themselves. Just helped spread jam on the bread for Tia, who got a bit of color back in her face.

Pepper woke up and busied herself in front of the fire, gnawing at the large bone Marie had given her from the soup pot, and Elsie wolfed down her bread, then nibbled at the figs from inside her blanket cocoon.

"Are you ready to tell us now?" Marie asked impatiently.

Elsie nodded. "Thomas, did you know Kit was one of the fae?"

Marie gasped. "He wasn't!" Then flashed an accusing look at Thomas.

Thomas' cheeks reddened. "I admit, I did know. But I knew you were in no danger. Kit is an honorable man."

Marie glared at Thomas. "How could you not mention that this whole time?"

"It was of no concern." He held his hands up, then turned to Elsie. "Was it? He didn't wrong you, did he?"

"I'm still trying to figure that out," Elsie admitted aloud. She wanted to believe he had thrown her in prison to help her.

"His brother helped us escape," Tia spoke up, looking much better after having some food and drink.

"Why did you have to escape? What happened? I must know the whole story." Marie wrung her hands together.

"To summarize: Mum was caught by the Winterfae Kingdom guards stealing from their sacred forest and got thrown in prison. I went with Kit to a fae ball at the palace to try to break her out. Oh, and Kit is one of the crown princes of the Winterfae Kingdom, Prince Christarel Whitewood." There, she said it.

Thomas' jaw could have dropped to the ground, it went so low. "Well, I never! That conniving imp!" Thomas had no wickedness in his words. In fact, he was grinning at the news.

Kit hadn't even told his travel companion of months who he was. That made her feel a little better, at least.

"You were in prison?" Marie's wide eyes settled on their mother in shock. Then she turned to Elsie. "A prince. A fae prince?"

"I know, it's a lot to take in," Elsie said, waiting for Marie to explode at her, to tell her she was right all along about the fae.

"But you are okay, Mother?" Marie's eyes softened.

Tia nodded. "Thanks to Elsie."

"You will start at the beginning and tell us everything," Marie demanded, ever the logical one.

"Very well." Elsie snuggled into the chair and began right from the start on the first day they set out and how she suspected Kit was fae that day they left Winterfrost.

They sat there for a good hour, enraptured by Elsie's story, both Thomas and Marie stopping her frequently to ask questions. Eventually, she got through the entire tale, some of which was news to her mother as well.

Elsie was nearly asleep in her chair. "I think we ought to get Mum to bed," she said to stop the questions.

"I must get to the tea house," Tia said, drowsy with sleep.

"It's all under control, Mum. I'll stop in soon and make sure the day is off to a good start, but I hired another girl, and she is quite competent." Marie took the cups and stood up.

Elsie was relieved to hear Marie hadn't taken everything on in their absence as she was prone to doing. She had handled things extremely well but looked like she needed a rest herself. There were dark rings under her eyes, and she was thinner than when Elsie left only those few weeks before.

Marie bustled them both off to bed with the promise of flat cakes and decorating the Midwinter log once they awoke. Elsie fell asleep as soon as her head hit the pillow.

After several hours of much-needed sleep, Elsie emerged into the living area bleary-eyed and not believing she had made it back to the cottage and on Midwinter of all days.

Pepper was once more asleep by the fire, and Marie returned from the tea house not long after Elsie woke. Marie made their traditional Midwinter's Day fried flat cakes and coated them in a thick layer of golden syrup.

Tia emerged just in time to eat them while they were still hot.

Elsie's heart warmed at the simple act of sitting around the table with her mum and sister, with the bonus of Pepper sitting beside them, drooling as she eyed the flat cakes.

Swallowing the thickness in her throat, Elsie marveled at the fact that they made it back. At several points in the past days, it seemed this was an unattainable dream. But here they were.

Elsie cleared her throat. "I got you Midwinter gifts." She dashed to her room and opened the pocket where she had squirreled away the gifts.

A lump formed in her chest when she pulled out the snow globe she had bought for Kit with the little finch. She pushed her feelings aside as she set it on the table. As she reached for the dream pillow for Marie, a piece of paper drifted onto the bed.

She picked it up and opened it. It was written in an elegant hand.

My dearest Elsie,

If you are reading this, it means I had to resort to Plan B. I offer my deepest apologies for the deception. You must understand it was the only way I could help you and your mother and save Midwinter Haven.

I do not know if my plan will work. But if you have it in your heart, please forgive me knowing that I care for you deeply and do not wish for our time together to end so soon.

I will wait for you by the Midwinter tree in Winterfrost Market Square at sundown on Midwinter's night.

I pray you will be there.

Your humble servant,

Kit

Elsie's heart squeezed in her chest, and she sank onto the bed, letting the chill of the room seep into her. He had planned it all.

CHAPTER 39

KIT

K it awoke, groggy and confused, as if he were trapped in a dream. His arms were heavy but supported by clouds of some sort.

A bitter liquid wet his lips. Horrid. Medicine tea.

His eyes refused to open.

This time, he was determined to open his eyes.

The light was harsh, and they wanted to close again, but he would not let them.

"I need to get to Winterfrost." He tried to sit up.

"If you stop being such a bother and just drink the bloody tea and this potion, you can go there," a frustrated voice said.

"Liri?" Kit cracked open an eye. Fae light burned into his skull, but he forced his eyes open.

"Yes, now if you'd listen to me and sit up, we can get you on the road."

Kit's eyes flashed wide. "What is the hour?" He glanced around. He was in his room at The Fae's Folly.

"It is not yet sunrise on Midwinter morn," Liri said. "You've gone and slept the night away and don't go blaming me. I tried to get you to drink the medicine."

Kit forced himself up and glanced at his arm. "You did this?"

"No, Healer August was kind enough to make a discrete visit. I found some coin in your bag." Liri held out the cup. "Drink up."

Kit took the tea from her with shaking hands and forced it down, trying his best not to choke, then took the small vial of potion. He was going to get to Winterfrost by nightfall, even if it bloody well killed him.

"That's one way to do it," Liri let out a sigh. "Now eat something."

CHAPTER 40

ELSIE

Realization washed over her. Elsie scrunched the edge of the letter in her hand with trembling fingers, then straightened it out. Her lips parted, allowing them to curl into a small smile.

She had been pretending since the ball, trying to convince herself he was not the one for her, but she was being a coward, running from what might be everything she ever wanted.

Pepper nudged her hand as if she knew what the letter said.

Elsie let out a shaky laugh. He wanted her. He had planned it.

She would go to the square and meet him. Yes, she could do that. A simple walk to the square to see the Midwinter hymns, and if Kit was there, she would hear him out.

"What's taking you so long, Elsie!" Marie called. "Did you find the presents?"

"Coming!" Elsie called back.

She stepped out of the room with the paper in hand.

"You're as white as snow, what is it?" her mum said.

Elsie didn't have the words to explain, so she simply handed her mum the letter to read.

"Did you forget the presents?" Marie crossed her arms.

Oh, right. Elsie spun around to go back into the room and came back out with the gifts.

"Oh, Elsie. Will you go?" her mum said, her eyes misty.

Elsie allowed herself a small smile. "I will."

"What? I want to see." Marie took the letter from their mother's hand.

Elsie placed the gifts on the table, waiting for Marie's reaction.

Her mum took Elsie's hands in hers. "You must take risks to find out what the heart truly wants. Only then can you live with no regrets."

Elsie's chest tightened. Then turned to Marie as she placed the letter down.

"But he is fae. What if it is another trick?" Marie frowned at the paper.

"Why would he do such a thing? If he is a prince, he must have better things than coming all this way to have a jest with a mortal," Tia said.

Marie handed the letter back and glanced at the star resting on Elsie's chest over her dress. "I suppose that is true."

"Besides, I want to meet this prince myself," Tia said seriously.

"You will come with me?" Elsie felt a little relieved at the prospect of having backup, even if her family weren't quite sure about Kit.

Marie crossed her arms. "If you are doing this, I shall ask Thomas to come too, just in case."

Elsie glanced at the clock. It was still several hours until sundown, which somehow seemed both too soon and too long to wait. But if this was her shot at happiness, she could not throw it away so easily and live to regret it for the rest of her life.

"I think this calls for tea." Tia slowly made her way to the kitchen area and set about making tea. Elsie wasn't about to stop her, but she had hoped her mother would take it easy.

Once the tea was sitting in front of them at the table, Elsie handed Marie and her mother the gifts she'd gotten in Midwinter Haven.

Marie was unsure about the dream pillow but wanted to know everything about it and gave Elsie a heartfelt thanks despite her mistrust of the barely magical object. Tia loved the teacup with the peony and transferred her hot tea into it right away.

Marie gifted Elsie with a beautiful collection of soaps filled with dried summer wildflowers that smelled delicious enough to eat.

Elsie couldn't have asked for anything more for Midwinter, though her mind drifted to Kit, and she wondered if she was ungrateful for what she had.

They sat nibbling fruitcake and started decorating the Midwinter log with ribbons, bundles of fragrant herbs, and dried oranges. Tia recounted her adventure, and Elsie zoned in and out, unable to stop thinking about meeting Kit in just a few hours.

CHAPTER 41

ELSIE

Elsie got to the square a little early, dressed in her usual red coat and green dress that she had brushed and left to air by the fire for the afternoon. Then she had taken an abnormal amount of time in arranging her hair into two perfect plaits with red bows.

It was not long until sunset. She pulled her bag close to her side, gripping it a little too tightly while Marie and their mother discussed a new tea blend.

The food stalls were in full swing for dinner, but despite usually being drawn to all the smells of smoky grilled meats and garlic bread, Elsie couldn't face eating due to the butterflies causing a riot in her stomach. She hadn't a clue what she was going to say to Kit, but she wanted to be there first, so she had time to think.

She nibbled her lip and glanced around. What if he was early? He could be there watching her.

Taking a breath, she forced herself to listen to the music and try to enjoy the Midwinter celebrations. The tree at the edge of the square was lit up with candles that glittered like stars. Beside it, a small choir sang familiar Midwinter hymns that conjured memories from past Midwinters across many towns and cities all over the Celestial Isles.

She allowed her shoulders to relax a little as she basked in the atmosphere of the happy faces all around her.

"Els!" Nell's voice sounded behind her, and she was nearly bowled over in a hug. "You're back!"

Elsie hugged her friend. A welcome distraction from waiting. "Nell! Gosh, it is good to see your face. A blessed Midwinter to you!"

Nell pulled away and grinned. "And to you! You look different, Els. Your cheeks are so rosy and bright." She tilted her head, studying Elsie's face.

"I know. I have had little sleep these past few days. It's a long story."

"You weren't enchanted in the north, were you?" Nell took off her glove and felt Elsie's forehead with the back of her hand.

Elsie shook her head. Not wanting to get into that conversation. "I don't think so," she lied. Nell would make way too big a deal of it.

"I see you found your mother." Nell grinned.

"She had quite the adventure." Elsie forced a smile, but couldn't muster the enthusiasm she rightly should have.

Nell frowned. "I am so glad for you. But that isn't it."

"I assure you; I am just tired."

"I know what it is!" Nell exclaimed. "It's that tracker, is it not? You tamed him and fell in love!"

Elsie did her best to keep her face neutral. Nell was a little too intuitive and also a little dramatic when it came to romance. She did not want her friend here when Kit turned up. But she still had a wee while before sunset.

"I certainly did not tame him, but I admit, I do not know what to make of him. It's become complicated." Elsie glanced around once more, both looking for Kit and hoping not to see him. She didn't know what she wanted.

"I knew it!" Nell said. "You must have had quite the adventure. You must tell me everything!"

Elsie had no intention of doing so right now. Her mind was buzzing, and she couldn't stop her eyes darting around, hunting for that familiar face in the growing crowds.

A figure stumbled onto the square. The crowd parted at the same time someone screamed.

Elsie's stomach dropped, and she grasped Nell's arm. The man trudged toward the magnificent tree, his gait unsteady with a limp on one side.

That couldn't be Kit. Could it?

Elsie wasn't sure at first, but wings snapped from the shadows, and cries echoed through the crowd.

Oh, angels have mercy. It was Kit.

All the singing stopped, and the square went strangely silent.

"It is one of the fae." Nell gripped Elsie's arm.

"No, Kit," she gasped. A sea of eyes turned to her in horror. Had she said that aloud? Not caring, Elsie stepped forward, dragging Nell with her.

"The fae have come! Gather weapons!" someone cried.

The crowd jostled, people stumbling over one another to get away from Kit as he trudged across the square, clutching his arm and heading for the large tree like the crazed townsfolk didn't even exist.

Every instinct told her to go to him. She glanced around, looking for Thomas. He appeared beside her.

"We must do something." Thomas' voice was panicked.

"He looks hurt, come with me," Elsie said to Thomas, unable to take her eyes off Kit, and she was walking before she realized it, Nell still attached to her arm.

"Elsie!" Nell kept a strong hold. "Don't go!"

Her eyes never left Kit, the world disappeared, and her whole body ached to be near him.

A hand gripped Elsie's arm and spun her around. Marie. "Don't go, Elsie," Marie said.

Kit's wings trailed down his back like wilted leaves. He clutched his arm to his chest and his gait slowed with an increasing limp.

"What is happening?" Nell demanded, her eyes wide with fear.

Elsie tried to shake off their arms, but Marie refused to let go.

Around them, the crowd had turned to yelling at Kit, but none dared get close. Many had left, no doubt to seek safety or gather weapons.

Tia rested her hand on Elsie's shoulder. "Are you sure this is what you want?"

"Yes. He didn't do anything. He isn't bad." Elsie's eyes pleaded silently for her mum to let her go.

"I trust you know what you are doing. Be careful, my love." Tia's eyes were wide with the same fear, but she did not stop Elsie.

Nell's eyes fixed on Kit, her mouth open in disbelief as she looked between Elsie and Kit as if unable to comprehend the situation.

But Elsie couldn't worry about anyone else right now, she hitched up her skirts and set off at a run. Her gaze narrowed like a tunnel only on Kit as he arrived at the tree, not having spotted them yet.

He swayed precariously, his wings giving a silent beat as if to help stabilize him, but it just sent him more off balance and into a lamp post by the great tree.

Thomas ran next to her, both of them ignoring the cries of the townspeople telling them to go back. The flash of torches and metal tools already in their hands glinted on the edge of her vision.

As they darted across the square, her heart thundered in her chest. She didn't know what she would say to him, but he'd walked into this wolf's den seeking her. She could not leave him to the wolves.

Leaning on a lamppost, Kit gripped it to pull himself up and looked around. His eyes locked with Elsie's, and relief flooded his glamour-free face that he didn't even try to mask.

Butterflies filled Elsie's stomach. How she loved that face, his true face, her Kit. She came to a halt right in front of him, her breath heavy.

"You came." Kit's grip slipped on the pole.

CHAPTER 42

ELSIE

Elsie and Thomas rushed to Kit's side as his grip on the lamp post failed. She tried to catch him under his arm, but he fell so fast. Thomas eased the descent, lowering Kit in a gentle slump to the ground.

Around them, people were yelling but keeping a safe distance from the fae that had wandered into their perfect Midwinter celebrations.

"Oh, Kit. What have you gotten yourself into?" Elsie helped Thomas lean Kit against the lamppost. His skin as pale as frost. Kit leaned back, his head resting on the cold pole in exhaustion, then his eyes flashed open and locked on hers. They were ice blue like the frozen lake and flooded her with memories of the past weeks.

"I'm so sorry for everything, Elsie," Kit said. "But you are here. You got my note?"

Elsie crouched beside him; her dress bunched around her as she kept a hand on his shoulder to stop him from toppling. He was shaking all over. How in the heavens had he made it so far in this condition? Where was his potion?

She took off her gloves and wrapped his hands in hers. Warmth seeped into their joined hands, and she realized how close his face was to hers, his breath misting into the night air combining with her own.

"I got your note. But I didn't expect an entrance quite like this." She glanced around. A crowd was forming. One with blades and farm tools being wielded as weapons. Thomas was standing guard with his back to them, yelling something at the crowds, but there was little he could do if the people charged.

"My apologies. I may have overdone it trying to get here in time. I also fell over a log somehow."

She quirked a smile. She couldn't even picture Kit stumbling over a log. He was always so graceful, the exact opposite of clumsy. "Do you have any crystals? Your potion?" Elsie dug into his coat pocket, aware of the closeness of her fingers to his skin—but she found nothing. She would have to try them all.

"Oh, right. Potion.... Liri put one somewhere." He reached into his inner pocket and plucked out the small vial.

Elsie helped him take off the stopper. Their hands brushed, sending heat rushing through her as she handed it back. Her eyes never left him as he drained the vial.

"What were you thinking coming in here without a glamour?" Her heart raced at seeing him after everything that happened. She wanted to hold him, to tell him how foolish he was—to kiss him.

"I had to see you. Knowing what you must think of me..." His voice trailed off.

He better not pass out now. *Hurry up, potion. Work!*

His hand folded around hers. By the angels, his skin felt good against hers. "Elsie, I know you must hate me."

She stared at his hands encasing hers in warmth.

"I don't hate you, Kit. But you left me there. You could have told me what you were planning. I would have understood." She did her best to keep the shake out of her voice.

"I needed it to be believable, for my father to know it was real."

Tears stung at the corner of her eyes, and she inhaled slowly through her nose. "Did you manage to get the stone away from him?" She held her breath, praying it was all worth it as her throat grew thick.

A brief smile ghosted across his lips. "My father cannot get to the stone. I stopped him, and Midwinter Haven is safe."

Elsie's heart glowed with quiet pride. He had done what he had been most terrified of, standing up to his father. "Oh, Kit. I am glad for you." She meant it. A fluttering spread through her stomach. She wanted to hug him, to kiss him, and show him how she felt, but that would not be wise. Not with this crowd of armed townspeople watching.

He had saved Midwinter Haven. Her chest grew tight with pride as she let the information wash over her. Her thoughts turned to Liri, Runa, all the nice stallholders she had met, all the people at the Great Northern Citadel studying. This was so much bigger than her, and they were all safe because of Kit.

The ice she had encased around her heart melted. She threw herself on him in a hug, nearly knocking him over. But he held onto the pole, and the warmth of his free arm coiled around her, pulling her in closer.

"Get that girl away from him!" someone yelled behind her.

"Stay back," Thomas warned. "Leave 'em be."

Elsie pulled away. "Kit, they're going to hurt you. We need to get out of here." She stood up and held his arm as he stabilized himself against the pole and stood to his full height. She took a breath, determined not to let panic take hold. She had to keep Kit safe.

Kit took her hand once more as if an angry mob wasn't gathering. "Can you forgive me, Elsie?"

Elsie's heart leaped to her throat. His wings sprang open, and she gasped. The emerald green shimmering the glow of the setting sun. He hadn't even attempted to reinstate his glamour. She wasn't sure if it was because he was too weak, or if he simply didn't care anymore.

Warmth spread through her. This was his face that she liked the most. Real, not hiding who he was.

"Of course I forgive you." Elsie's breath caught; her chest tightened as if she had forgotten how to breathe.

Kit gripped her hand even tighter, his palms sweaty. "I love you, Elsie. The only place I want to be in this world is by your side."

"Oh, Kit." Her heart drummed in her chest. She wanted this. Not a life with some farmer in a quiet town where magic was despised. Apparently, what she wanted was a rebellious fae prince who would stumble into a town of angry mortals for her and not care.

Kit tucked her hair behind her ear. "I will go wherever you choose if you will have me."

The world around her dulled, and her cheeks heated as her heart raced even faster than before, if that was possible. "Of course I will. I love you too, Kit." She rose onto her toes and pressed a brief, chaste kiss to his lips, but it was enough to set off the crowd.

The clang of metal on cobblestones wrenched her from the moment.

"Time to leave!" Thomas yelled over the noise.

Elsie gently pulled away from Kit and took his hand in hers, their fingers intertwining.

"Not sure that wee display helped the situation." Thomas stepped in front of them.

"Sorry," Elsie squeaked. Perhaps kissing him was a little too much for this crowd. The townspeople glared at them with pure hatred.

They walked slowly toward Tia, Marie, and Nell who were huddled together along with Mrs. Baker, their loyal customer from the tea house, and Hob, the butcher, who seemed very friendly with Mrs. Baker.

All had a wary eye on Kit, including Nell and Marie. But Thomas did a wonderful job of bellowing at the townspeople to keep back as her family and friends formed their own small mob. Pepper stayed close to Kit, barking at anyone who so much as looked at her owner.

Mrs. Baker was shaking her cane and glaring at everyone with a wonderful death stare. Hob didn't seem to know what was going on but made an excellent barrier to the side with his enormous frame.

A group of men blocked their path as they tried to leave.

"This fae's got you bewitched. Let us take him, and we will free you from his enchantment," a large man toting a scythe said from the front of the mob.

"I am not enchanted, and he is no danger to you. Kit is brave and loyal, selfless!" Elsie clung to Kit protectively. The heat of his skin melded with hers, giving her a rush of energy. No one would touch him.

"Step away and worry yourself no more," the man bellowed, probably thinking himself quite heroic.

Had the man even heard her?

Old Mrs. Baker stepped forward.

"This is ridiculous. There used to be a time when we accepted fae in this town. This one means no harm and is no threat to you." Her voice boomed across the square. "You will let the girl and her fae pass, and the fae will ensure no harm comes to our town. Isn't that right?" Mrs. Baker shot a look at Kit.

"You have my word. No harm will come to anyone," Kit said far too calmly.

"He's a fae, he twists words," scythe man said.

Elsie glared at the man, trying to quell the anger in her blood. She admired Kit's patience. If she had any of his powers, she might have blasted them all away by now.

"Let them pass," the woman ordered, and the crowd stepped aside in the confusion as if they hadn't realized what they were doing.

Mrs. Baker winked at Elsie as they passed.

They wasted no time in getting to the edge of the square and parted ways with Mrs. Baker and Hob. Neither of whom seemed afraid of the townspeople.

Elsie was shaking all over, or it could have been Kit. It was hard to tell. But a giddiness washed over her as if they had escaped death once again. Thomas walked behind them to make sure no one followed, while Pepper remained at Kit's side. Tia and Marie walked ahead with Nell, each of them occasionally glancing back, presumably to check Kit hadn't done anything to her.

"You could have added your princely titles at the end to really throw them off on that vow," she teased and curled her arm around his waist.

The comforting weight of his arm fell over her shoulder, and he whispered in her ear, "I didn't need to. That woman was fae, a powerful one by the look of it." A shiver tracked up her spine as his breath tickled her ear.

She bit her lip and smiled. "Well, I'll be damned." Mrs. Baker had been fae all that time, and no one knew it. Elsie wouldn't be the one to spill her secret.

Kit smiled. Angels. It was good to see that smile again. Now all she wanted to do was get him alone somehow.

Kit's chuckle reverberated pleasantly through her. "Anyway, I am not sure I am a prince any longer. I am all yours."

Elsie's cheeks grew warm. She rather liked the sound of that.

CHAPTER 43

KIT

The fire crackled, and the smell of roasting meat and garlic filled the tiny cottage with a comfortable warmth. Outside the paned window, silent snow fell, and Kit almost felt like he could relax.

He had lost nearly everything: his title, his family, endless riches, a privileged life in a palace, even his health, but he couldn't care less. He had Elsie and Pepper, and that was all that mattered.

Though he was on edge being around Elsie's family. Marie kept glancing at him, and he wasn't sure what Elsie's mother thought of him.

Pepper sat at his feet, occasionally lifting her large head to check that he was still there. Kit still shivered, despite being right next to the fire in a chair Elsie had dragged close to the flames for him. He struggled to keep his eyes open but refused to fall asleep, his gaze always returning to Elsie. By the gods, he was lucky to have her.

She glided around the small kitchen with a smile dancing on her lips as she blended tea from various jars. She was everything he wanted, everything he needed to survive. She was the most thoughtful, generous, and warm-hearted person he had ever met. His blood rushed hot at the very thought of holding her in his arms.

Kit's thoughts snapped back to reality when Elsie's mother sank into the chair across from his, her back rigid, and she cleared her throat. Kit attempted to sit up but failed to move an inch, exhaustion overwhelming him as he let his heavy arms fall back to the blanket covering his legs.

"I want to apologize for taking the mushroom from your peoples' forest. It was foolish of me, and I hate myself for putting Elsie in such a position." She shook her head, the anguish clear on her face. "I thank you for everything you did for her. I would not be here with my family if it were not for you. You have my gratitude."

Kit swallowed. He had not been expecting that. If anything, he expected Elsie's family to hate him and throw him out.

"I believe it is Elsie you should thank. She was most determined to find you." He wanted them to accept him, for Elsie's sake.

A smile cracked the corner of Tia's lips. "She is more than I deserve."

"I apologize for my father. He wanted to make an example of you."

She rubbed her forehead. Her eyes had dark shadows under them, and her face was hollow, evidence of what even a short time in Snowspire prison could do to a mortal.

"I was so foolish, but I got the answers I was seeking," Tia spoke quietly and glanced over at Marie.

"Oh." Kit presumed she was referring to her missing husband. Should he enquire further? It couldn't be good news. He glanced over at Elsie pouring tea.

Fortunately, she spoke without him having to ask. "It was as I feared. He was foolish and paid the price. I nearly suffered the same fate."

"You are fortunate Elsie did not give up." Kit sensed she did not want Marie to hear. Nor did she want pity, it seemed.

"I thought she was not real when I heard her voice. I prayed to the angels she was not real." Tears tracked down Tia's cheek. "The only thing worse than being condemned to such a fate was knowing I had caused the same for my daughter."

Kit leaned in, hoping she would stop crying before Marie noticed and blamed him. "Elsie cares for you. But you must know as well as I that she could not be stopped. She is a credit to you." He wasn't sure what else to say. Crying people made him extremely uncomfortable.

"I suspect you will be a good thing for her." Tia studied him. "As long as you do not use your fae trickery on her," she added with narrowed eyes.

He had no intention of ever tricking Elsie or using any magic on her unless she asked. He had learned that lesson and glanced at Elsie as she walked over.

"What are you two whispering about?" Elsie sidled up next to him with a teacup steaming and a familiar medicinal scent. She must have put it in his coat when they were packing. Gods, all he wanted was to touch her. To feel the warmth of her skin and know she was real.

Tia rose from her chair. "Nothing, my love, just getting to know the prince."

Elsie raised a questioning eyebrow at the two of them and handed Kit the cup.

"Drink the tea, Kit. Dinner will be ready soon." Elsie's hand rested on his shoulder for a brief moment. As she stood up, she trailed her fingers along the back of his neck sending a spark of shivers up his spine.

Tea, he needed the tea to stop thinking about the feel of her fingers on his skin. He put the cup to his lips and sipped. Elsie glanced back with a gleam of mischief in her eyes and winked. He nearly spat out his tea.

Dinner was a simple affair, comprising a modest cut of pork shared between all of them, including Pepper, along with a decent serving of herb-coated potatoes and carrots, and brandy-soaked fruitcake for pudding—he couldn't have asked for a better Midwinter feast.

Kit sat on the rug by the fire, relishing the warmth of the flames. He didn't dare look at Elsie, not wanting his thoughts to give him away.

He wanted to get Elsie alone.

His skin was practically buzzing, both with returning magic and the need to feel her. To know that she wanted him as much as he wanted her.

Conveniently, due to Elsie's insistence and not-so-subtle suggestions, Elsie's family, Nell, and Thomas all happened to want to go for a walk to welcome the Midwinter moon. It was most considerate and very unsubtle, but they all went along with it.

Elsie took her time making after-dinner tea and made her way over to the fire. Pepper was sound asleep at one end of the hearth. She handed him a second teacup that smelled of unfamiliar spices and apple.

He set the cup down beside his other one. "I may have just turned all the people of Winterfrost against you. I'm sorry, I know you wanted to stay here and make a life for yourself." Was it selfish of him to ask her to leave with him? Did she want this, want him? He had to be sure.

She stared into the flames, taking time to warm both sides of her hands. "It's okay, Kit. Towns come and go. I really should be more used to it by now."

She turned around with a smile and sank to the floor on the rug next to Kit, nestling into his side. He lifted his arm and wound it around her shoulders, pulling her in close, his heart racing as her breath ghosted across his neck.

This was real. "I was so afraid you wouldn't make it across the mountain."

"If not for Pepper, I might not have." Elsie narrowed her eyes at Pepper as if pondering something.

Kit smiled. "That's the nice thing about having a magical dog."

"Pepper's magic?" Her eyes widened.

He nodded, a smile tugged at the corner of his mouth, surprised Elsie hadn't asked sooner.

She breathed off an easy laugh. "Of course she is."

The warmth of her hand fell to his chest, and she looked up at him, her brown eyes sparkling with mischief. "Are you going to kiss me?" Her gaze moved to his lips.

"Gods, yes," he breathed. This was happening. She wanted him. He was suddenly aware of every inch of her body pressed against his side as his heart hammered in his chest.

His skin felt like it sparked when his fingers brushed her cheek. Tilting her head back, he kissed her softly at first, but it awakened something in both of them. The fire between them roared. Her lips burned against his, and he took her in his arms and lowered her into the rug.

She knotted her fists in his shirt, pulling him down to her, their lips crashing together. But, as if on cue, footsteps outside broke the spell, and he pulled away, breathless. "I don't think this was the reason your family left us alone together." He strained his ears, listening for the click of the door.

Elsie didn't seem worried, or she didn't hear the footsteps. "Probably not. No hurry, we have all the time in the world." She smiled, then traced her thumb over Kit's jawline as her eyes saddened. "I thought I'd lost you."

He hovered over her and dipped down brushing the faintest of kisses across her lips when the footsteps faded away. "You will never lose me. In fact, you won't be able to get rid of me now. I'm a spoiled exiled prince who needs someone to look after him," he teased. Hoping it would bring the smile back to her face.

She hit him in the chest and laughed, pushing him away. "A prince who is more than capable of looking after himself. But you needn't worry, I promise I will always be there to tell you're being a royal arrogant git." She beamed at him.

He pushed himself up to sit with his back against the armchair. Elsie eased herself up on her elbows and looked at him. Her raven hair fuzzing around her head like a halo.

"Seriously, Kit. I'd love to go back to Midwinter Haven with you. If that's what you were trying to ask me before we got so pleasantly distracted." She sat up and slid her legs to the side under her.

He swallowed. She would really do that for him? "But it was your dream to stay here. Are you sure this is what you want?" He was hyperaware of her movements, wanting her to be closer.

"Dreams can change, and mine is to open a tea shop. I'll find the perfect place one day." She shrugged and once more snuggled into Kit's side and leaned her head on his shoulder. He drank in her warmth and her scent, cinnamon and smokiness.

"I just wanted you to be sure you know what you're signing up for." He kissed the side of her head. This felt so right. Even if she said she wanted to stay here, he would make it work somehow.

"I'm aware you're not very popular here in Winterfrost or at Snowspire." She scrunched up her nose and laughed. "Midwinter Haven on the other hand..."

She looked up at him with those inquisitive, beautiful brown eyes.

"We will be safe there," Kit assured her.

She eyed him hungrily, like she was having the exact same thoughts he was. Ones certainly inappropriate for her family to walk in on. "I won't get arrested again?"

"Midwinter Haven laws will protect you as long as you stay within the borders. You should be safe there, but whatever challenges we face, from now on, we face them together."

She snuggled closer to his side, and he drew circles along her forearm with his finger.

Pepper plodded over and rested her head on Elsie's feet. "You did well, Kit. The people of Midwinter Haven don't know how lucky they are to have you." Then she looked up at him. The familiar sparkle of more questions danced in her eyes. "Did you know it was Anders who got us out? You didn't send him?"

Kit shook his head. "He took great delight in informing me of the fact. Turns out he forced Fenn to take a message to the border watch on Frosthaven Keep."

"Of course he did," Elsie said, and he could practically hear the eye roll. "He was a great help, though."

"What did he ask in return?" Kit sat up straight. He wasn't sure he wanted to know. Elsie was smart, but Anders was notorious for getting what he wanted from people.

Elsie slid out from under his arm and moved to a cross-legged position with her back to the fire. "I might tell you one day." She shuffled her skirts around, trying to awkwardly find her pocket while seated.

"Fine, keep your secrets." It couldn't be all that bad if she was smiling.

"Oh, and he gave me a magic compass." She pulled out Anders' wayfind, of all things, from her pocket.

"He gave you his wayfind?" Kit's mouth flew open. That was Anders' most prized possession. A rare artifact from their great, great grandfather. Perhaps he had changed, perhaps he had been helping all along. In his own special way of course.

"I promised I would return it, and I intend to." She twisted the wish bracelet around her wrist, the one he had given her.

"It worked." He nodded toward the bracelet. "It brought your mother back to you." He shifted to sit cross-legged in front of Elsie. Their knees touching, he took her hands in his, running his thumb across the silver charms.

"You said this bracelet was to *find one's heart.*' I believe it brought you to me." She leaned in and skimmed his lips with hers, then pulled away, leaving behind the taste of tea and fruitcake. Before he could savor the kiss, her hands slipped from his grasp, and she stood up.

"I have a Midwinter present for you!" She skipped away playfully, and Pepper jumped up, barking and leaping around Elsie as she laughed.

She got him a present? After everything he had put her through. He hadn't thought to get her anything. He hadn't even dared think that far ahead or allow himself to think they might be together.

She settled in front of him once more, her knee pressing against his, her eyes bright with excitement.

"Open it!"

The gift was wrapped in a lace handkerchief. He slid it off to reveal a snow globe with a tiny finch, a redpoll, with a scarlet berry in its beak at the center.

The words caught in his throat as his chest tightened. "It's perfect." His voice came out as a whisper. She'd remembered. No one had ever chosen him such a thoughtful gift. He shook it and watched the snow fall lazily. "I don't deserve you."

"And I never thought I would fall for an exiled fae prince, but here we are." She grinned and caught his hand, entwining their fingers.

He pulled her in close for a proper kiss, and when he pulled away, she was smiling as loud footsteps sounded up the path.

"Wherever you are is my home, Kit. And you, Pepper," she added, patting Pepper's sleepy head. "Let's make a home in Midwinter Haven."

Just as he was about to kiss her, the door swung open. Marie, Tia, and Thomas stomped in loudly.

"Not interrupting anything are we?" Thomas yelled, despite being in the same room.

Elsie took Kit's hand in hers and smiled at him. "Not at all. We were just about to add the final touches to the Midwinter log before we light it."

We were? Kit turned to see them all staring at him and Elsie by the fire. Thomas was beaming. Tia smiled in approval at Elsie. Marie was frowning.

"You better teach Kit how to do it properly then," Marie ordered. "I'll get more ribbons."

Acceptance. Or as much as he could hope for, and a lot more than he deserved.

"Let's decorate this Midwinter log then, shall we?" Kit locked eyes with Elsie.

She entwined her fingers with his and shook her head with a growing smile. "Yes, let's. We actually made it to Midwinter, together."

Epilogue

Two weeks later

T he floorboards creaked as Elsie descended the stairs. No matter how quietly she stepped, she could never get close to as silent as Kit. Only two weeks had passed since they were last at The Fae's Folly, yet so much had changed it could have been a lifetime ago.

Kit's arm had improved slightly, but Healer August said it would be an ongoing recovery. They returned to Midwinter Haven with only a small delay. A small 'snowstorm' had meant they needed to stay the night in their cozy cave. Fortunately, they were well prepared with blankets, candles, and elvish brandy.

Elsie and Kit spent a glorious night wrapped in one another's arms and pleasantly discovered that humans and fae are very compatible indeed. Just as she suspected.

So far, Elsie hadn't regretted any of her decisions, and it had felt like returning home when they arrived back at Midwinter Haven.

Warmth filled her heart whenever she thought of the future, building a life for herself and Kit in Midwinter Haven. Plus, Marie and

Thomas planned to visit, having both decided to stay in Winterfrost for the foreseeable future.

Tia was not keen to return, understandably, and planned to take Tia's Traveling Teas down to Middlemarch for the spring festivals.

"There you are." Kit's voice sounded from the darkness.

She rested her hand over her racing heart. "You're getting far too good at that."

Kit chuckled and stepped out of the shadows, pulling her into a heated kiss. "Those blasted reporters are still waiting out front. Best use the back door again." Kit stepped back and held his arm out with a gentlemanly bow. Elsie, with her blood still searing from the kiss, entwined her arm with his as they turned away from the main entrance of Fae's Folly.

Elsie squeezed his arm, in a loving way, of course. "You'll have to face them at some point."

"Doesn't have to be today." Kit leaned over and kissed her cheek sending a flood of warmth to her belly.

Did they have time to go back to bed? Kit had said he wanted to show her something, but perhaps it could wait.

No, she had promised she would go. She pushed those thoughts aside for later. "Very well. I'm sure the Haven Peacekeepers will have you make a public statement, anyway." Once news had spread that Prince Christarel had returned to Midwinter Haven, not only had The Fae's Folly attracted a horde of reporters, but the Haven Peacekeepers had offered Kit a job. He had accepted straight away, making him the newest adviser to the force.

Kit opened the door. Elsie let go of Kit's arm and squealed as Pepper jumped up on her, showering her with wet dog kisses. "Yes, we're going for a walk, you clever dog!"

They set off in the crisp morning air down the main street. Midwinter decorations still hung in windows, and the smell of fried dough mingled with coffee and woodsmoke. Someone had recently swept the path from the light sprinkling of snow they'd had overnight, and it had not yet turned to slush, making the street pleasant to walk on.

"Where are we going?" Elsie asked, a tingle of nerves rushing through her. She wasn't sure she liked surprises.

A sly grin crept to Kit's lips. "You'll see."

They passed through the Midwinter Haven market, the ice walls glistening in the bright morning sun. Elsie greeted each early-bird shop owner they came across with a smile and a hearty, "Good morrow." She was already making friends. She'd even spoken several times with a vampire!

They left the market and followed the curve of a cobbled lane Elsie hadn't yet been down, passing signs for a bookshop, a cobbler, a chandlery, and stopped at a boarded-up window right next to a pie shop that smelled wonderful.

"What's this?" Elsie asked, her muscles twitchy with nerves as Kit stopped at the black door of the closed shop.

"You've still got that coin you saved?"

"Yes, some of it." Why was he asking? Did he find them a place to live? Is that what this was?

He held up a shiny brass key. "The landlord lent me this." Kit put the key in the lock without further explanation.

"For what purpose?" Elsie narrowed her eyes. Did Kit want them to live in a shop? He was still getting used to not being a prince and learning the ways of 'peasants' as he sometimes liked to tease. Perhaps there was a room above the shop.

"You'll see." There was that same grin again.

Kit opened the door and gestured for Elsie to enter. She stepped into the cool darkness that smelled of dust and dried lavender. Pulling her coat tighter around her, Elsie waited as her eyes adjusted to the dimness. Shards of morning light sent stark lines across the floor from the gaps in the boarded-up windows, and when she stepped, the dust danced like starlight in the sunbeam.

"What is this place?" she whispered into the quiet space.

The warmth of Kit's arm folded around her shoulder. "It's for rent if you want it."

Kit snapped his fingers, and a fae light on a nearby bench lit up, sending a soft glow around the room.

Elsie's breath hitched. It was a shop, a beautiful shop.

Warm wood shelving lined the two side walls of the long room, with tables and chairs stacked in front. The bench with the light was actually a counter, and behind it, more shelves of stained wood.

"It could be a tea shop," Elsie breathed as visions of customers, steaming tea, and cheerful faces flooded her mind.

"That's what I was hoping you would say." Kit walked to the counter and lit the tiny burner he must have set up there earlier, Elsie's travel kettle and tea set all ready to go.

Pepper set about sniffing everything in the shop as Elsie grinned, spinning in a circle to take in the shop once more, then ran to Kit and threw herself on him.

"It is perfect!" She kissed him hard and felt his smile beneath her lips as he kissed her back.

He pulled away. "You'll have to negotiate with the landlord, but I think he will give you a fair price."

Pepper barked in approval.

Elsie nearly squealed with excitement. Kit pulled up two chairs and dusted them off as Elsie made tea and poured it into her two familiar cups.

Elsie sat at the edge of her chair, buzzing as she looked around. She visualized where she would place tables and where she would stack her jars of tea as she held the warm cup in her palms with both hands. Steam drifted across her face, and she took in the sweet smell of cinnamon, knowing this was the last time she would have this blend.

Kit hadn't mentioned why it was her mother's spiced tea he selected for this moment, but Elsie appreciated the gesture. She relished the sweetness and the calming warmth that trickled through to her limbs. The last of the special tea, but the start of a new era.

After they had finished the tea and Elsie finished rambling on about where she would place everything, how she would decorate, and how they would have a big opening day celebration, Kit pulled out a lunch bag and set it on the bench.

"What's this?" Elsie craned her head to take a peek.

The mouthwatering smell of fennel and sausage drifted from the bag. "Pepper and I owe you."

He pulled out a bun and handed it to Elsie.

"You owe me lunch, at breakfast time?" Was she missing something?

"Yes." He placed a sausage in the bun and dove back into the bag.

Elsie tilted her head. The sausage looked delicious. It was still steaming, as if it were right out of the cooker, and the bun was fluffy and light. *What was this about?*

Pepper sat at her feet, drooling unashamedly, her eyes locked on the sausage. "Oh no you don't." Memories of the day she met Kit flashed before her eyes. *That's what this was about.*

Kit held out a jar of Elsie's favorite sweet mustard with a tiny spoon. "Want some?"

"I see what this is. You finally realized I was right that night." She beamed. This made this wonderful morning that much better.

"I wouldn't go that far. But we owe you for ruining your dinner that night, and did I mention I love you?" His fingers trailed up her arm suggestively.

"You're lucky I love you too. Yes, mustard please, and I hope you bought something for Pepper. I'm not sharing this one." Elsie grinned.

Kit leaned over and planted a kiss on her cheek. "Of course, I didn't forget Pepper." He rummaged in the bag and took out two more sausages and placed them on a piece of waxed paper on the floor.

"Well, if we're in the business of balancing things out. I believe I owe you for your tracking services. You did, after all, succeed in your task." She put down the bun and went to reach for her purse. Maybe it could help get his book printed.

He folded his hand over hers. "Your forgiveness is payment enough for me." He looked around. "Though we may need to live in this shop until I get a wage and your shop is running."

"I couldn't think of anything better." She grinned. Yes, they could make this work.

Even in the chilling air, Elsie's heart warmed. This was home, wherever Kit was. She couldn't hold it in any longer and threw herself on him in the biggest hug of her life.

"I think I'll call it 'The Tea Cozy.'"

Acknowledgements

Thank you to everyone who got excited about this book! It was such a pleasure to write, and I hope it brought you the same sense of coziness reading it as I felt while writing it.

A huge thank you to all my amazing beta readers: Nicole, Beth, Liz, Sean, and Elena. Of course, a special thanks to my editor, Mandi Oyster, and to my proofreader, Amy McKenna.

I hope *Winterfrost Market* brought a touch of Midwinter magic into your life, no matter the season. If you loved the book, I'd be so grateful if you could share the love by leaving a review on your favorite platform.

I look forward to sharing more magical tales from Midwinter Haven with you in the future!

ALSO BY JENNY SANDIFORD

The Shadow Atlas
Initiate (The Shadow Atlas #1)
Apprentice (The Shadow Atlas #2)
Captive (The Shadow Atlas #3)

Read The Shadow Atlas Prequel for Free!
House of Ravens (The Shadow Atlas 0.5)
Go to jennysandiford.com

Tales of Midwinter Haven
Winterfrost Market (Tales of Midwinter Haven #1)

About The Author

Jenny Sandiford

Jenny grew up in small town New Zealand on a steady diet of fairytales and fantasy books. She lived in Mongolia for nine years with her husband where they spent the unfrozen months of the year living on the edge of the Gobi Desert mining gold. When she isn't writing, Jenny enjoys hiking, meeting new animals, and loves to curl up in a sunny corner with a cup of tea, a cat, and a book. She lives in Darwin, Australia, with her husband and their two street cats from Mongolia.

CONNECT WITH JENNY ON:

Website: jennysandiford.com
Instagram: instagram.com/JennySandifordAuthor
Facebook: facebook.com/JennySandifordAuthor
Goodreads: Jenny Sandiford

WANT THE LATEST BOOK RELEASE NEWS?
Sign up for monthly updates!

jennysandiford.com/subscribe